It began as a simple gathering of friends.

In one night, it became a desperate struggle for survival.

Surviving was easy. Now the Companions have to save the world from ultimate destruction.

In the autumn twilight, the Dark Queen awakens, bringing . . .

A Rumor of Dragons

CHRONICLES

By Margaret Weis & Tracy Hickman

A Rumor of Dragons

Night of the Dragons

The Nightmare Lands
(Available October 2003)

To the Gates of Palanthas
(Available December 2003)

Hope's Flame
(Available January 2004)

A Dawn of Dragons
(Available March 2004)

CHRONICLES

PART 1

A RUMOR OF DRAGONS

MARGARET WEIS & TRACY HICKMAN

COVER ART
Glen Angus

INTERIOR ART
Vinod Rams

MIRROR
STONE

A RUMOR OF DRAGONS
©2003 Wizards of the Coast, Inc.

Distributed in the United States by Holtzbrinck Publishing. Distributed in Canada by Fenn Ltd.

Distributed to the hobby, toy, and comic trade in the United States and Canada by regional distributors.

Distributed worldwide by Wizards of the Coast, Inc. and regional distributors.

Cover art by Glen Angus
Cartography by Dennis Kauth
First Printing: June 2003
Library of Congress Catalog Card Number: 2002114092

9 8 7 6 5 4

US ISBN: 0-7869-3087-X
UK ISBN: 0-7869-3088-8
620-86000-001-EN

U.S., CANADA,
ASIA, PACIFIC, & LATIN AMERICA
Wizards of the Coast, Inc.
P.O. Box 707
Renton, WA 98057-0707
+1-800-324-6496

EUROPEAN HEADQUARTERS
Wizards of the Coast, Belgium
T. Hosfveld 6d
1702 Groot-Bijgaarden
Belgium
+322 457 3350

Visit our web site at **www.mirrorstonebooks.com**

To Laura, the true Laurana
—Tracy Raye Hickman

To my children, David and Elizabeth Baldwin, for their
courage and support
—Margaret Weis

The Lands of Abanasinia

Table of Contents

CANTICLE OF THE DRAGON

Hear the sage as his song descends
like heaven's rain or tears,
and washes the years, the dust of the many stories
from the High Tale of the Dragonlance.
For in ages deep, past memory and word,
in the first blush of the world
when the three moons rose from the lap of the forest,
dragons, terrible and great,
made war on this world of Krynn.

Yet out of the darkness of dragons,
out of our cries for light
in the blank face of the black moon soaring,
a banked light flared in Solamnia,
a knight of truth and of power,
who called down the gods themselves
and forged the mighty Dragonlance, piercing the soul
of dragonkind, driving the shade of their wings
from the brightening shores of Krynn.

Thus Huma, Knight of Solamnia,
Lightbringer; First Lancer;
followed his light to the foot of the Khalkist Mountains,
to the stone feet of the gods,
to the crouched silence of their temple.
He called down the Lancemakers, he took on
their unspeakable power to crush the unspeakable evil,
to thrust the coiling darkness
back down the tunnel of the dragon's throat.

Paladine, the Great God of Good,
shone at the side of Huma,
strengthening the lance of his strong right arm,
and Huma, ablaze in a thousand moons,
banished the Queen of Darkness,

banished the swarm of her shrieking hosts
back to the senseless kingdom of death, where their curses
swooped upon nothing and nothing
deep below the brightening land.

Thus ended in thunder the Age of Dreams
and began the Age of Might,
When Istar, kingdom of light and truth, arose in the east,
where minarets of white and gold
spired to the sun and to the sun's glory,
announcing the passing of evil,
and Istar, who mothered and cradled
the long summers of good,
shone like a meteor
in the white skies of the just.

Yet in the fullness of sunlight
the Kingpriest of Istar saw shadows:
At night he saw the trees as things with daggers, the streams
blackened and thickened under the silent moon.
He searched books for the paths of Huma,
for scrolls, signs, and spells
so that he, too, might summon the gods, might find
their aid in his holy aims,
might purge the world of sin.

Then came the time of dark and death
as the gods turned from the world.
A mountain of fire crashed like a comet through Istar,
the city split like a skull in the flames,
mountains burst from once-fertile valleys,
seas poured into the graves of mountains,
the deserts sighed on abandoned floors of the seas,
the highways of Krynn erupted
and became the paths of the dead.

Thus began the Age of Despair.
The roads were tangled.
The winds and the sandstorms dwelt in the husks of cities.
The plains and mountains became our home.
As the old gods lost their power,
we called to the blank sky
into the cold, dividing gray to the ears of new gods.
The sky is calm, silent, unmoving.
We have yet to hear their answer.

THE OLD MAN

Tika Waylan straightened her back with a sigh, flexing her shoulders to ease her cramped muscles. She tossed the soapy bar rag into the water pail and glanced around the empty room.

It was getting harder to keep up the old inn. There was a lot of love rubbed into the warm finish of the wood, but even love and tallow couldn't hide the cracks and splits in the well-used tables or prevent a customer from sitting on an occasional splinter. The Inn of the Last Home was not fancy, not like some she'd heard about in Haven. It was comfortable. The living tree in which it was built wrapped its ancient arms around it lovingly, while the walls and fixtures were crafted around the boughs of the tree with such care as to make it impossible to tell where nature's work left off and man's began. The bar seemed to ebb and flow like a polished wave around the living wood that supported it. The stained glass in the window panes cast welcoming flashes of vibrant color across the room.

Shadows were dwindling as noon approached. The Inn of the Last Home would soon be open for business. Tika looked around and smiled in satisfaction. The tables were clean and polished. All she had left to do was sweep the floor. She began to shove aside the heavy wooden benches, as Otik emerged from the kitchen, enveloped in fragrant steam.

"Should be another brisk day—for both the weather and business," he said, squeezing his stout body behind the bar. He began to set out mugs, whistling cheerfully.

"I'd like the business cooler and the weather warmer," said Tika, tugging at a bench. "I walked my feet off yesterday and got little thanks and less tips! Such a gloomy crowd! Everybody nervous, jumping at every sound. I dropped a mug last night and—I swear—Retark drew his sword!"

"Pah!" Otik snorted. "Retark's a Solace Seeker Guard. They're always nervous. You would be too if you had to work for Hederick, that faint—"

"Watch it," Tika warned.

Otik shrugged. "Unless the High Theocrat can fly now, he won't be listening to us. I'd hear his boots on the stairs before he could hear me." But Tika noticed he lowered his voice as he continued. "The residents of Solace won't put up with much more, mark my words. People disappearing, being dragged off to who knows where. It's a sad time." He shook his head. Then he brightened. "But it's good for business."

"Until he closes us down," Tika said gloomily. She grabbed the broom and began sweeping briskly.

"Even theocrats need to fill their bellies and wash the fire and brimstone from their throats." Otik chuckled. "It must be thirsty work, haranguing people about the New Gods day in and day out—he's in here every night."

Tika stopped her sweeping and leaned against the bar.

"Otik," she said seriously, her voice subdued. "There's other talk, too—talk of war. Armies massing in the north. And there are these strange, hooded men in town, hanging around with the High Theocrat, asking questions."

Otik looked at the nineteen-year-old girl fondly, reached out, and patted her cheek. He'd been father to her, ever since her own had vanished so mysteriously. He tweaked her red curls.

"War. Pooh." He sniffed. "There's been talk of war ever since the Cataclysm. It's just talk, girl. Maybe the Theocrat makes it up just to keep people in line."

"I don't know," Tika frowned. "I—"

The door opened.

Both Tika and Otik started in alarm and turned to the door. They had not heard footsteps on the stairs, and that was uncanny! The Inn of the Last Home was built high in the branches of a mighty vallenwood tree, as was every other building in Solace, with the exception of the blacksmith shop. The townspeople had decided to take to the trees during the terror and chaos following the Cataclysm. And thus Solace became a tree town, one of the few truly beautiful wonders left on Krynn. Sturdy wooden bridge-walks connected the houses and businesses perched high above the ground where five hundred people went about their daily lives. The Inn of the Last Home was the largest building in Solace and stood forty feet off the ground. Stairs ran around the ancient vallenwood's gnarled trunk. As Otik had said, any visitor to the Inn would be heard approaching long before he was seen.

But neither Tika nor Otik had heard the old man.

He stood in the doorway, leaning on a worn oak staff, and peered around the Inn. The tattered hood of his plain, gray robe was drawn over his head, its shadow obscuring the features of his face except for his hawkish, shining eyes.

"Can I help you, Old One?" Tika asked the stranger, exchanging worried glances with Otik. Was this old man a Seeker spy?

"Eh?" The old man blinked. "You open?"

"Well . . ." Tika hesitated.

"Certainly," Otik said, smiling broadly. "Come in, Gray-beard. Tika, find our guest a chair. He must be tired after that long climb."

"Climb?" Scratching his head, the old man glanced around the porch, then looked down to the ground below. "Oh, yes. Climb. A great many stairs . . ." He hobbled inside, then made a playful swipe at Tika with his staff. "Get along with your work, girl. I'm capable of finding my own chair."

Tika shrugged, reached for her broom, and began sweeping, keeping her eyes on the old man.

He stood in the center of the Inn, peering around as though confirming the location and position of each table and chair in the room. The common room was large and bean-shaped, wrapping around the trunk of the vallenwood. The tree's smaller limbs supported the floor and ceiling. He looked with particular interest at the fireplace, which stood about three-quarters of the way back into the room. The only stonework in the Inn, it was obviously crafted by dwarven hands to appear to be part of the tree, winding naturally through the branches above. A bin next to the side of the firepit was stacked high with cordwood and pine logs brought down from the high mountains. No resident of Solace would consider burning the wood of their own great trees. There was a back route out the kitchen; it was a forty-foot drop, but a few of Otik's customers found this setup very convenient. So did the old man.

He muttered satisfied comments to himself as his eyes went from one area to another. Then, to Tika's astonishment, he suddenly dropped his staff, hitched up the sleeves of his robes, and began rearranging the furniture!

Tika stopped sweeping and leaned on her broom. "What are you doing? That table's always been there!"

A long, narrow table stood in the center of the common room. The old man dragged it across the floor and shoved it up against the trunk of the huge vallenwood, right across from the firepit, then stepped back to admire his work.

"There," he grunted. "S'posed to be closer to the firepit. Now bring over two more chairs. Need six around here."

Tika turned to Otik. He seemed about to protest, but, at that moment, there was a flaring light from the kitchen. A scream from the cook indicated that the grease had caught fire again. Otik hurried toward the swinging kitchen doors.

"He's harmless," he puffed as he passed Tika. "Let him do what he wants—within reason. Maybe he's throwing a party."

Tika sighed and took two chairs over to the old man as requested. She set them where he indicated.

"Now," the old man said, glancing around sharply. "Bring two more chairs—comfortable ones, mind you—over here. Put them next to the firepit, in this shadowy corner."

" 'Tisn't shadowy," Tika protested. "It's sitting in full sunlight!"

"Ah"—the old man's eyes narrowed—"but it will be shadowy tonight, won't it? When the fire's lit . . ."

"I—I suppose so . . ." Tika faltered.

"Bring the chairs. That's a good girl. And I want one, right here." The old man gestured at a spot in front of the firepit. "For me."

"Are you giving a party, Old One?" Tika asked as she carried over the most comfortable, well-worn chair in the Inn.

"A party?" The thought seemed to strike the old man as funny. He chuckled. "Yes, girl. It will be a party such as the world of Krynn has not seen since before the Cataclysm! Be ready, Tika Waylan. Be ready!"

He patted her shoulder, tousled her hair, then turned and lowered himself, bones creaking, into the chair.

"A mug of ale," he ordered.

Tika went to pour the ale. It wasn't until she had brought the old man his drink and gone back to her sweeping that she stopped, wondering how he knew her name.

Old Friends Meet.
A Rude Interruption.

1

Flint Fireforge collapsed on a moss-covered boulder. His old dwarven bones had supported him long enough and were unwilling to continue without complaint.

"I should never have left." Flint grumbled, looking down into the valley below. He spoke aloud, though there was no sign of another living person about. Long years of solitary wandering had forced the dwarf into the habit of talking to himself. He slapped both hands on his knees. "And I'll be hanged if I'm ever leaving again!" he announced vehemently.

Warmed by the afternoon sun, the boulder felt comfortable to the ancient dwarf, who had been walking all day in the chill autumn air. Flint relaxed and let the warmth seep into his bones—the warmth of the sun and the warmth of his thoughts. Because he was home.

He looked around him, his eyes lingering fondly over the familiar landscape. The mountainside below him formed one side of a high mountain bowl carpeted in autumn splendor. The vallenwood trees in the valley were ablaze in the season's colors, the brilliant reds and golds fading into the purple of the Kharolis peaks beyond. The flawless, azure sky among the trees was repeated in the waters of Crystalmir Lake. Thin columns of smoke curled among the treetops, the only sign of the presence of Solace. A soft, spreading haze blanketed the vale with the sweet aroma of home fires burning.

As Flint sat and rested, he pulled a block of wood and a gleaming dagger from his pack, his hands moving without conscious thought. Since time uncounted, his people had always had the need to shape the shapeless to their liking. He himself had been a metalsmith of some renown before his retirement some years earlier. He put the knife to the wood, then, his attention caught, Flint's hands remained idle as he watched the smoke drift up from the hidden chimneys below.

"My own home fire's gone out," Flint said softly. He shook himself, angry at feeling sentimental, and began slicing at the wood with a vengeance. He grumbled loudly, "My house has been sitting empty. Roof probably leaked, ruined the furniture. Stupid quest. Silliest thing I ever did. After one hundred and forty-eight years, I ought to have learned!"

"You'll never learn, dwarf," a distant voice answered him. "Not if you live to be *two* hundred and forty-eight!"

Dropping the wood, the dwarf's hand moved with calm assurance from the dagger to the handle of his axe as he peered down the path. The voice sounded familiar, the first familiar voice he'd heard in a long time. But he couldn't place it.

Flint squinted into the setting sun. He thought he saw the figure of a man striding up the path. Standing, Flint drew back into the shadow of a tall pine to see better. The man's walk was marked by an easy grace—an elvish grace, Flint would have said; yet the man's body had the thickness and tight muscles of a human, while the facial hair was definitely humankind's. All the dwarf could see of the man's face beneath a green hood was tan skin and a brownish-red beard. A longbow was slung over one shoulder and a sword hung at his left side. He was dressed in soft leather, carefully tooled in the intricate designs the elves loved. But no elf in the world of Krynn could grow a beard . . . no elf, but . . .

"Tanis?" said Flint hesitantly as the man neared.

"The same." The newcomer's bearded face split in a wide grin. He held open his arms and, before the dwarf could stop him, engulfed Flint in a hug that lifted him off the ground. The dwarf clasped his old friend close for a brief instant, then, remembering his dignity, squirmed and freed himself from the half-elf's embrace.

"Well, you've learned no manners in five years," the dwarf grumbled. "Still no respect for my age or my station. Hoisting me around like a sack of potatoes." Flint peered down the road. "I hope no one who knows us saw us."

"I doubt there are many who'd remember us," Tanis said, his eyes studying his stocky friend fondly. "Time doesn't pass for you and me, old dwarf, as it does for humans. Five years is a long time for them, a few moments for us." Then he smiled. "You haven't changed."

"The same can't be said of others." Flint sat back down on the stone and began to carve once more. He scowled up at Tanis. "Why the beard? You were ugly enough."

Tanis scratched his chin. "I have been in lands that were not friendly to those of elven blood. The beard—a gift from my human father," he said with bitter irony, "did much to hide my heritage."

Flint grunted. He knew that wasn't the complete truth. Although the half-elf abhorred killing, Tanis would not be one to hide from a fight behind a beard. Wood chips flew.

"I have been in lands that were not friendly to anyone of any kind of blood." Flint turned the wood in his hand, examining it. "But we're home now. All that's behind us."

"Not from what I've heard," Tanis said, drawing his hood up over his face again to keep the sun out of his eyes. "The High-seekers in Haven appointed a man named Hederick to govern as High Theocrat in Solace, and he's turned the town into a hotbed of fanaticism with his new religion."

Tanis and the dwarf both turned and looked down into the quiet valley. Lights began to wink on, making the homes in the trees visible among the vallenwood. The night air was still and calm and sweet, tinged with the smell of wood smoke from the home fires. Now and again they could hear the faint sound of a mother calling her children to dinner.

"I've heard of no evil in Solace," Flint said quietly.

"Religious persecution . . . inquisitions . . ." Tanis's voice sounded ominous coming from the depths of his hood. It was deeper, more somber than Flint remembered. The dwarf frowned. His friend had changed in five years. And elves never change! But then Tanis was only half-elven, a child of violence, his mother having been raped by a human warrior during one of the many wars that had divided the different races of Krynn in the chaotic years following the Cataclysm.

"Inquisitions! That's only for those who defy the new High Theocrat, according to rumor." Flint snorted. "I don't believe in the Seeker gods—never did—but I don't parade my beliefs in the street. Keep quiet and they'll let you alone, that's my motto. The Highseekers in Haven are still wise and virtuous men. It's just this one rotten apple in Solace that's spoiling the whole barrel. By the way, did you find what you sought?"

"Some sign of the ancient, true gods?" Tanis asked. "Or peace of mind? I went seeking both. Which did you mean?"

"Well, I assume one would go with the other," Flint growled. He turned the piece of wood in his hands, still not satisfied with its proportions. "Are we going to stand here all night, smelling the cooking fires? Or are we going to go into town and get some dinner?"

"Go." Tanis waved. The two started down the path together, Tanis's long strides forcing the dwarf to take two steps to his one. Though it had been many years since they had journeyed together, Tanis unconsciously slowed his pace, while Flint unconsciously quickened his.

"So you found nothing?" Flint pursued.

"Nothing," Tanis replied. "As we discovered long ago, the only clerics and priests in this world serve false gods. I heard tales of healing, but it was all trickery and magic. Fortunately, our friend Raistlin taught me what to watch—"

"Raistlin!" Flint puffed. "That pasty-faced, skinny magician. He's more than half charlatan himself. Always sniveling and whining and poking his nose where it doesn't belong. If it weren't for his twin brother looking after him, someone would've put an end to his magic long ago."

Tanis was glad his beard hid his smile. "I think the young man was a better magician than you give him credit for," he said. "And, you must admit, he worked long and tirelessly to help those who were taken in by the fake clerics—as I did." He sighed.

"For which you got little thanks, no doubt," the dwarf muttered.

"Very little," Tanis said. "People want to believe in something—even if, deep inside, they know it is false. But what of you? How was your journey to your homelands?"

Flint stumped along without answering, his face grim. Finally he muttered, "I should never have gone," and glanced up at Tanis, his eyes, barely visible through the thick, over-hanging, white eyebrows—informing the half-elf that this turn of the conversation was not welcome. Tanis saw the look but asked his questions anyhow.

"What of the dwarven clerics? The stories we heard?"

"Not true. The clerics vanished three hundred years ago during the Cataclysm. So say the elders."

"Much like the elves," Tanis mused.

"I saw—"

"Hsst!" Tanis held out a warning hand.

Flint came to a dead stop. "What?" he whispered.

Tanis motioned. "Over in that grove."

Flint peered toward the trees, at the same time reaching for the battle-axe that was strapped behind his back.

The red rays of the setting sun glistened briefly on a piece of metal flashing among the trees. Tanis saw it once, lost it, then saw it again. At that moment, though, the sun sank, leaving the sky glowing a rich violet, and causing night's shadows to creep through the forest trees.

Flint squinted into the gloom. "I don't see anything."

"I did," Tanis said. He kept staring at the place where he'd seen the metal, and gradually his elvensight began to detect the warm red aura cast by all living beings but visible only to the elves. "Who goes there?" Tanis called.

The only answer for long moments was an eerie sound that made the hair rise on the half-elf's neck. It was a hollow, whirring sound that started out low, then grew higher and higher and eventually attained a high-pitched, screaming whine. Soaring with it, came a voice.

"Elven wanderer, turn from your course and leave the dwarf behind. We are the spirits of those poor souls Flint Fireforge left on the barroom floor. Did we die in combat?"

The spirit voice soared to new heights, as did the whining, whirring sound accompanying it.

"No! We died of shame, cursed by the ghost of the grape for not being able to outdrink a hill dwarf."

Flint's beard was quivering with rage, and Tanis, bursting out laughing, was forced to grab the angry dwarf's shoulder to keep him from charging headlong into the brush.

"Curse the eyes of the elves!" The spectral voice turned merry. "And blast the beards of the dwarves!"

"Wouldn't you know it?" Flint groaned. "Tasslehoff Burrfoot!"

There was a faint rustle in the underbrush, then a small figure stood on the path. It was a kender, one of a race of people considered by many on Krynn to be as much a nuisance as mosquitoes. Small-boned, the kender rarely grew over four feet tall. This particular kender was about Flint's height, but his slight build and perpetually childlike face made him seem smaller. He wore bright blue leggings that stood out in sharp contrast to his furred vest and plain, home-spun tunic. His brown eyes glinted with mischief and fun; his smile seemed to reach to the tips of his pointed ears. He dipped his head in a mock bow, allowing a long tassel of brown hair—his pride and joy—to flip forward over his nose. Then he straightened up, laughing. The metallic gleam Tanis's quick eyes had spotted came from the buckle of one of the numerous packs strapped around his shoulders and waist.

Tas grinned up at them, leaning on his hoopak staff. It was this staff that had created the eerie noise. Tanis should have recognized it at once, having seen the kender scare off many would-be attackers by whirling his staff in the air, producing that screaming whine. A kender invention, the hoopak's bottom end was copper-clad and sharply pointed; the top end was forked and held a leather sling. The staff itself was made out of a single piece of supple willow wood. Although scorned by every other race on Krynn, the hoopak was more than a useful tool or weapon to a kender—it was his symbol. "New roads demand a hoopak," was a popular saying among kenderkind. It was always followed immediately by another of their sayings: "No road is ever old."

Tasslehoff suddenly ran forward, his arms open wide.

"Flint!" The kender threw his arms around the dwarf and hugged him. Flint, embarrassed, returned the embrace reluctantly, then quickly stepped back. Tasslehoff grinned, then looked up at the half-elf.

"Who's this?" He gasped. "Tanis! I didn't recognize you with a beard!" He held out his short arms.

"No, thanks," said Tanis, grinning. He waved the kender away. "I want to keep my money pouch."

With a sudden look of alarm, Flint felt under his tunic. "You rascal!" He roared and leaped at the kender, who was doubled over, laughing. The two went down in the dust.

Tanis, chuckling, started to pull Flint off the kender. Then he stopped and turned in alarm. Too late, he heard the silvery jingle of harness and bridle and the whinny of a horse. The half-elf put his hand on the hilt of his sword, but he had already lost any advantage he might have gained through alertness.

Swearing under his breath, Tanis could do nothing but stand and stare at the figure emerging from the shadows. It was seated on a small, furry-legged pony that walked with its head down as if it were ashamed of its rider. Gray, mottled skin sagged into folds about the rider's face. Two pig-pink eyes stared out at them from beneath a military-looking helmet. Its fat, flabby body leaked out between pieces of flashy, pretentious armor.

A peculiar odor hit Tanis, and he wrinkled his nose in disgust. "Hobgoblin!" his brain registered. He loosened his sword and kicked at Flint, but at that moment the dwarf gave a tremendous sneeze and sat up on the kender.

"Horse!" said Flint, sneezing again.

"Behind you," Tanis replied quietly.

Flint, hearing the warning note in his friend's voice, scrambled to his feet. Tasslehoff quickly did the same.

The hobgoblin sat astride the pony, watching them with a sneering, supercilious look on his flat face. His pink eyes reflected the last lingering traces of sunlight.

"You see, boys," the hobgoblin stated, speaking the Common tongue with a thick accent, "what fools we are dealing with here in Solace."

There was gritty laughter from the trees behind the hobgoblin. Five goblin guards, dressed in crude uniforms, came out on foot. They took up positions on either side of their leader's horse.

"Now . . ." The hobgoblin leaned over his saddle. Tanis watched with a kind of horrible fascination as the creature's huge belly completely engulfed the pommel. "I am Fewmaster Toede, leader of the forces that are keeping Solace protected from undesirable elements. You have no right to be walking in the city limits after dark. You are under arrest." Fewmaster Toede leaned down to speak to a goblin near him. "Bring me the blue crystal staff, if you find it on them," he said in the croaking goblin tongue. Tanis, Flint, and Tasslehoff all looked at each other questioningly. Each of them could speak some goblin, Tas better than the others. Had they heard right? A blue crystal staff?

"If they resist," added Fewmaster Toede, switching back to Common for grand effect, "kill them."

With that, he yanked on the reins, flicked his mount with a riding crop, and galloped off down the path toward town.

"Goblins! In Solace! This new Theocrat has much to answer for!" Flint spat. Reaching up, he swung his battle-axe from its holder on his back and planted his feet firmly on the path, rocking back and forth until he felt himself balanced. "Very well," he announced. "Come on."

"I advise you to retreat," Tanis said, throwing his cloak over one shoulder and drawing his sword. "We have had a long journey. We are hungry and tired and late for a meeting with friends we have not seen in a long time. We have no intention of being arrested."

"Or of being killed," added Tasslehoff. He had drawn no weapon but stood staring at the goblins with interest.

A bit taken aback, the goblins glanced at each other nervously. One cast a baleful look down the road where his leader had vanished. The goblins were accustomed to bullying peddlers and farmers traveling to the small town, not to challenging armed and obviously skilled fighters. But their hatred of the other races of Krynn was long-standing. They drew their long, curved blades.

Flint strode forward, his hands getting a firm grip on the axe handle. "There's only one creature I hate worse than a gully dwarf," he muttered, "and that's a goblin!"

The goblin dove at Flint, hoping to knock him down. Flint swung his axe with deadly accuracy and timing. A goblin head rolled into the dust, the body crashing to the ground.

"What are you slime doing in Solace?" Tanis asked, meeting the clumsy stab of another goblin skillfully. Their swords crossed and held for a moment, then Tanis shoved the goblin backward. "Do you work for the High Theocrat?"

"Theocrat?" The goblin gurgled with laughter. Swinging its weapon wildly, it ran at Tanis. "That fool? Our Fewmaster works for the—ugh!" The creature impaled itself on Tanis's sword. It groaned, then slid off onto the ground.

Tanis stared at the dead goblin in frustration. "The clumsy idiot! I didn't want to kill it, just find out who hired it."

"You'll find out who hired us, sooner than you'd like!" snarled another goblin, rushing at the distracted half-elf. Tanis turned quickly and disarmed the creature. He kicked it in its stomach and the goblin crumpled over.

Another goblin sprang at Flint before the dwarf had time to recover from his lethal swing. He staggered backward, trying to regain his balance.

Then Tasslehoff's shrill voice rang out. "These scum will fight for anyone, Tanis. Throw them some dog meat once in a while and they're yours forev—"

"Dog meat!" The goblin croaked and turned from Flint in a rage. "How about kender meat, you little squeaker!" The goblin flapped toward the apparently unarmed kender, its purplish red hands grasping for his neck. Tas, without ever losing the innocent, childlike expression on his face, reached into his fleecy vest, whipped out a dagger, and threw it—all in one motion. The goblin

clutched his chest and fell with a groan. There was a sound of
flapping feet as the remaining goblin fled. The battle was over.

Tanis sheathed his sword, grimacing in disgust at the stinking bodies; the smell reminded him of rotting fish. Flint wiped
black goblin blood from his axe blade. Tas stared mournfully at
the body of the goblin he killed. It had fallen facedown, his
dagger buried underneath.

"I'll get it for you," Tanis offered, preparing to roll the body
over.

"No." Tas made a face. "I don't want it back. You can never get
rid of the smell, you know."

Tanis nodded. Flint fastened his axe in its carrier again, and
the three continued on down the path.

The lights of Solace grew brighter as darkness deepened. The
smell of the wood smoke on the chill night air brought thoughts
of food and warmth—and safety. The companions hurried their
steps. They did not speak for a long time, each hearing Flint's
words echo in his mind: Goblins. In Solace.

Finally, however, the irrepressible kender giggled.

"Besides," he said, "that dagger was Flint's!"

RETURN TO THE INN.
A SHOCK. THE OATH IS BROKEN.

2

Nearly everyone in Solace managed to drop into the Inn of the Last Home sometime during the evening hours these days. People felt safer in crowds.

Solace had long been a crossroads for travelers. They came northeast from Haven, the Seeker capital. They came from the elven kingdom of Qualinesti to the south. Sometimes they came from the east, across the barren Plains of Abanasinia. Throughout the civilized world, the Inn of the Last Home was known as a traveler's refuge and center for news. It was to the Inn that the three friends turned their steps.

The huge, convoluted trunk rose through the surrounding trees. Against the shadow of the vallenwood, the colored panes of the Inn's stained-glass windows glittered brightly, and sounds of life drifted down from the windows. Lanterns, hanging from the tree limbs, lit the winding stairway. Though the autumn night was settling chill amid the vallenwoods of Solace, the travelers felt the companionship and memories warm the soul and wash away the aches and sorrows of the road.

The Inn was so crowded on this night that the three were continually forced to stand aside on the stairs to let men, women, and children pass them. Tanis noticed that people glanced at him and his companions with suspicion—not with the welcoming looks they would have given five years ago.

Tanis's face grew grim. This was not the homecoming he had dreamed about. Never in the fifty years he had lived in Solace had he felt such tension. The rumors he had heard about the malignant corruption of the Seekers must be true.

Five years ago, the men calling themselves "seekers" ("we seek the new gods") had been a loose-knit organization of clerics practicing their new religion in the towns of Haven, Solace, and Gateway. These clerics had been misguided, Tanis believed, but at least they had been honest and sincere. In the intervening years, however, the clerics had gained more and more status as their religion flourished. Soon they became concerned not so much with glory in the afterlife as with power on Krynn. They took over the governing of the towns with the people's blessing.

A touch on Tanis's arm interrupted his thoughts. He turned and saw Flint silently pointing below. Looking down, Tanis saw guards marching past, walking in parties of four. Armed to the teeth, they strutted with an air of self-importance.

"At least they're human—not goblin," Tas said.

"That goblin sneered when I mentioned the High Theocrat," Tanis mused. "As if they were working for someone else. I wonder what's going on."

"Maybe our friends will know," Flint said.

"If they're here," Tasslehoff added. "A lot could have happened in five years."

"They'll be here—if they're alive," Flint added in an undertone. "It was a sacred oath we took—to meet again after five years had passed and report what we had found out about the evil spreading in the world. To think we should come home and find evil on our very doorsteps!"

"Hush! Shhh!" Several passersby looked so alarmed at the dwarf's words that Tanis shook his head.

"Better not talk about it here," the half-elf advised.

Reaching the top of the stairs, Tas flung the door open wide. A wave of light, noise, heat, and the familiar smell of Otik's spicy potatoes hit them full in the face. It engulfed them and washed over them soothingly. Otik, standing behind the bar as they always remembered him, hadn't changed, except maybe to grow stouter. The Inn didn't appear to have changed either, except to grow more comfortable.

Tasslehoff, his quick kender eyes sweeping the crowd, gave a yell and pointed across the room. Something else hadn't changed either—the firelight gleaming on a brightly polished, winged dragon helm.

"Who is it?" asked Flint, straining to see.

"Caramon," Tanis replied.

"Then Raistlin'll be here, too," Flint said without a great deal of warmth in his voice.

Tasslehoff was already sliding through the muttering knots of people, his small, lithe body barely noticed by those he passed. Tanis hoped fervently the kender wasn't "acquiring" any objects from the Inn's customers. Not that he stole things—Tasslehoff would have been deeply hurt if anyone had accused him of theft. But the kender had an insatiable curiosity, and various interesting items belonging to other people had a way of falling into Tas's possession. The last thing Tanis wanted tonight was trouble. He made a mental note to have a private word with the kender.

The half-elf and the dwarf made their way through the crowd with less ease than their little friend. Nearly every chair was taken, every table filled. Those who could not find room to sit down were standing, talking in low voices. People looked at Tanis and Flint darkly, suspiciously, or curiously. No one greeted Flint, although there were several who had been long-standing customers of the dwarven metalsmith. The people of Solace had their own problems, and it was apparent that Tanis and Flint were now considered outsiders.

A roar sounded from across the room, from the table where the dragon helm lay reflecting light from the firepit. Tanis's grim face relaxed into a smile as he saw the giant Caramon lift little Tas off the floor in a bear hug.

Flint, wading through a sea of belt buckles, could only imagine the sight as he listened to Caramon's booming voice answering Tasslehoff's piping greeting. "Caramon better look to his purse," Flint grumbled. "Or count his teeth."

The dwarf and the half-elf finally broke through the press of people in front of the long bar. The table where Caramon sat was shoved back against the tree trunk. In fact, it was sitting in an odd position. Tanis wondered why Otik had moved it when everything else remained exactly the same. But the thought was crushed out of him, for it was his turn to receive the big warrior's affectionate greeting. Tanis hastily removed the longbow and quiver of arrows from his back before Caramon hugged them into kindling.

"My friend!" Caramon's eyes were wet. He seemed about to say more but was overcome by emotion. Tanis was also momentarily unable to talk, but this was because he'd had his breath squeezed out of him by Caramon's muscular arms.

"Where's Raistlin?" he asked when he could talk. The twins were never far apart.

"There." Caramon nodded toward the end of the table. Then he frowned. "He's changed," the warrior warned Tanis.

The half-elf looked into a corner formed by an irregularity of the vallenwood tree. The corner was shrouded in shadow, and for a moment he couldn't see anything after the glare of the firelight. Then he saw a slight figure sitting huddled in red robes, even in the heat of the nearby fire. The figure had a hood cast over its face.

Tanis felt a sudden reluctance to speak to the young mage alone, but Tasslehoff had flitted away to find the barmaid and Flint was being lifted off his feet by Caramon. Tanis moved to the end of the table.

"Raistlin?" he said, feeling a strange sense of foreboding.

The robed figure looked up. "Tanis?" the man whispered as he slowly pulled the hood off his head.

The half-elf sucked in his breath and fell back a pace. He stared in horror.

The face that turned toward him from the shadows was a face out of a nightmare. Changed, Caramon had said! Tanis shuddered. "Changed" wasn't the word! The mage's white skin had turned a golden color. It glistened in the firelight with a faintly metallic quality, looking like a gruesome mask. The flesh had melted from the face, leaving the cheekbones outlined in dreadful shadows.

The lips were pulled tight in a dark straight line. But it was the man's eyes that arrested Tanis and held him pinned in their terrible gaze. For the eyes were no longer the eyes of any living human Tanis had ever seen. The black pupils were now the shape of hourglasses! The pale blue irises Tanis remembered now glittered gold!

"I see my appearance startles you," Raistlin whispered. There was a faint suggestion of a smile on his thin lips.

Sitting down across from the young man, Tanis swallowed. "In the name of the true gods, Raistlin—"

Flint plopped into a seat next to Tanis. "I've been hoisted into the air more times today than—*Reorx!*" Flint's eyes widened. "What evil's at work here? Are you cursed?" The dwarf gasped, staring at Raistlin.

Caramon took a seat next to his brother. He picked up his mug of ale and glanced at Raistlin. "Will you tell them, Raist?" he said in a low voice.

"Yes," Raistlin said, drawing the word out into a hiss that made Tanis shiver. The young man spoke in a soft, wheezing voice, barely above a whisper, as if it were all he could do to force the words out of his body. His long, nervous hands, which were the same golden color as his face, toyed absently with uneaten food on a plate before him.

"Do you remember when we parted five years ago?" Raistlin began. "My brother and I planned a journey so secret I could not even tell you, my dear friends, where we were going."

There was a faint note of sarcasm in the gentle voice. Tanis bit his lip. Raistlin had never, in his entire life, had any "dear friends."

"I had been selected by Par-Salian, the head of my order, to take the Test," Raistlin continued.

"The Test!" Tanis repeated, stunned. "But you were too young. What, twenty? The Test is given only to mages who have studied years and years—"

"You can imagine my pride," Raistlin said coldly, irritated at the interruption—"My brother and I traveled to the secret place, the fabled Towers of High Sorcery. And there I passed the Test." The mage's voice sank. "And there I nearly died!"

Caramon choked, obviously in the grip of some strong emotion. "It was awful," the big man began, his voice shaking. "I found him in that horrible place, blood flowing from his mouth, dying! I picked him up and—"

"Enough, brother!" Raistlin's soft voice flicked like a whip. Caramon flinched. Tanis saw the young mage's golden eyes narrow, the thin hands clench. Caramon fell silent and gulped down his ale, glancing nervously at his brother. There was clearly a new strain, a tension between the twins.

Raistlin drew a deep breath and continued. "When I awoke," the mage said, "my skin had turned this color—a mark of my suffering. My body and my health are irretrievably shattered. And my eyes! I see through hourglass pupils and therefore I see time, as it affects all things. Even as I look at you now, Tanis," the mage whispered, "I see you dying, slowly, by inches. And so I see every living thing."

Raistlin's thin, clawlike hand gripped Tanis's arm. The half-elf shivered at the cold touch and started to pull away, but the golden eyes and the cold hand held him fast.

The mage leaned forward, his eyes glowing feverishly. "But I have power now!" he whispered. "Par-Salian told me the day would come when my strength would shape the world! I have power and"—he gestured—"the Staff of Magius."

Tanis looked to see a staff leaning against the vallenwood trunk within easy reach of Raistlin's hand. It was a plain wooden staff. A ball of bright crystal, clutched in a disembodied golden claw carved to resemble the talon of a dragon, gleamed at the top.

"Was it worth it?" Tanis asked quietly.

Raistlin stared at him, then his lips parted in a caricature of a grin. He withdrew his hand from Tanis's arm and folded his arms in the sleeves of his robe. "Of course!" the mage hissed. "Power is what I have long sought—and still seek." He leaned back and his thin figure melted into the dark shadow until all Tanis could see were the golden eyes, glittering in the firelight.

"Ale," said Flint, clearing his throat and licking his lips as if he would wash a bad taste out of his mouth. "Where is that kender? I suppose he stole the barmaid—"

"Here we are," cried Tas's cheerful voice. A tall, young, red-haired girl loomed behind him, carrying a tray of mugs.

Caramon grinned. "Now, Tanis," he boomed, "guess who this is. You, too, Flint. If you win, I'll buy this round."

Glad to take his mind off Raistlin's dark tale, Tanis stared at the laughing girl. Red hair curled around her face, her green eyes danced with fun, freckles were lightly smattered across her nose and cheeks. Tanis seemed to remember the eyes, but beyond that he was blank.

"I give up," he said. "But then, to elves humans seem to change so rapidly that we lose track. I am one hundred and two, yet seem no more than thirty to you. And to me those hundred years seem as thirty. This young woman must have been a child when we left."

"I was fourteen." The girl laughed and set the tray down on the table. "And Caramon used to say I was so ugly my father would have to pay someone to marry me."

"Tika!" Flint slammed his fist on the table. "You're buying, you great oaf!" He pointed at Caramon.

"No fair!" The giant laughed. "She gave you a clue."

"Well, the years have proved him wrong," Tanis said, smiling. "I've traveled many roads and you're one of the prettiest girls I've seen on Krynn."

Tika blushed with pleasure. Then her face darkened. "By the way, Tanis"—she reached in her pocket and drew forth a cylindrical object—"this arrived for you today. Under strange circumstances."

Tanis frowned and reached for the object. It was a small scroll-case made of black, highly polished wood. He slowly removed a thin piece of parchment and unrolled it. His heart thudded painfully at the sight of the bold, black handwriting.

"It's from Kitiara," he said finally, knowing his voice sounded strained and unnatural. "She's not coming."

There was a moment's silence. "That's done it," Flint said. "The circle is broken, the oath denied. Bad luck." He shook his head. "Bad luck."

Knight of Solamnia.
The old man's party.

3

Raistlin leaned forward. He and Caramon exchanged glances as thoughts passed wordlessly between them. It was a rare moment, for only great personal difficulty or danger ever made the twins' close kinship apparent. Kitiara was their older half-sister.

"Kitiara would not break her oath unless another, stronger oath bound her." Raistlin spoke their thoughts aloud.

"What does she say?" Caramon asked.

Tanis hesitated, then licked his dry lips. "Her duties with her new lord keep her busy. She sends her regrets and best wishes to all of us and her love—" Tanis felt his throat constrict. He coughed. "Her love to her brothers and to—" He paused, then rolled up the parchment. "That's all."

"Love to who?" Tasslehoff asked brightly. "Ouch!" He glared at Flint who had trod upon his foot. The kender saw Tanis flush. "Oh," he said, feeling stupid.

"Do you know who she means?" Tanis asked the brothers. "What new lord does she talk about?"

"Who knows with Kitiara?" Raistlin shrugged his thin shoulders. "The last time we saw her was here, in the Inn, five years ago. She was going north with Sturm. We have not heard from her since. As for the new lord, I'd say we now know why she broke her oath to us: she has sworn allegiance to another. She is, after all, a mercenary."

"Yes," Tanis admitted. He slipped the scroll back into its case and looked up at Tika. "You say this arrived under strange circumstances? Tell me."

"A man brought it in, late this morning. At least I think it was a man." Tika shivered. "He was wrapped head to foot in clothing of every description. I couldn't even see his face. His voice was hissinglike and he spoke with a strange accent. 'Deliver this to one Tanis Half-Elven,' he said. I told him you weren't here and hadn't been here for several years. 'He will be,' the man said. Then he left." Tika shrugged. "That's all I can tell you. The old man over there saw him." She gestured to an old man sitting in a chair before the fire. "You might ask him if he noticed anything else."

Tanis turned to look at an old man who was telling stories to a dreamy-eyed child staring into the flames. Flint touched his arm.

"Here comes one who can tell you more," the dwarf said.

"Sturm!" Tanis said warmly, turning toward the door.

Everyone except Raistlin turned. The mage relapsed into the shadows once more.

At the door stood a straight-backed figure dressed in full plate armor and chain mail, the symbol of the Order of the Rose on the breastplate. A great many people in the Inn turned to stare, scowling. The man was a Solamnic knight, and the Knights of Solamnia had fallen into ill-repute up north. Rumors of their corruption had spread even this far south. The few who recognized Sturm as a long-time former resident of Solace shrugged and turned back to their drinking. Those who did not, continued to stare. In these days of peace, it was unusual enough to see a knight in full armor enter the Inn. But it was still more unusual to see a knight in full armor that dated back practically to the Cataclysm!

Sturm received the stares as accolades due his rank. He carefully smoothed his great, thick moustaches, which, being the ages-old symbol of the Knights, were as obsolete as his armor. He bore the trappings of the Solamnic Knights with unquestioned pride, and he had the sword-arm and the skill to defend that pride. Although people in the Inn stared, no one, after one look at the knight's calm, cold eyes, dared snicker or make a derogatory comment.

The knight held the door open for a tall man and a woman heavily cloaked in furs. The woman must have spoken a word of thanks to Sturm, for he bowed to her in a courtly, old-fashioned manner long dead in the modern world.

"Look at that." Caramon shook his head in admiration. "The gallant knight helps the lady fair. I wonder where he dragged up those two?"

"They're barbarians from the Plains," said Tas, standing on a chair, waving his arms to his friend. "That's the dress of the Que-shu tribe."

Apparently the two Plainsmen declined any offer Sturm made, for the knight bowed again and left them. He walked across the crowded Inn with a proud and noble air, such as he might have worn walking forward to be knighted by the king.

Tanis rose to his feet. Sturm came to him first and threw his arms around his friend. Tanis gripped him tightly, feeling the knight's strong, sinewy arms clasp him in affection. Then the two stood back to look at each other for a brief moment.

Sturm hasn't changed, Tanis thought, except that there are more lines around the sad eyes, more gray in the brown hair. The cloak is a little more frayed. There are a few more dents in the ancient armor. But the knight's flowing moustaches—his pride and joy—were as long and sweeping as ever, his shield was polished just as brightly, his brown eyes were just as warm when he saw his friends.

"And you have a beard," Sturm said with amusement.

Then the knight turned to greet Caramon and Flint. Tasslehoff dashed off after more ale, Tika having been called away to serve others in the growing crowd.

"Greetings, Knight," whispered Raistlin from his corner.

Sturm's face grew solemn as he turned to greet the other twin. "Raistlin," he said.

The mage drew back his hood, letting the light fall on his face. Sturm was too well-bred to let his astonishment show beyond a slight exclamation. But his eyes widened. Tanis realized the young mage was getting a cynical pleasure out of seeing his friends' discomfiture.

"Can I get you something, Raistlin?" Tanis asked.

Margaret Weis & Tracy Hickman

"No, thank you," the mage answered, moving into the shadows once again.

"He eats practically nothing," Caramon said in a worried tone. "I think he lives on air."

"Some plants live on air," Tasslehoff stated, returning with Sturm's ale. "I've seen them. They hover up off the ground. Their roots suck food and water out of the atmosphere."

"Really?" Caramon's eyes were wide.

"I don't know who's the greater idiot," said Flint in disgust. "Well, we're all here. What news?"

"All?" Sturm looked at Tanis questioningly.

"Kitiara?"

"Not coming," Tanis replied steadily. "We were hoping perhaps you could tell us something."

"Not I." The knight frowned. "We traveled north together and parted soon after crossing the Sea Narrows into Old Solamnia. She was going to look up relatives of her father, she said. That was the last I saw of her."

"Well, I suppose that's that." Tanis sighed. "What of your relatives, Sturm? Did you find your father?"

Sturm began to talk, but Tanis only half-listened to Sturm's tale of his travels in his ancestral land of Solamnia. Tanis's thoughts were on Kitiara. Of all his friends, she had been the one he most longed to see. After five years of trying to get her dark eyes and crooked smile out of his mind, he discovered that his longing for her grew daily. Wild, impetuous, hot-tempered— the swordswoman was everything Tanis was not. She was also human, and love between human and elf always ended in tragedy. Yet Tanis could no more get Kitiara out of his heart than he could get his human half out of his blood. Wrenching his mind free of memories, he began listening to Sturm.

"I heard rumors. Some say my father is dead. Some say he's alive." His face darkened. "But no one knows where he is."

"Your inheritance?" Caramon asked.

Sturm smiled, a melancholy smile that softened the lines in his proud face. "I wear it," he replied simply. "My armor and my weapon."

Tanis looked down to see that the knight wore a splendid, if old-fashioned, two-handed sword.

Caramon stood up to peer over the table. "That's a beauty," he said. "They don't make them like that these days. My sword broke in a fight with an ogre. Theros Ironfeld put a new blade on it today, but it cost me dearly. So you're a knight now?"

Sturm's smile vanished. Ignoring the question, he caressed the hilt of his sword lovingly. "According to the legend, this sword will break only if I do," he said. "It was all that was left of my father's—"

Suddenly Tas, who hadn't been listening, interrupted. "Who are those people?" the kender asked in a shrill whisper.

Tanis looked up as the two barbarians walked past their table, heading for empty chairs that sat in the shadows of a corner near the firepit. The man was the tallest man Tanis had ever seen. Caramon—at six feet—would come only to this man's shoulder. But Caramon's chest was probably twice as big around, his arms three times as big. Although the man was bundled with the furs barbarian tribesmen live in, it was obvious that he was thin for his great height. His face, though dark-skinned, had the pale cast of one who has been ill or suffered greatly.

His companion—the woman Sturm had bowed to—was so muffled in a fur-trimmed cape and hood that it was difficult to tell much about her. Neither she nor her tall escort glanced at Sturm as they passed. The woman carried a plain staff trimmed with feathers in barbaric fashion. The man carried a well-worn knapsack. They sat down in the chairs, huddled in their cloaks, and talked together in low voices.

"I found them wandering around on the road outside of town," Sturm said. "The woman appeared near exhaustion, the man just as bad. I brought them here, told them they could get food and rest for the night. They are proud people and would have refused my help, I think, but they were lost and tired and"—Sturm lowered his voice—"there are things on the road these days that it is better not to face in the dark."

"We met some of them, asking about a staff," Tanis said grimly. He described their encounter with Fewmaster Toede.

Although Sturm smiled at the description of the battle, he shook his head. "A Seeker guard questioned me about a staff outside," he said. "Blue crystal, wasn't it?"

Caramon nodded and put his hand on his brother's thin arm. "One of the slimy guards stopped us," the warrior said. "They were going to impound Raist's staff, if you'll believe that—'for further investigation,' they said. I rattled my sword at them and they thought better of the notion."

Raistlin moved his arm from his brother's touch, a scornful smile on his lips.

"What would have happened if they had taken your staff?" Tanis asked Raistlin.

The mage looked at him from the shadows of his hood, his golden eyes gleaming. "They would have died horribly," the mage whispered, "and *not* by my brother's sword!"

The half-elf felt chilled. The mage's softly spoken words were more frightening than his brother's bravado. "I wonder what is so important about a blue crystal staff that goblins would kill to get it?" Tanis mused.

"There are rumors of worse to come," Sturm said quietly. His friends moved closer to hear him. "Armies are gathering in the north. Armies of strange creatures, not human. There is talk of war."

"But what? Who?" Tanis asked. "I've heard the same."

"And so have I," Caramon added. "In fact, I heard—"

As the conversation continued, Tasslehoff yawned and turned away. Easily bored, the kender looked around the Inn for some new amusement. His eyes went to the old man, still spinning tales for the child by the fire. The old man had a larger audience now—the two barbarians were listening, Tas noted. Then his jaw dropped.

The woman had thrown her hood back and the firelight shone on her face and hair. The kender stared in admiration. The woman's face was like the face of a marble statue—classic, pure, cold.

But it was her hair that captured the kender's attention. Tas had never before seen such hair, especially on the Plainsmen, who were usually dark-haired and dark-skinned. No jeweler spinning molten strands of silver and gold could have created the effect of this woman's silver-gold hair shining in the firelight.

One other person listened to the old man. This was a man dressed in the rich brown and golden robes of a Seeker. He sat at a small round table, drinking mulled wine. Several mugs stood empty before him and, even as the kender watched, he called sourly for another.

"That's Hederick," Tika whispered as she passed the companions' table. "The High Theocrat."

The man called out again, glaring at Tika. She bustled quickly over to help him. He snarled at her, mentioning poor service. She seemed to start to answer sharply, then bit her lip and kept silent.

The old man came to an end of his tale. The boy sighed. "Are all your stories of the ancient gods true, Old One?" he asked curiously.

Tasslehoff saw Hederick frown. The kender hoped he wouldn't bother the old man. Tas touched Tanis's arm to catch his attention, nodding his head toward the Seeker with a look that meant there might be trouble.

The friends turned. All were immediately overwhelmed by the beauty of the Plainswoman. They stared in silence.

The old man's voice carried clearly over the drone of the other conversation in the common room. "Indeed, my stories are true, child." The old man looked directly at the woman and her tall escort. "Ask these two. They carry such stories in their hearts."

"Do you?" The boy turned to the woman eagerly. "Can you tell me a story?"

The woman shrank back into the shadows, her face filled with alarm as she noticed Tanis and his friends staring at her. The man drew near her protectively, his hand reaching for his weapon. He glowered at the group, especially the heavily armed warrior, Caramon.

"Nervous fool," Caramon commented, his hand straying to his own sword.

"I can understand why," Sturm said. "Guarding such a treasure. He *is* her bodyguard, by the way. I gathered from their conversation that she's some kind of royal person in their tribe. Though I imagine from the looks they exchanged that their relationship goes a bit deeper than that."

The woman raised her hand in a gesture of protest. "I'm sorry." The friends had to strain to hear her low voice. "I am not a teller of tales. I have not the art." She spoke the Common tongue, her accent thick.

The child's eager face filled with disappointment. The old man patted him on the back, then looked directly into the woman's eyes. "You may not be a teller of tales," he said pleasantly, "but you are a singer of songs, aren't you, Chieftain's Daughter? Sing the child your song, Goldmoon. You know the one."

From out of nowhere, apparently, a lute appeared in the old man's hands. He gave it to the woman who stared at him in fear and astonishment.

"How . . . do you know me, sir?" she asked.

"That is not important." The old man smiled gently. "Sing for us, Chieftain's Daughter."

The woman took the lute with hands that trembled visibly. Her companion seemed to make a whispered protest, but she did not hear him. Her eyes were held fast by the glittering black eyes of the old man. Slowly, as if in a trance, she began to strum the lute. As the melancholy chords drifted through the common room, conversations ceased. Soon, everyone was watching her, but she did not notice. Goldmoon sang for the old man alone.

The grasslands are endless,
And summer sings on,
And Goldmoon the princess
Loves a poor man's son.
Her father the chieftain
Makes long roads between them:
The grasslands are endless, and summer sings on.

The grasslands are waving,
The sky's rim is gray,
The chieftain sends Riverwind
East and away,

To search for strong magic
At the lip of the morning,
The grasslands are waving, the sky's rim is gray.

O Riverwind, where have you gone?
O Riverwind, autumn comes on.
I sit by the river
And look to the sunrise,
But the sun rises over the mountains alone.

The grasslands are fading,
The summer wind dies,
He comes back, the darkness
Of stones in his eyes.

He carries a blue staff
As bright as a glacier:
The grasslands are fading, the summer wind dies.

The grasslands are fragile,
As yellow as flame,
The chieftain makes mockery
Of Riverwind's claim.

He orders the people
To stone the young warrior:
The grasslands are fragile, as yellow as flame.

The grassland has faded,
And autumn is here.
The girl joins her lover,
The stones whistle near,

The staff flares in blue light
And both of them vanish:
The grasslands are faded, and autumn is here.

There was heavy silence in the room as her hand struck the
final chord. Taking a deep breath, she handed the lute back to
the old man and withdrew into the shadows once more.

"Thank you, my dear," the old man said, smiling.

"Now can I have a story?" the little boy asked wistfully.

"Of course," the old man answered and settled back in his chair. "Once upon a time, the great god, Paladine—"

"Paladine?" the child interrupted. "I've never heard of a god named Paladine."

A snorting sound came from the High Theocrat sitting at the nearby table. Tanis looked at Hederick, whose face was flushed and scowling. The old man appeared not to notice.

"Paladine is one of the ancient gods, child. No one has worshiped him for a long time."

"Why did he leave?" the little boy asked.

"He did not leave us," the old man answered, and his smile grew sad. "Men left him after the dark days of the Cataclysm. They blamed the destruction of the world on the gods, instead of on themselves, as they should have done. Have you ever heard the 'Canticle of the Dragon'?"

"Oh, yes," the boy said eagerly. "I love stories about dragons, though papa says dragons never existed. I believe in them, though. I hope to see one someday!"

The old man's face seemed to age and grow sorrowful. He stroked the young boy's hair. "Be careful what you wish, my child," he said softly. Then he fell silent.

"The story—" the boy prompted.

"Oh, yes. Well, once upon a time Paladine heard the prayer of a very great knight, Huma—"

"Huma from the Canticle?"

"Yes, that's the one. Huma became lost in the forest. He wandered and wandered until he despaired because he thought he would never see his homeland again. He prayed to Paladine for help, and there suddenly appeared before him a white stag."

"Did Huma shoot it?" the boy asked.

"He started to, but his heart failed him. He could not shoot an animal so magnificent. The stag bounded away. Then it stopped and looked back at him, as if waiting. Huma began to follow it. Day and night, he followed the stag until it led him to his homeland. He offered thanks to the god, Paladine."

"Blasphemy!" snarled a voice loudly. A chair crashed back.

Tanis put down his mug of ale, looking up. Everyone at the table stopped drinking to watch the drunken Theocrat.

"Blasphemy!" Hederick, weaving unsteadily on his feet, pointed at the old man. "Heretic! Corrupting our youth! I'll bring you before the counshel, old man." The Seeker fell back a step, then staggered forward again. He looked around the room with a pompous air. "Call the guardsh!" He made a grandiose gesture. "Have them arresht thish man and thish woman for singing lewd songsh. Obviously a witch! I'll confishcate thish staff!"

The Seeker lurched across the floor to the barbarian woman, who was staring at him in disgust. He reached clumsily for her staff.

"No," the woman called Goldmoon spoke coolly. "That is mine. You cannot take it."

"Witch!" the Seeker sneered. "I am the High Theocrat! I take what I want."

He started to make another grab for the staff. The woman's tall companion rose to his feet. "The Chieftain's Daughter says you will not take it," the man said harshly. He shoved the Seeker backward.

The tall man's push was not rough, but it knocked the drunken Theocrat completely off balance. His arms flailing wildly, he tried to catch himself. He lurched forward, too far, tripped over his official robes, and fell headfirst into the roaring fire.

There was a whoosh and a flare of light, then a sickening smell of burning flesh. The Theocrat's scream tore through the stunned silence as the crazed man leaped to his feet and started whirling around in a frenzy. He had become a living torch!

Tanis and the others sat, unable to move, paralyzed with the shock of the incident. Only Tasslehoff had wits enough to run forward, anxious to try and help the man. But the Theocrat was screaming and waving his arms, fanning the flames that were consuming his clothes and his body. There seemed no way that the little kender could help him.

"Here!" The old man grabbed the barbarian's feather-decorated staff and handed it to the kender. "Knock him down. Then we can smother the fire."

Tasslehoff took the staff. He swung it, using all his strength, and hit the Theocrat squarely in the chest. The man fell to the ground. There was a gasp from the crowd. Tasslehoff himself stood, open-mouthed, the staff clutched in his hand, staring down at the amazing sight at his feet.

The flames had died instantly. The man's robes were whole, undamaged. His skin was pink and healthy. He sat up, a look of fear and awe on his face. He stared down at his hands and his robes. There was not a mark on his skin. There was not the smallest cinder smoking on his robes.

"It healed him!" the old man proclaimed loudly. "The staff! Look at the staff!"

Tasslehoff's eyes went to the staff in his hands. It was made of blue crystal and was glowing with a bright blue light!

The old man began shouting. "Call the guards! Arrest the kender! Arrest the barbarians! Arrest their friends! I saw them come in with this knight." He pointed at Sturm.

"What?" Tanis leaped up. "Are you crazy, old man?"

"Call the guards!" The word spread. "Did you see—? The blue crystal staff? We've found it. Now they'll leave us alone. Call the guards!"

The Theocrat staggered to his feet, his face pale, blotched with red. The barbarian woman and her companion stood up, fear and alarm in their faces.

"Foul witch!" Hederick's voice shook with rage. "You have cured me with evil! Even as I burn to purify my flesh, you will burn to purify your soul!" With that, the Seeker reached out, and before anyone could stop him, he plunged his hand back into the flames! He gagged with the pain but did not cry out. Then, clutching his charred and blackened hand, he turned and staggered off through the murmuring crowd, a wild look of satisfaction on his pain-twisted face.

"You've got to get out of here!" Tika came running over to Tanis, her breath coming in gasps. "The whole town's been hunting for that staff! Those hooded men told the Theocrat they'd destroy Solace if they caught someone harboring the staff. The townspeople will turn you over to the guards!"

"But it's not our staff!" Tanis protested. He glared at the old man and saw him settle back into his chair, a pleased smile on his face. The old man grinned at Tanis and winked.

"Do you think they'll believe you!" Tika wrung her hands. "Look!"

Tanis looked around. People were glaring at them balefully. Some took a firm grip on their mugs. Others eased their hands onto the hilts of their swords. Shouts from down below drew his eyes back to his friends.

"The guards are coming!" exclaimed Tika.

Tanis rose. "We'll have to go out through the kitchen."

"Yes!" She nodded. "They won't look back there yet. But hurry. It won't take them long to surround the place."

Years of being apart had not affected the companions' ability to react as a team to threat of danger. Caramon had pulled on his shining helm, drawn his sword, shouldered his pack, and was helping his brother to his feet. Raistlin, his staff in his hand, was moving around the table. Flint had hold of his battle-axe and was frowning darkly at the onlookers, who seemed hesitant about rushing to attack such well-armed men. Only Sturm sat, calmly drinking his ale.

"Sturm!" Tanis said urgently. "Come on! We've got to get out of here!"

"Run?" The knight appeared astonished. "From this rabble?"

"Yes." Tanis paused; the knight's code of honor forbade running from danger. He had to convince him. "That man is a religious fanatic, Sturm. He'll probably burn us at the stake! And"—a sudden thought rescued him—"there is a lady to protect."

"The lady, of course." Sturm stood up at once and walked over to the woman. "Madam, your servant." He bowed; the courtly knight would not be hurried. "It seems we are all in this together. Your staff has placed us in considerable danger—you most of all. We are familiar with the area around here: we grew up here. You, I know, are strangers. We would be honored to accompany you and your gallant friend and guard your lives."

"Come on!" Tika urged, tugging on Tanis's arm. Caramon and Raistlin were already at the kitchen door.

"Get the kender," Tanis told her.

Tasslehoff stood, rooted to the floor, staring at the staff. It was rapidly fading back to its nondescript brown color. Tika grabbed Tas by his topknot and pulled him toward the kitchen. The kender shrieked, dropping the staff.

Goldmoon swiftly picked it up, clutching it close to her. Although frightened, her eyes were clear and steady as she looked at Sturm and Tanis; she was apparently thinking rapidly. Her companion said a harsh word in their language. She shook her head. He frowned and made a slashing motion with his hand. She snapped a quick reply and he fell silent, his face dark.

"We will go with you," Goldmoon said to Sturm in the Common tongue. "Thank you for the offer."

"This way!" Tanis herded them out through the swinging kitchen doors, following Tika and Tas. He glanced behind him and saw some of the crowd move forward, but in no great hurry.

The cook stared at them as they ran through the kitchen. Caramon and Raistlin were already at the exit, which was nothing more than a hole cut in the floor. A rope hung from a sturdy limb above the hole and dropped forty feet to the ground.

"Ah!" exclaimed Tas, laughing. "Here the ale comes up and the garbage goes down." He swung out onto the rope and shinnied down easily.

"I'm sorry about this," Tika apologized to Goldmoon, "but it is the only way out of here."

"I can climb down a rope." Then the woman smiled and added, "Though I admit it has been many years."

She handed her staff to her companion and grasped the stout rope. She began to descend, moving skillfully hand over hand. When she reached the bottom, her companion tossed the staff down, swung on the rope, and dropped through the hole.

"How are you going to get down, Raist?" Caramon asked, his face lined with concern. "I can carry you on my back—"

Raistlin's eyes flashed with an anger that startled Tanis. "I can get down myself!" the mage hissed. Before anyone could stop him, he stepped to the edge of the hole and leaped out into the air. Everyone gasped and peered down, expecting to see Raistlin splattered all over the ground. Instead, they saw the young mage gently floating down, his robes fluttering around him. The crystal on his staff glowed brightly.

"He shivers my skin!" Flint growled to Tanis.

"Hurry!" Tanis shoved the dwarf forward. Flint grabbed hold of the rope. Caramon followed, the big man's weight causing the limb the rope was tied around to creak.

"I will go last," Sturm said, his sword drawn.

"Very well." Tanis knew it was useless to argue. He slung the longbow and quiver of arrows over his shoulder, grabbed the rope, and started down. Suddenly his hands slipped. He slid down the rope, unable to stop it tearing the skin off his palms. He landed on the ground and looked, wincing, at his hands. His palms were raw and bleeding. But there was no time to think about them. Glancing up, he watched as Sturm descended.

Tika's face appeared in the opening. "Go to my house!" she mouthed, pointing through the trees. Then she was gone.

"I know the way," Tasslehoff said, his eyes glowing with excitement. "Follow me."

They hurried off after the kender, hearing the sounds of the guards climbing the stairway into the Inn. Tanis, unused to walking on the ground in Solace, was soon lost. Above him he could see the bridge-walks, the street lamps gleaming among the tree leaves. He was completely disoriented, but Tas kept pushing forward confidently, weaving in and out among the huge trunks of the vallenwood trees. The sounds of the commotion at the Inn faded.

"We'll hide at Tika's for the night," Tanis whispered to Sturm as they plunged through the underbrush. "Just in case someone recognized us and decides to search our homes. Everyone will have forgotten about this by morning. We'll take the Plainsmen to my house and let them rest a few days. Then we can send the barbarians on to Haven where the Council of High Seekers can talk with them. I think I might even go along—I'm curious about this staff."

Sturm nodded. Then he looked at Tanis and smiled his rare, melancholy smile. "Welcome home," the knight said.

"Same to you." The half-elf grinned.

They both came to a sudden halt, bumping into Caramon in the dark.

"We're here, I think," Caramon said.

In the light of the street lamps that hung in the tree limbs, they could see Tasslehoff climbing tree branches like a gully dwarf. The rest followed more slowly, Caramon assisting his brother. Tanis, gritting his teeth from the pain in his hands, climbed up slowly through the rapidly thinning autumn foliage. Tas pulled himself up over the porch railing with the skill of a burglar. The kender slipped over to the door and peered up and down the bridge-walk. Seeing no one on it, he motioned to the others. Then he studied the lock and smiled to himself in satisfaction. The kender slid something out of one of his pouches. Within seconds, the door of Tika's house swung open.

"Come in," he said, playing host.

They crowded inside the little house, the tall barbarian being forced to duck his head to avoid hitting the ceiling. Tas pulled the curtains shut. Sturm found a chair for the lady, and the tall barbarian went to stand behind her. Raistlin stirred up the fire.

"Keep watch," Tanis said. Caramon nodded. The warrior had already posted himself at a window, staring out into the darkness. The light from a street lamp gleamed through the curtains into the room, casting dark shadows on the walls. For long moments no one spoke, each staring at the others.

Tanis sat down. His eyes turned to the woman. "The blue crystal staff," he said quietly. "It healed that man. How?"

"I do not know." She faltered. "I—I haven't had it very long."

Tanis looked down at his hands. They were bleeding from where the rope had peeled off his skin. He held them out to her. Slowly, her face pale, the woman touched him with the staff. It began to glow blue. Tanis felt a slight shock tingle through his body. Even as he watched, the blood on his palms vanished, the skin became smooth and unscarred, the pain eased and soon left him completely.

"True healing!" he said in awe.

THE OPEN DOOR.
FLIGHT INTO DARKNESS.

4

Raistlin sat down on the hearth, rubbing his thin hands in the warmth of the small fire. His golden eyes seemed brighter than the flames as he stared intently at the blue crystal staff resting across the woman's lap.

"What do you think?" asked Tanis.

"If she's a charlatan, she's a good one," Raistlin commented thoughtfully.

"Worm! You dare to call the Chieftain's Daughter charlatan!" The tall barbarian stepped toward Raistlin, his dark brows contracted in a vicious scowl. Caramon made a low, rumbling sound in his throat and moved from the window to stand behind his brother.

"Riverwind . . ." The woman laid her hand on the man's arm as he drew near her chair. "Please. He meant no harm. It is right that they do not trust us. They do not know us."

"And we do not know them," the man growled.

"If I might examine it?" Raistlin said.

Goldmoon nodded and held out the staff. The mage stretched out his long, bony arm, his thin hands grasping for it eagerly. As Raistlin touched the staff, however, there was a bright flash of blue light and a crackling sound. The mage jerked his hand back, crying out in pain and shock. Caramon jumped forward, but his brother stopped him.

"No, Caramon," Raistlin whispered hoarsely, wringing his injured hand. "The lady had nothing to do with that."

The woman, indeed, was staring at the staff in amazement.

"What is it then?" Tanis asked in exasperation. "A staff that heals and injures at the same time?"

"It merely knows its own." Raistlin licked his lips, his eyes glittering. "Watch. Caramon, take the staff."

"Not me!" The warrior drew back as if from a snake.

"Take the staff!" Raistlin demanded.

Reluctantly, Caramon stretched out a trembling hand. His arm twitched as his fingers came closer and closer. Closing his eyes and gritting his teeth in anticipation of pain, he touched the staff. Nothing happened.

Caramon opened his eyes wide, startled. He gripped the staff, lifted it in his huge hand, and grinned.

"See there." Raistlin gestured like an illusionist showing off a trick to the crowd. "Only those of simple goodness, pure in heart"—his sarcasm was biting—"may touch the staff. It is truly a sacred staff of healing, blessed by some god. It is not magic. No magic objects that I have ever heard about have healing powers."

"Hush!" ordered Tasslehoff, who had taken Caramon's place by the window. "The Theocrat's guards!" he warned softly.

No one spoke. Now they could all hear goblin footsteps flapping on the bridge-walks that ran among the branches of the vallenwood trees.

"They're conducting a house-to-house search!" Tanis whispered incredulously, listening to fists banging on a neighboring door.

"The Seekers demand right of entry!" croaked a voice. There was a pause, then the same voice said, "No one home, do we kick the door in?"

"Naw," said another voice. "We'd better just report to the Theocrat, let him kick the door down. Now if it was unlocked, that'd be different, we're allowed to enter then."

Tanis looked at the door opposite him. He felt the hair rise on the back of his neck. He could have sworn they had shut and bolted the door . . . now it stood slightly open!

"The door!" he whispered. "Caramon—"

But the warrior had already moved over to stand behind the door, his back to the wall, his giant hands flexing.

The footsteps flapped to a stop outside. "The Seekers demand right of entry." The goblins began to bang on the door, then stopped in surprise as it swung open.

"This place is empty," said one. "Let's move on."

"You got no imagination, Grum," said the other. "Here's our chance to pick up a few pieces of silver."

A goblin head appeared around the open door. Its eyes focused on Raistlin, sitting calmly, his staff on his shoulder. The goblin grunted in alarm, then began to laugh.

"Oh, ho! Look what we've found! A staff!" The goblin's eyes gleamed. It took a step toward Raistlin, its partner crowding close behind. "Hand me that staff!"

"Certainly," the mage whispered. He held his own staff forth. "*Shirak*," he said. The crystal ball flared into light. The goblins shrieked and shut their eyes, fumbling for their swords. At that moment, Caramon jumped from behind the door, grabbed the goblins around their necks, and swept their heads together with a sickening thud. The goblin bodies crumpled into a stinking heap.

"Dead?" asked Tanis as Caramon bent over them, examining them by the light of Raistlin's staff.

"I'm afraid so." The big man sighed. "I hit them too hard."

"Well, that's torn it," Tanis said grimly. "We've murdered two more of the Theocrat's guards. He'll have the town up in arms. Now we can't just lie low for a few days—we've got to get out of here! And you two"—he turned to the barbarians—"had better come with us."

"Wherever we're going," muttered Flint irritably.

"Where were you headed?" Tanis asked Riverwind.

"We were traveling to Haven," the barbarian answered reluctantly.

"There are wise men there," Goldmoon said. "We hoped they could tell us about this staff. You see, the song I sang—it was true: the staff saved our lives—"

"You'll have to tell us later," Tanis interrupted. "When these guards don't report back, every goblin in Solace will be swarming up the trees. Raistlin, put out that light."

The mage spoke another word, *"Dumak."* The crystal glimmered, then the light died.

"What'll we do with the bodies?" Caramon asked, nudging a dead goblin with his booted foot. "And what about Tika? Won't she get into trouble?"

"Leave the bodies." Tanis's mind was working quickly. "And hack up the door. Sturm, knock over a few tables. We'll make it look as if we broke in here and got into a fight with these fellows. That way, Tika shouldn't be in too much trouble. She's a smart girl—she'll manage."

"We'll need food," Tasslehoff stated. He ran into the kitchen and began rummaging through the shelves, stuffing loaves of bread and anything else that looked edible into his pouches. He tossed Flint a full skin of wine. Sturm overturned a few chairs. Caramon arranged the bodies to make it look as if they had died in a ferocious battle. The Plainsmen stood in front of the dying fire, looking at Tanis uncertainly.

"Well?" said Sturm. "Now what? Where are we going?"

Tanis hesitated, running over the options in his mind. The Plainsmen had come from the east and—if their story was true and their tribe *had* been trying to kill them—they wouldn't want to go back that way. The group could travel south, into the elven kingdom, but Tanis felt a strange reluctance to go back to his homelands. He knew, too, that the elves would not be pleased to see these strangers enter their hidden city.

"We will travel north," he said finally. "We will escort these two until we come to the crossroads, then we can decide what to do from there. They can go on southwest to Haven, if they wish. I plan to travel farther north and see if the rumors about armies gathering are true."

"And perhaps run into Kitiara," Raistlin whispered slyly.

Tanis flushed. "Is that plan all right?" he asked, looking around.

"Though not the eldest among us, Tanis, you are the wisest," Sturm said. "We follow you—as always."

Caramon nodded. Raistlin was already heading for the door. Flint shouldered the wine skin, grumbling.

Tanis felt a gentle hand touch his arm. He turned and looked down into the clear blue eyes of the beautiful barbarian.

"We are grateful," Goldmoon said slowly, as if unused to expressing appreciation. "You risk your lives for us, and we are strangers."

Tanis smiled and clasped her hand. "I am Tanis. The brothers are Caramon and Raistlin. The knight is Sturm Brightblade. Flint Fireforge carries the wine and Tasslehoff Burrfoot is our clever locksmith. You are Goldmoon and he is Riverwind. There—we are strangers no longer."

Goldmoon smiled wearily. She patted Tanis's arm, then started out the door, leaning on the staff that once again seemed plain and nondescript. Tanis watched her, then glanced up to see Riverwind staring at him, the barbarian's dark face an impenetrable mask.

"Well," Tanis amended silently, "*some* of us are no longer strangers."

Soon everyone had gone, Tas leading the way. Tanis stood alone for a moment in the wrecked living room, staring at the bodies of the goblins. This was supposed to have been a peaceful homecoming after bitter years of solitary travel. He thought of his comfortable house. He thought of all the things he had planned to do—things he had planned to do together with Kitiara. He thought of long winter nights, with storytelling around the fire at the Inn, then returning home, laughing together beneath the fur blankets, sleeping through the snow-covered mornings.

Tanis kicked at the smoldering coals, scattering them. Kitiara had not come back. Goblins had invaded his quiet town. He was fleeing into the night to escape a bunch of religious fanatics, with every likelihood he could never return.

Elves do not notice the passage of time. They live for hundreds of years. For them, the seasons pass like brief rain showers. But Tanis was half human. He sensed change coming, felt the disquieting restlessness men feel before a thunderstorm.

He sighed and shook his head. Then he went out the shattered door, leaving it swinging crazily on one hinge.

Farewell to Flint. Arrows fly.
Message in the stars.

5

Tanis swung over the porch and dropped down through the tree limbs to the ground below. The others waited, huddled in the darkness, keeping out of the light cast by street lamps swinging in the branches above them. A chill wind had sprung up, blowing out of the north. Tanis glanced behind him and saw other lights, lights of the search parties. He pulled his hood over his head and hurried forward.

"Wind's switched," he said. "There'll be rain by morning." He looked around at the small group, seeing them in the eerie, wildly dancing light of the wind-tossed lamps. Goldmoon's face was scarred with weariness. Riverwind's was a stoic mask of strength, but his shoulders sagged. Raistlin, shivering, leaned against a tree, wheezing for breath.

Tanis hunched his shoulders against the wind. "We've got to find shelter," he said. "Some place to rest."

"Tanis—" Tas tugged on the half-elf's cloak. "We could go by boat. Crystalmir Lake's only a short way. There're caves on the other side, and it will cut walking time tomorrow."

"That's a good idea, Tas, but we don't have a boat."

"No problem." The kender grinned. His small face and sharply pointed ears made him look particularly impish in the eerie light. Tas is enjoying all of this immensely, Tanis realized. He felt like shaking the kender, lecturing him sternly on how much danger they were in. But the half-elf knew it was useless: kender are totally immune to fear.

"The boat's a good idea," Tanis repeated, after a moment's thought. "You guide. And don't tell Flint," he added. "I'll take care of that."

"Right!" Tas giggled, then slipped back to the others. "Follow me," he called out softly, and he started off once more. Flint, grumbling into his beard, stumped after the kender. Goldmoon followed the dwarf. Riverwind cast a quick, penetrating glance around at everyone in the group, then fell into step behind her.

"I don't think he trusts us," Caramon observed.

"Would you?" Tanis asked, glancing at the big man. Caramon's dragon helm glinted in the flickering lights; his ring-mail armor was visible whenever the wind blew his cape back. A longsword clanked against his thick thighs, a short bow and a quiver of arrows were slung over his shoulder, a dagger protruded from his belt. His shield was battered and dented from many fights. The giant was ready for anything.

Tanis looked over at Sturm, who proudly wore the coat of arms of a knighthood that had fallen into disgrace three hundred years before. Although Sturm was only four years older than Caramon, the knight's strict, disciplined life, hardships brought on by poverty, and his melancholy search for his beloved father had aged the knight beyond his years. Only twenty-nine, he looked forty.

Tanis thought, I don't think I'd trust us either.

"What's the plan?" Sturm asked.

"We're going by boat," Tanis answered.

"Oh, ho!" Caramon chuckled. "Told Flint yet?"

"No. Leave that to me."

"Where are we getting the boat?" Sturm asked suspiciously.

"You'll be happier not knowing," the half-elf said.

The knight frowned. His eyes followed the kender, who was far ahead of them, flitting from one shadow to another. "I don't like this, Tanis. First we're murderers, now we're about to become thieves."

"I don't consider myself a murderer." Caramon snorted. "Goblins don't count."

Tanis saw the knight glare at Caramon. "I don't like any of this, Sturm," he said hastily, hoping to avoid an argument. "But it's a matter of necessity. Look at the Plainsmen—pride's the only thing keeping them on their feet. Look at Raistlin . . ." Their eyes went to the mage, who was shuffling through the dry leaves, keeping always in the shadows. He leaned heavily upon his staff. Occasionally, a dry cough racked his frail body.

Caramon's face darkened. "Tanis is right," he said softly. "Raist can't take much more of this. I must go to him." Leaving the knight and the half-elf, he hurried forward to catch up with the robed, bent figure of his twin.

"Let me help you, Raist," they heard Caramon whisper.

Raistlin shook his hooded head and flinched away from his brother's touch. Caramon shrugged and dropped his arm. But the big warrior stayed close to his frail brother, ready to help him if necessary.

"Why does he put up with that?" Tanis asked softly.

"Family. Ties of blood." Sturm sounded wistful. He seemed about to say more, then his eyes went to Tanis's elven face with its growth of human hair and he fell silent. Tanis saw the look, knew what the knight was thinking. Family, ties of blood—they were things the orphaned half-elf wouldn't know about.

"Come on," Tanis said abruptly. "We're dropping behind."

They soon left the vallenwood trees of Solace and entered the pine forest surrounding Crystalmir Lake. Tanis could faintly hear muffled shouts far behind them. "They've found the bodies," he guessed. Sturm nodded gloomily. Suddenly Tasslehoff seemed to materialize out of the darkness right beneath the half-elf's nose.

"The trail runs a little over a mile to the lake," Tas said. "I'll meet you where it comes out." He gestured vaguely, then disappeared before Tanis could say a word. The half-elf looked back at Solace. There seemed to be more lights, and they were moving in this direction. The roads were probably already blocked.

"Where's the kender?" Flint grumbled as they plunged through the forest.

"Tas is meeting us at the lake," Tanis replied.

"Lake?" Flint's eyes grew wide in alarm. "What lake?"

"There's only one lake around here, Flint," Tanis said, trying hard not to smile at Sturm. "Come on. We'd better keep going." His elvensight showed him the broad red outline of Caramon and the slighter red shape of his brother disappearing into the thick woods ahead.

"I thought we were just going to lie low in the woods for a while." Flint shoved his way past Sturm to complain to Tanis.

"We're going by boat." Tanis moved forward.

"Nope!" Flint growled. "I'm not getting in any boat!"

"That accident happened ten years ago!" Tanis said, exasperated. "Look, I'll make Caramon sit still."

"Absolutely not!" the dwarf said flatly. "No boats. I took a vow."

"Tanis," Sturm's voice whispered behind him. "Lights."

"Blast!" The half-elf stopped and turned. He had to wait a moment before catching sight of lights glittering through the trees. The search had spread beyond Solace. He hurried to catch up with Caramon, Raistlin, and the Plainsmen.

"Lights!" he called out in a piercing whisper. Caramon looked back and swore. Riverwind raised his hand in acknowledgment. "I'm afraid we're going to have to move faster, Caramon—" Tanis began.

"We'll make it," the big man said, unperturbed. He was supporting his brother now, his arm around Raistlin's thin body, practically carrying him. Raistlin coughed softly, but he was moving. Sturm caught up with Tanis. As they forced their way through the brush, they could hear Flint, puffing along behind, muttering angrily to himself.

"He won't come, Tanis," Sturm said. "Flint's been in mortal fear of boats ever since Caramon almost accidentally drowned him that time. You weren't there. You didn't see him after we hauled him out."

"He'll come," Tanis said, breathing hard. "He can't let us youngsters go off into danger without him."

Sturm shook his head, unconvinced.

Tanis looked back again. He saw no lights, but he knew they were too deep in the forest now to see them. Fewmaster Toede may not have impressed anybody with his brains, but it wouldn't take much intelligence to figure out that the group might take to the water. Tanis stopped abruptly to keep from bumping into someone. "What is it?" he whispered.

"We're here," Caramon answered. Tanis breathed a sigh of relief as he stared out across the dark expanse of Crystalmir Lake. The wind whipped the water into frothy whitecaps.

"Where's Tas?" He kept his voice low.

"There, I think." Caramon pointed at a dark object floating close to shore. Tanis could barely make out the warm red outline of the kender sitting in a large boat.

The stars gleamed with icy brightness in the blue-black sky. The red moon, Lunitari, was rising like a bloody fingernail from the water. Its partner in the night sky, Solinari, had already risen, marking the lake with molten silver.

"What wonderful targets we're going to make!" Sturm said irritably.

Tanis could see Tasslehoff turning this way and that, searching for them. The half-elf reached down, fumbling for a rock in the darkness. Finding one, he lobbed it into the water. It splashed just a few yards ahead of the boat. Tas, reacting to Tanis's signal, propelled the boat to shore.

"You're going to put all of us in one boat!" Flint said in horror. "You're mad, half-elf!"

"It's a big boat," Tanis said.

"No! I won't go. If it were one of the legendary white-winged boats of Tarsis, I still wouldn't go! I'd rather take my chances with the Theocrat!"

Tanis ignored the fuming dwarf and motioned to Sturm. "Get everyone loaded up. We'll be along in a moment."

"Don't take too long," Sturm warned. "Listen."

"I can hear," Tanis said grimly. "Go on."

"What are those sounds?" Goldmoon asked the knight as he came up to her.

"Goblin search parties," Sturm answered. "Those whistles keep them in contact when they're separated. They're moving into the woods now."

Goldmoon nodded in understanding. She spoke a few words to Riverwind in their own language, apparently continuing a conversation Sturm had interrupted. The big Plainsman frowned and gestured back toward the forest with his hand.

He's trying to convince her to split with us, Sturm realized. Maybe he's got enough woodslore to hide from goblin search parties for days, but I doubt it.

"*Riverwind, gue-lando!*" Goldmoon said sharply. Sturm saw Riverwind scowl in anger. Without a word, he turned and stalked toward the boat. Goldmoon sighed and looked after him, deep sorrow in her face.

"Can I do anything to help, lady?" Sturm asked gently.

"No," she replied. Then she said sadly, as if to herself, "He rules my heart, but I am his ruler. Once, when we were young, we thought we could forget that. But I have been 'Chieftain's Daughter' too long."

"Why doesn't he trust us?" Sturm asked.

"He has all the prejudices of our people," Goldmoon replied. "The Plainsmen do not trust those who are not human." She glanced back. "Tanis cannot hide his elven blood beneath a beard. Then there are the dwarf, the kender."

"And what of you, lady?" Sturm asked. "Why do you trust us? Don't you have these same prejudices?"

Goldmoon turned to face him. He could see her eyes, dark and shimmering as the lake behind her. "When I was a girl," she said in her deep, low voice, "I was a princess of my people. I was a priestess. They worshiped me as a goddess. I believed in it. I adored it. Then something happened—" She fell silent, her eyes filled with memories.

"What was that?" Sturm prompted softly.

"I fell in love with a shepherd," Goldmoon answered, looking at Riverwind. She sighed and walked toward the boat.

Sturm watched Riverwind wade into the water to drag the boat closer to shore as Raistlin and Caramon reached the water's edge. Raistlin clutched his robes around him, shivering.

"I can't get my feet wet," he whispered hoarsely. Caramon did not reply. He simply put his huge arms around his brother, lifted him as easily as he would have lifted a child, and set Raistlin in the boat. The mage huddled in the aft part of the boat, not saying a word of thanks.

"I'll hold her steady," Caramon told Riverwind. "You get in." Riverwind hesitated a moment, then climbed quickly over the side. Caramon helped Goldmoon into the boat. Riverwind caught hold of her and steadied her as the boat rocked gently. The Plainsmen moved to sit in the stern, behind Tasslehoff.

Caramon turned to Sturm as the knight drew near. "What's happening back there?"

"Flint says he'll burn before he'll get in a boat—at least then he'll die warm instead of wet and cold."

"I'll go up and haul him down here," Caramon said.

"You'd only make things worse. You were the one that nearly drowned him, remember? Let Tanis handle it—he's the diplomat."

Caramon nodded. Both men stood, waiting in silence. Sturm saw Goldmoon look at Riverwind in mute appeal, but the Plainsman did not heed her glance. Tasslehoff, fidgeting on his seat, started to call out a shrill question, but a stern look from the knight silenced him. Raistlin huddled in his robes, trying to suppress an uncontrollable cough.

"I'm going up there," Sturm said finally. "Those whistles are getting closer. We don't dare take any more time." But at that moment, he saw Tanis shake hands with the dwarf, and begin to run toward the boat alone. Flint stayed where he was, near the edge of the woods. Sturm shook his head. "I told Tanis the dwarf wouldn't come."

"Stubborn as a dwarf, so the old saying goes," Caramon grunted. "And that one's had one hundred and forty-eight years to grow stubborner." The big man shook his head sadly. "Well, we'll miss him, that's for certain. He's saved my life more than once. Let me go get him. One punch on the jaw and he won't know whether he's in a boat or his own bed."

Tanis ran up, panting, and heard the last comment. "No, Caramon," he said. "Flint would never forgive us. Don't worry about him. He's going back to the hills. Get in the boat. There are more lights coming this way. We left a trail through the forest a blind gully dwarf could follow."

"No sense all of us getting wet," Caramon said, holding the side of the boat. "You and Sturm get in. I'll shove off."

Sturm was already over the side. Tanis patted Caramon on the back, then climbed in. The warrior pushed the boat out into the lake. He was up to his knees in water when they heard a call from the shore.

"Hold it!" It was Flint, running down from the trees, a vague moving shape of blackness against the moonlit shoreline. "Hang on! I'm coming!"

"Stop!" Tanis cried. "Caramon! Wait for Flint!"

"Look!" Sturm half-rose, pointing. Lights had appeared in the trees, smoking torches held by goblin guards.

"Goblins, Flint!" Tanis yelled. "Behind you! Run!" The dwarf, never questioning, put his head down and pumped for the shore, one hand on his helm to keep it from flying off.

"I'll cover him," Tanis said, unslinging his bow. With his elven sight, he was the only one who could see the goblins behind the torches. Fitting an arrow to his bow, Tanis stood as Caramon held the big boat steady. Tanis fired at the outline of the lead goblin. The arrow struck it in the chest and it pitched forward on its face. The other goblins slowed slightly, reaching for their own bows. Tanis fitted another arrow to his bow as Flint reached the shoreline.

"Wait! I'm coming!" the dwarf gasped and he plunged into the water and sank like a rock.

"Grab him!" Sturm yelled. "Tas, row back. There he is! See? The bubbles—" Caramon was splashing frantically in the water, hunting for the dwarf. Tas tried to row back, but the weight in the boat was too much for the kender. Tanis fired again, missed his mark, and swore beneath his breath. He reached for another arrow. The goblins were swarming down the hillside.

"I've got him!" Caramon shouted, pulling the dripping, spluttering dwarf out by the collar of his leather tunic. "Quit struggling," he told Flint, whose arms were flailing out in all directions. But the dwarf was in a complete state of panic. A goblin arrow thunked into Caramon's chain mail and stuck there like a scrawny feather.

"That does it!" The warrior grunted in exasperation and, with a great heave of his muscular arms, he pitched the dwarf into the boat as it moved out away from him. Flint caught hold of a seat and held on, his lower half sticking out over the edge. Sturm grabbed him by the belt and dragged him aboard as the boat rocked alarmingly. Tanis nearly lost his balance and was forced to drop his bow and catch hold of the side to keep from being thrown into the water. A goblin arrow stuck into the gunwale, just barely missing Tanis's hand.

"Row back to Caramon, Tas!" Tanis yelled.

"I can't!" shouted the struggling kender. One swipe of an out-of-control oar nearly knocked Sturm overboard.

The knight yanked the kender from his seat. He grabbed the oars and smoothly brought the boat around to where Caramon could get hold of the side.

Tanis helped the warrior climb in, then yelled to Sturm, "Pull!" The knight pulled on the oars with all his strength, leaning over backward as he thrust the oars deep into the water. The boat shot away from shore, accompanied by the howls of angry goblins. More arrows whizzed around the boat as Caramon, dripping wet, plopped down next to Tanis.

"Goblin target practice tonight," Caramon muttered, pulling the arrow from his mail shirt. "We show up beautifully against the water."

Tanis was fumbling for his dropped bow when he noticed Raistlin sitting up. "Take cover!" Tanis warned, and Caramon started to reach for his brother, but the mage, scowling at both of them, slipped his hand into a pouch on his belt. His delicate fingers drew out a handful of something as an arrow struck the seat next to him. Raistlin did not react. Tanis started to pull the mage down, then realized he was lost in the concentration necessary to a magic-user casting a spell. Disturbing him now might have drastic consequences, causing the mage to forget the spell or worse—to miscast the spell.

Tanis gritted his teeth and watched. Raistlin lifted his thin, frail hand and allowed the spell component he had taken from his pouch to fall slowly from between his fingers onto the deck of the boat. Sand, Tanis realized.

"*Ast tasarak sinuralan krynawi*," Raistlin murmured, and then moved his right hand slowly in an arc parallel to the shore. Tanis looked back toward land. One by one, the goblins dropped their bows and toppled over, as though Raistlin were touching each in turn. The arrows ceased. Goblins farther away howled in rage and ran forward. But by that time, Sturm's powerful strokes had carried the boat out of range.

"Good work, little brother!" Caramon said heartily. Raistlin blinked and seemed to return to the world, then the mage sank forward. Caramon caught him and held him for a moment. Then Raistlin sat up and sucked in a deep breath, which caused him to cough.

"I'll be all right," he whispered, withdrawing from Caramon.

"What did you do to them?" asked Tanis as he searched for enemy arrows to drop them overboard; goblins occasionally poisoned the arrowtips.

"I put them to sleep," Raistlin hissed through teeth that clicked together with the cold. "And now I must rest." He sank back against the side of the boat.

Tanis looked at the mage. Raistlin had, indeed, gained in power and skill. I wish I could trust him, the half-elf thought.

The boat moved across the star-filled lake. The only sounds to be heard were the soft, rhythmic splashing of the oars in the water and Raistlin's dry, wracking cough. Tasslehoff uncorked the wineskin, which Flint had somehow retained on his wild dash, and tried to get the chilled, shivering dwarf to swallow a mouthful. But Flint, crouched at the bottom of the boat, could only shudder and stare out across the water.

Goldmoon sank deeper into her fur cape. She wore the soft doeskin breeches of her people with a fringed overskirt and belted tunic. Her boots were made of soft leather. Water had sloshed over the edge of the boat when Caramon had thrown Flint aboard. The water made the doeskin cling to her, and soon she was chilled and shivering.

"Take my cape," Riverwind said in their language, starting to remove his bearskin cloak.

"No." She shook her head. "You have been suffering from the fever. I never get sick, you know that. But"—she looked up at him and smiled—"you may put your arm around me, warrior.

The heat from our bodies will warm us both."

"Is that a royal command, Chieftain's Daughter?" Riverwind whispered teasingly, drawing her close to him.

"It is," she said, leaning against his strong body with a sigh of contentment. She looked up into the starry heavens, then stiffened and caught her breath in alarm.

"What is it?" Riverwind asked, staring up.

The others in the boat, although they had not understood the exchange, heard Goldmoon's gasp and saw her eyes transfixed by something in the night sky.

Caramon poked his brother and said, "Raist, what is it? I don't see anything."

Raistlin sat up, cast back his hood, then coughed. When the spasm passed, he searched the night sky. Then he stiffened, and his eyes widened. Reaching out with his thin, bony hand, Raistlin clutched Tanis's arm, holding onto it tightly as the half-elf involuntarily tried to pull away from the mage's skeletal grip. "Tanis . . ." Raistlin wheezed, his breath nearly gone. "The constellations . . ."

"What?" Tanis was truly startled by the pallor of the mage's metallic gold skin and the feverish luster of his strange eyes. "What about the constellations?"

"Gone!" rasped Raistlin and lapsed into a fit of coughing. Caramon put his arm around him, holding him close, almost as if the big man were trying to hold his brother's frail body together. Raistlin recovered, wiped his mouth with his hand. Tanis saw that his fingers were dark with blood. Raistlin took a deep breath, then spoke.

"The constellation known as the Queen of Darkness and the one called Valiant Warrior. Both gone. She has come to Krynn, Tanis, and he has come to fight her. All the evil rumors we have heard are true. War, death, destruction . . ." His voice died in another fit of coughing.

Caramon held him. "C'mon, Raist," he said soothingly. "Don't get so worked up. It's only a bunch of stars."

"Only a bunch of stars," Tanis repeated flatly. Sturm began to row again, pulling swiftly for the opposite bank.

58

NIGHT IN A CAVE.
DISSENSION. TANIS DECIDES.

6

A chill wind began to blow across the lake. Storm clouds rolled across the sky from the north, obliterating the gaping black holes left by the fallen stars. The companions hunched down in the boat, pulling their cloaks tighter around them as the rain spattered down. Caramon joined Sturm at the oars. The big warrior tried to talk to the knight, but Sturm ignored him. He rowed in grim silence, occasionally muttering to himself in Solamnic.

"Sturm! There—between the great rocks to the left!" Tanis called out, pointing.

Sturm and Caramon pulled hard. The rain made sighting the landmark rocks difficult and, for a moment, it seemed that they had lost their way in the darkness. Then the rocks suddenly loomed ahead. Sturm and Caramon brought the boat around. Tanis sprang out over the side and pulled it to shore. Torrents of rain lashed down. The companions climbed from the boat, wet and chilled. They had to lift the dwarf out—Flint was stiff as a dead goblin from fear. Riverwind and Caramon hid the boat in the thick underbrush. Tanis led the rest up a rocky trail to a small opening in the cliff face.

Goldmoon looked at the opening dubiously. It seemed to be no more than a large crack in the surface of the cliff. Inside, however, the cave was large enough for all of them to stretch out comfortably.

"Nice home." Tasslehoff glanced around. "Not much in the way of furniture."

Tanis grinned at the kender. "It will do for the night. I don't think even the dwarf will complain about this. If he does, we'll send him back to sleep in the boat!"

Tas flashed his own smile back at the half-elf. It was good to see the old Tanis back. He had thought his friend unusually moody and indecisive, not the strong leader he had remembered from earlier days. Yet, now that they were on the road, the glint was back in the half-elf's eyes. He had come out of his brooding shell and was taking charge, slipping back into his accustomed role. He needed this adventure to get his mind off his problems—whatever those might be. The kender, who had never been able to understand Tanis's inner turmoil, was glad this adventure had come along.

Caramon carried his brother from the boat and laid him down as gently as he could on the soft warm sand that covered the floor of the cave while Riverwind started a fire. The wet wood crackled and spit, but soon caught fire. The smoke curled up toward the ceiling and drifted out through a crack. The Plainsman covered the cave's entrance with brush and fallen tree branches, hiding the light of the fire and effectively keeping out the rain.

He fits in well, Tanis thought as he watched the barbarian work. He could almost be one of us. Sighing, the half-elf turned his attention to Raistlin. Kneeling down beside him, he looked at the young mage with concern. Raistlin's pale face reflected in the flickering firelight reminded the half-elf of the time he and Flint and Caramon had barely rescued Raistlin from a vicious mob, intent on burning the mage at the stake. Raistlin had attempted to expose a charlatan cleric who was bilking the villagers out of their money. Instead of turning on the cleric, the villagers had turned on Raistlin. As Tanis had told Flint—people wanted to believe in something.

Caramon busied himself around his brother, placing his own heavy cloak over his shoulders. Raistlin's body was wracked by coughing spasms, and blood trickled from his mouth. His eyes gleamed feverishly. Goldmoon knelt beside him, a cup of wine in her hand.

"Can you drink this?" she asked him gently.

Raistlin shook his head, tried to speak, coughed and pushed her hand away. Goldmoon looked up at Tanis. "Perhaps—my staff?" she asked.

"No." Raistlin choked. He motioned for Tanis to come near him. Even sitting next to him, Tanis could barely hear the mage's words; his broken sentences were interrupted by great gasps for air and fits of coughing. "The staff will not heal me, Tanis," he whispered. "Do not waste it on me. If it is a blessed artifact . . . its sacred power is limited. My body was my sacrifice . . . for my magic. This damage is permanent. Nothing can help. . . ." His voice died, his eyes closed.

The fire suddenly flared as wind whirled around the cavern. Tanis looked up to see Sturm pulling the brush aside and entering the cave, half-carrying Flint, who stumbled along on unsteady feet. Sturm dumped him down beside the fire. Both were soaking wet. Sturm was clearly out of patience with the dwarf and, as Tanis noted, with the entire group. Tanis watched him with concern, recognizing the signs of a dark depression that sometimes overwhelmed the knight. Sturm liked the orderly, the well-disciplined. The disappearance of the stars, the disturbance of the natural order of things, had shaken him badly.

Tasslehoff wrapped a blanket around the dwarf who sat huddled on the cave floor, his teeth chattering in his head so that his helm rattled. "B-b-b-boat . . ." was all he could say. Tas poured him a cup of wine which the dwarf drank greedily.

Sturm looked at Flint in disgust. "I'll take the first watch," he said and moved toward the mouth of the cave.

Riverwind rose to his feet. "I will watch with you," he said harshly.

Sturm froze, then turned slowly to face the tall Plainsman. Tanis could see the knight's face, etched in sharp relief by the firelight, dark lines carved around the stern mouth. Although shorter in stature than Riverwind, the knight's air of nobility and the rigidity of his stance made the two appear almost equal.

"I am a knight of Solamnia," Sturm said. "My word is my honor and my honor is my life. I gave my word, back in the Inn, that I would protect you and your lady. If you choose to dispute my word, you dispute my honor and therefore you insult me. I cannot allow that insult to remain between us."

"Sturm!" Tanis was on his feet.

Never taking his eyes from the Plainsman, the knight raised his hand. "Don't interfere, Tanis," Sturm said. "Well, what will it be, swords, knives? How do you barbarians fight?"

Riverwind's stoic expression did not change. He regarded the knight with intense, dark eyes. Then he spoke, choosing his words carefully. "I did not mean to question your honor. I do not know men and their cities, and I tell you plainly—I am afraid. It is my fear that makes me speak thus. I have been afraid ever since the blue crystal staff was given to me. Most of all, I am afraid for Goldmoon." The Plainsman looked over at the woman, his eyes reflecting the glowing fire. "Without her, I die. How could I trust—" His voice failed. The stoic mask cracked and crumbled from pain and weariness. His knees buckled and he pitched forward. Sturm caught him.

"You couldn't," the knight said. "I understand. You are tired, and you have been sick." He helped Tanis lay the Plainsman at the back of the cave. "Rest now. I will stand watch." The knight shoved aside the brush, and without saying another word, stepped outside into the rain.

Goldmoon had listened to the altercation in silence. Now she moved their meager possessions to the back of the cave and knelt down by Riverwind's side. He put his arm around her and held her close, burying his face in her silver-gold hair. The two settled in the shadows of the cave. Wrapped in Riverwind's fur cape, they were soon asleep, Goldmoon's head resting on her warrior's chest.

Tanis breathed a sigh of relief and turned back to Raistlin. The mage had fallen into a fitful sleep. Sometimes he murmured strange words in the language of magic, his hand reaching out to touch his staff. Tanis glanced around at the others. Tasslehoff was sitting near the fire, sorting through his "acquired" objects. He sat cross-legged, the treasures on the cave floor in front of him. Tanis could make out glittering rings, a few unusual coins, a feather from the goatsucker bird, pieces of twine, a bead necklace, a soap doll, and a whistle. One of the rings looked familiar. It was a ring of elven make, given Tanis a long time ago by someone he kept on the borders of his mind. It was a finely carved, delicate ring of golden, clinging ivy leaves.

Tanis crept over to the kender, walking softly to keep from waking the others. "Tas . . . " He tapped the kender on the shoulder and pointed. "My ring . . ."

"Is it?" asked Tasslehoff with wide-eyed innocence. "Is this yours? I'm glad I found it. You must have dropped it at the Inn."

Tanis took the ring with a wry smile, then settled down next to the kender. "Have you got a map of this area, Tas?"

The kender's eyes shone. "A map? Yes, Tanis. Of course." He swept up all his valuables, dumped them back into a pouch, and pulled a hand-carved, wooden scroll case from another pouch. He drew forth a sheaf of maps. Tanis had seen the kender's collection before, but it never failed to astonish him. There must have been a hundred, drawn on everything from fine parchment to soft kid leather to a huge palmetto leaf.

"I thought you knew every tree personally around these parts, Tanis." Tasslehoff sorted through his maps, his eyes occasionally lingering on a favorite.

The half-elf shook his head. "I've lived here many years," he said. "But, let's face it, I don't know any of the dark and secret paths."

"You won't find many to Haven." Tas pulled a map from his pile and smoothed it out on the cave floor. "The Haven Road through Solace Vale is quickest, that's for certain."

Tanis studied the map by the light of the dying campfire. "You're right," he said. "The road is not only quickest—it seems to be the only passable route for several miles ahead. Both south and north of us lie the Kharolis Mountains—no passes there." Frowning, Tanis rolled up the map and handed it back. "Which is exactly what the Theocrat will figure."

Tasslehoff yawned. "Well," he said, putting the map back carefully into the case, "it's a problem that will be solved by wiser heads than mine. I'm along for the fun." Tucking the case back into a pouch, the kender lay down on the cave floor, drew his legs up beneath his chin, and was soon sleeping the peaceful sleep of small children and animals.

Tanis looked at him with envy. Although aching with weariness, he couldn't relax enough for sleep. Most of the others had dropped off, all but the warrior watching over his brother. Tanis walked over to Caramon.

"Turn in," he whispered. "I'll watch Raistlin."

"No," the big warrior said. Reaching out, he gently pulled a cloak up closer around his brother's shoulders. "He might need me."

"But you've got to get some sleep."

"I will." Caramon grinned. "Go get some sleep yourself, nursemaid. Your children are fine. Look—even the dwarf is out cold."

"I don't have to look," Tanis said. "The Theocrat can probably hear him snoring in Solace. Well, my friend, this reunion was not much like we planned five years ago."

"What is?" Caramon asked softly, glancing down at his brother.

Tanis patted the man's arm, lay down and rolled up in his own cloak and, at last, fell asleep.

The night passed—slowly for those on watch, swiftly for those asleep. Caramon relieved Sturm. Tanis relieved Caramon. The storm continued unabated all night, the wind whipping the lake into a white-capped sea. Lightning branched through the darkness like flaming trees. Thunder rumbled continually. The storm finally blew itself out by morning, and the half-elf watched day dawn, gray and chill. The rain had ended, but storm clouds still hung low. No sun appeared in the sky. Tanis felt a growing sense of urgency. He could see no end to the storm clouds massing to the north. Autumn storms were rare, especially ones with this ferocity. The wind was bitter, too, and it seemed odd that the storm came out of the north, when they generally swept east, across the Plains. Sensitive to the ways of nature, the strange weather upset Tanis nearly as much as Raistlin's fallen stars. He felt a need to get going, even though it was early morning yet. He went inside to wake the others.

The cave was chill and gloomy in the gray dawn, despite the crackling fire. Goldmoon and Tasslehoff were fixing breakfast.

Riverwind stood in the back of the cave, shaking out Goldmoon's fur cloak. Tanis glanced at him. The Plainsman had been about to say something to Goldmoon as Tanis entered, but fell silent, contenting himself with staring at her meaningfully as he continued his work. Goldmoon kept her eyes lowered, her face pale and troubled. The barbarian regrets having let himself go last night, Tanis realized.

"There is not much food, I'm afraid," Goldmoon said, tossing cereal into a pot of boiling water.

"Tika's larder wasn't well stocked," Tasslehoff added in apology. "We've got a loaf of bread, some dried beef, half a moldy cheese, and the oatmeal. Tika must eat her meals out."

"Riverwind and I didn't bring any provisions," Goldmoon said. "We really didn't expect to make this trip."

Tanis was about to ask her more about her song and the staff, but the others started waking up as they smelled food. Caramon yawned, stretched, and stood up. Walking over to peer into the cook-pot, he groaned. "Oatmeal? Is that all?"

"There'll be less for dinner." Tasslehoff grinned. "Tighten your belt. You're gaining weight anyhow."

The big man sighed dismally.

The sparse breakfast was cheerless in the cold dawn. Sturm, refusing all offers of food, went outside to keep watch. Tanis could see the knight, sitting on a rock, staring gloomily at the dark clouds that trailed wispy fingers along the still water of the lake. Caramon ate his share of the food quickly, gulped down his brother's portion, and then appropriated Sturm's when the knight walked out. Then the big man sat, watching wistfully while the rest finished.

"You gonna eat that?" he asked, pointing to Flint's share of bread. The dwarf scowled. Tasslehoff, seeing the warrior's eyes roam over to his plate, crammed his bread into his mouth, nearly choking himself in the process. At least it kept him quiet, Tanis thought, glad for the respite from the kender's shrill voice. Tas had been teasing Flint unmercifully all morning, calling him "Seamaster" and "Shipmate," asking him the price of fish, and how much he would charge to ferry them back across the lake.

Flint finally threw a rock at him, and Tanis sent Tas down to the lake to scrub out the pans.

The half-elf walked to the back of the cave.

"How are you this morning, Raistlin?" he asked. "We're going to have to be moving out soon."

"I am much better," the mage replied in his soft, whispering voice. He was drinking some herbal concoction of his own making. Tanis could see small, feathery green leaves floating in steaming water. It gave off a bitter, acrid odor and Raistlin grimaced as he swallowed it.

Tasslehoff came bounding back into the cave, pots and tin plates clattering loudly. Tanis gritted his teeth at the noise, started to reprimand the kender, then changed his mind. It wouldn't do any good.

Flint, seeing the tension on Tanis's face, grabbed the pots from the kender and began packing them away. "Be serious," the dwarf hissed at Tasslehoff. "Or I'll take you by the topknot and tie you to a tree as a warning to all kender—"

Tas reached out and plucked something from the dwarf's beard. "Look!" the kender held it up gleefully. "Seaweed!" Flint, roaring, made a grab for the kender, but Tas skipped out of his way agilely.

There was a rustling sound as Sturm shoved aside the brush covering the doorway. His face was dark and brooding.

"Stop this!" Sturm said, glowering at Flint and Tas, his moustaches quivering. His dour gaze turned on Tanis. "I could hear these two clear down by the lake. They'll have every goblin in Krynn on us. We've got to get out of here. Well, which way are we headed?"

An uneasy silence fell. Everyone stopped what he was doing and looked at Tanis, with the exception of Raistlin. The mage was wiping his cup out with a white cloth, cleaning it fastidiously. He continued working, eyes downcast, as though totally uninterested.

Tanis sighed and scratched his beard. "The Theocrat in Solace is corrupt. We know that now. He is using the goblin scum to take control. If he had the staff, he would use it for his own profit. We've searched for a sign of the true gods for years. It seems we may have found one. I am not about to hand it over to that Solace fraud. Tika said she believed the Highseekers in Haven were still interested in the truth. They may be able to tell us about the staff, where it came from, what its powers are. Tas, give me the map."

The kender, spilling the contents of several pouches onto the floor, finally produced the parchment requested.

"We are here, on the west bank of Crystalmir," Tanis continued. "North and south of us are branches of the Kharolis Mountains which form the boundaries of Solace Vale. There are no known passes through either range except through Gateway Pass south of Solace—"

"Almost certainly held by the goblins," muttered Sturm. "There are passes to the northeast—"

"That's across the lake!" Flint said in horror.

"Yes"—Tanis kept a straight face—"across the lake. But those lead to the Plains, and I don't believe you want to go that direction." He glanced at Goldmoon and Riverwind. "The west road goes through the Sentinel Peaks and Shadow Canyon to Haven. That seems to me the obvious direction to take."

Sturm frowned. "And if the Highseekers there are as bad as the one in Solace?"

"Then we continue south to Qualinesti."

"Qualinesti?" Riverwind scowled. "The Elven Lands? No! Humans are forbidden to enter. Besides, the way is hidden—"

A rasping, hissing sound cut into the discussion. Everyone turned to face Raistlin as he spoke. "There is a way." His voice was soft and mocking; his golden eyes glittered in the cold light of dawn. "The paths of Darken Wood. They lead right to Qualinesti."

"Darken Wood?" Caramon repeated in alarm. "No, Tanis!" The warrior shook his head. "I'll fight the living any day of the week—but not the dead!"

"The dead?" Tasslehoff asked eagerly. "Tell me, Caramon—"

"Shut up, Tas!" Sturm snapped. "Darken Wood is madness. None who enter have ever returned. You would have us take this prize there, mage?"

"Hold!" Tanis spoke sharply. Everyone fell silent. Even Sturm quieted. The knight looked at Tanis's calm, thoughtful face, the almond-shaped eyes that held the wisdom of his many years of wandering. The knight had often tried to resolve within himself why he accepted Tanis's leadership. He was nothing more than a bastard half-elf, after all. He did not come of noble blood. He wore no armor, carried no shield with a proud emblem. Yet Sturm followed him, and loved him and respected him as he respected no other living man.

Life was a dark shroud to the Solamnic knight. He could not pretend to ever know or understand it except through the code of the knights he lived by. "*Est Sularus oth Mithas*"—"My honor is life." The code defined honor and was more complete and detailed and strict than any known on Krynn. The code had held true for seven hundred years, but Sturm's secret fear was that, someday, in the final battle, the code would have no answers. He knew that if that day came, Tanis would be at his side, holding the crumbling world together. For while Sturm followed the code, Tanis lived it.

Tanis's voice brought the knight's thoughts back to the present. "I remind all of you that this staff is not our 'prize.' The staff rightfully belongs to Goldmoon—if it belongs to anyone. We have no more right to it than the Theocrat in Solace." Tanis turned to Goldmoon. "What is your will, lady?"

Goldmoon stared from Tanis to Sturm, then she looked at Riverwind. "You know my mind," he said coldly. "But—you are Chieftain's Daughter." He rose to his feet. Ignoring her pleading gaze, he stalked outside.

"What did he mean?" Tanis asked.

"He wants us to leave you, take the staff to Haven," Goldmoon answered, her voice low. "He says you are adding to our danger. We would be safer on our own."

"Adding to your danger!" Flint exploded. "Why we wouldn't be here, I wouldn't have nearly drowned—again!—if it hadn't been for—for—" The dwarf began to sputter in his rage.

Tanis held up his hand. "Enough." He scratched his beard. "You will be safer with us. Will you accept our help?"

"I will," Goldmoon answered gravely, "for a short distance at least."

"Good," Tanis said. "Tas, you know your way through Solace Vale. You are our guide. And remember, we're not on a picnic!"

"Yes, Tanis," the kender said, subdued. He gathered his many pouches, hung them around his waist and over his shoulders. Passing Goldmoon, he knelt swiftly and patted her hand, then he was out the cave entrance. The rest hastily gathered their gear together and followed.

"It's going to rain again," Flint grumbled, glancing up at the lowering clouds. "I should have stayed in Solace." Muttering, he walked off, adjusting his battle-axe on his back. Tanis, waiting for Goldmoon and Riverwind, smiled and shook his head. At least some things never changed, dwarves among them.

Riverwind took their packs from Goldmoon and slung them over his shoulder. "I have made certain the boat is well-hidden and secure," he told Tanis. The stoic mask was in place again this morning. "In case we need it."

"A good idea," Tanis said. "Thank—"

"If you will go ahead." Riverwind motioned. "I will come behind and cover our tracks."

Tanis started to speak, to thank the Plainsman. But Riverwind had already turned his back and was beginning his work. Walking up the path, the half-elf shook his head. Behind him, he could hear Goldmoon speaking softly in her own language. Riverwind replied—one, harsh word. Tanis heard Goldmoon sigh, then all other words were lost in the sound of crackling brush as Riverwind obliterated all traces of their passing.

The story of the staff.
Strange clerics. Eerie feelings.

7

The thick woods of Solace Vale were a green mass of vibrant life. Beneath the dense roof of the vallenwoods flourished thistlebrush and greenwall. The ground was crisscrossed with the bothersome tangleshoot vines. These had to be trod on with great care or they would suddenly snake around an ankle, trapping the helpless victim until he was devoured by one of the many predatory animals lurking in the Vale, thus providing tangleshoot with what it needed to live—blood.

It took over an hour of hacking and chopping through the brush to get to the Haven Road. All of them were scratched, torn, and tired, and the long stretch of smooth-packed dirt that carried travelers to Haven or beyond was a welcome sight. It wasn't until they stopped just in sight of the road and rested that they realized there were no sounds. A hush had fallen over the land, as if every creature were holding its breath, waiting. Now that they had reached the road, no one was particularly eager to step out of the shelter of the brush.

"Do you think it's safe?" Caramon asked, peering through a hedge.

"Safe or not, it's the way we have to go," Tanis snapped, "unless you can fly or unless you want to go back into the forest. It took us an hour to travel a few hundred yards. We ought to reach the crossroads next week at that pace."

70

The big man flushed, chagrined. "I didn't mean—"

"I'm sorry." Tanis sighed. He too looked down the road. The vallenwoods formed a dark corridor in the gray light. "I don't like it any better than you do."

"Do we separate or stay together?" Sturm interrupted what he considered idle chatter with cold practicality.

"We stay together," Tanis replied. Then, after a moment, he added, "Still, someone ought to scout—"

"I will, Tanis," Tas volunteered, popping up out of the brush beneath Tanis's elbow. "No one would ever suspect a kender traveling alone."

Tanis frowned. Tas was right—no one would suspect him. Kender were all afflicted with wanderlust, traveling throughout Krynn in search of adventure. But Tas had the disconcerting habit of forgetting his mission and wandering off if something more interesting caught his attention.

"Very well," Tanis said finally. "But, remember, Tasslehoff Burrfoot, keep your eyes open and your wits about you. No roaming off the road and above all"—Tanis fixed the kender's eye with his own sternly—"keep your hands out of other people's belongings."

"Unless they're bakers," Caramon added.

Tas giggled, pushed his way through the final few feet of brush, and started off down the road, his hoopak staff digging holes in the mud, his pouches jouncing up and down as he walked. They heard his voice lift in a kender trailsong.

Your one true love's a sailing ship
That anchors at our pier.
We lift her sails, we man her decks,
We scrub the portholes clear;
And yes, our lighthouse shines for her,
And yes, our shores are warm;
We steer her into harbor,
Any port in a storm.

The sailors stand upon the docks,
The sailors stand in line,

As thirsty as a dwarf for gold
Or centaurs for cheap wine.

For all the sailors love her,
And flock to where she's moored,
Each man hoping that he might
Go down, all hands on board.

Tanis, grinning, allowed a few minutes to pass after hearing the last verse of Tas's song before starting out. Finally they stepped out on the road with as much fear as a troupe of unskilled actors facing a hostile audience. It felt as if every eye on Krynn was on them.

The deep shade under the flame-colored leaves made it impossible to see anything in the woods even a few feet from the road. Sturm walked ahead of the group, alone, in bitter silence. Tanis knew that though the knight held his head proudly, he was slogging through his own darkness. Caramon and Raistlin followed. Tanis kept his eyes on the mage, concerned about his ability to keep up.

Raistlin had experienced some difficulty in getting through the brush, but he was moving along well now. He leaned on his staff with one hand, holding open a book with the other. Tanis at first wondered what the mage was studying, then realized it was his spellbook. It is the curse of the magi that they must constantly study and recommit their spells to memory every day. The words of magic flame in the mind, then flicker and die when the spell is cast. Each spell burns up some of the magician's physical and mental energy until he is totally exhausted and must rest before he can use his magic again.

Flint stumped along on the other side of Caramon. The two began to argue softly about the ten-year-old boating accident.

"Trying to catch a fish with your bare hands—" Flint grumbled his disgust.

Tanis came last, walking next to the Plainsmen. He turned his attention to Goldmoon. Seeing her clearly in the flecked gray light beneath the trees, he noticed lines around her eyes that made her appear older than her twenty-nine years.

"Our lives have not been easy," Goldmoon confided to him as they walked. "Riverwind and I have loved each other many years, but it is the law of my people that a warrior who wants to marry his chieftain's daughter must perform some great feat to prove himself worthy. It was worse with us. Riverwind's family was cast out of our tribe years ago for refusing to worship our ancestors. His grandfather believed in ancient gods who had existed before the Cataclysm, though he could find little evidence of them left on Krynn.

"My father was determined I should not marry so far beneath my station. He sent Riverwind on an impossible quest, to find some object with holy properties that would prove the existence of these ancient gods. Of course, my father didn't believe such an object existed. He hoped Riverwind would meet his death, or that I would come to love another." She looked up at the tall warrior walking beside her and smiled. But his face was hard, his eyes staring far away. Her smile faded. Sighing, she continued her story, speaking softly, more to herself than Tanis.

"Riverwind was gone long years. And my life was empty. I sometimes thought my heart would die. Then, just a week ago, he returned. He was half-dead, out of his mind with a raging fever. He stumbled into camp and fell at my feet, his skin burning to the touch. In his hand, he clutched this staff. We had to pry his fingers loose. Even unconscious, he would not release it.

"He raved in his fever about a dark place, a broken city where death had black wings. Then, when he was nearly wild with fear and terror and the servants had to tie his arms to the bed, he remembered a woman, a woman dressed in blue light. She came to him in the dark place, he said, and healed him and gave him the staff. When he remembered her, he grew calmer and his fever broke.

"Two days ago—" She paused, had it really been only two days? It seemed a lifetime! Sighing, she continued. "He presented the staff to my father, telling him it had been given to him by a goddess, though he did not know her name. My father looked at this staff"—Goldmoon held it up—"and commanded it to do something, anything. Nothing happened. He threw it back to Riverwind, proclaiming him a fraud, and ordered the people to stone him to death as punishment for his blasphemy!"

Goldmoon's face grew pale as she spoke, Riverwind's face dark and shadowed.

"The tribe bound Riverwind and dragged him to the Grieving Wall," she said, barely speaking above a whisper. "They started hurling rocks. He looked at me with so much love and he shouted that not even death would separate us. I couldn't bear the thought of living my life alone, without him. I ran to him. The rocks struck us—" Goldmoon put her hand to her forehead, wincing in remembered pain, and Tanis's attention was drawn to a fresh, jagged scar on her tanned skin. "There was a blinding flash of light. When Riverwind and I could see again, we were standing on the road outside of Solace. The staff glowed blue, then dimmed and faded until it is as you see it now. It was then we determined to go to Haven and ask the wise men at the temple about the staff."

"Riverwind," Tanis asked, troubled, "what do you remember of this broken city? Where was it?"

Riverwind didn't answer. He glanced at Tanis out of the corner of his dark eyes, and it was obvious his thoughts had been far away. Then he stared off into the shadowy trees.

"Tanis Half-Elven," he finally said. "That is your name?"

"Among humans, that is what I am called," Tanis answered. "My elvish name is long and difficult for humans to pronounce."

Riverwind frowned. "Why is it," he asked, "that you are called half-elf and not half-man?"

The question struck Tanis like a blow across the face. He could almost envision himself sprawling in the dirt and had to force himself to stop and swallow an angry retort. He knew Riverwind was asking this question for a reason. It had not been meant as an insult. This was a test, Tanis realized. He chose his words carefully.

"According to humans, half an elf is but part of a whole being. Half a man is a cripple."

Riverwind considered this, finally nodded once, abruptly, and answered Tanis's question.

"I wandered many long years," he replied. "Often I had no idea where I was. I followed the sun and the moons and the stars. My last journey is like a dark dream." He was silent for a moment. When he spoke, it was as if he were talking from some great distance. "It was a city once beautiful, with white buildings supported by tall columns of marble. But it is now as if some great hand had picked up the city and cast it down a mountainside. The city is now very old and very evil."

"Death on black wings," Tanis said softly.

"It rose like a god from the darkness, its creatures worshiped it, shrieking and howling." The Plainsman's face paled beneath his sun-baked skin. He was sweating in the chill morning air. "I can speak of it no more!" Goldmoon laid her hand on his arm, and the tension in his face eased.

"And out of the horror came a woman who gave you the staff?" Tanis pursued.

"She healed me," Riverwind said simply. "I was dying."

Tanis stared intently at the staff Goldmoon held in her hand. It was just a plain, ordinary staff that he never noticed until his attention was called to it. A strange device was carved on the top, and feathers—such as the barbarians admire—were tied around it. Yet he had seen it glow blue! He had felt its healing powers. Was this a gift from ancient gods—come to aid them in their time of need? Or was it evil? What did he know of these barbarians anyway? Tanis thought about Raistlin's claim that the staff could only be touched by those pure of heart. He shook his head. It sounded good. He wanted to believe it. . . .

Tanis, lost in thought, felt Goldmoon touch his arm. He looked up to see Sturm and Caramon signaling. The half-elf suddenly realized he and the Plainsmen had fallen far behind the others. He broke into a run.

"What is it?"

Sturm pointed. "The scout returns," he said dryly.

Tasslehoff was running down the road toward them. He waved his arm three times.

"Into the brush!" Tanis ordered. The group hurriedly left the road and plunged into the bushes and scrub trees growing along the south edge, all except Sturm.

"Come on!" Tanis put his hand on the knight's arm. Sturm pulled away from the half-elf.

"I will not hide in a ditch!" the knight stated coldly.

"Sturm—" Tanis began, fighting to control his rising anger. He choked back bitter words that would do no good and might cause irreparable harm. Instead, he turned from the knight, his lips compressed, and waited in grim silence for the kender.

Tas came dashing up, pouches and packs bouncing wildly as he ran. "Clerics!" he gasped. "A party of clerics. Eight."

Sturm sniffed. "I thought it was a battalion of goblin guards at the least. I believe we can handle a party of clerics."

"I don't know," Tasslehoff said, dubiously. "I've seen clerics from every part of Krynn and I've never seen any like these." He glanced down the road apprehensively, then gazed up at Tanis, unusual seriousness in his brown eyes. "Do you remember what Tika said about the strange men in Solace—hanging around with Hederick? How they were hooded and dressed in heavy robes? Well, that describes these clerics exactly! And, Tanis, they gave me an eerie feeling." The kender shuddered. "They'll be in sight in a few moments."

Tanis glanced at Sturm. The knight raised his eyebrows. Both of them knew that kenders did not feel the emotion of fear, yet were extremely sensitive to other creatures' natures. Tanis couldn't remember when the sight of any being on Krynn had ever given Tas an "eerie feeling"—and he had been with the kender in some tight spots.

"Here they come," Tanis said suddenly. He and Sturm and Tas moved back into the shadows of the trees to the left, watching as the clerics slowly rounded a bend in the road. They were too far away for the half-elf to be able to tell much about them, except that they were moving very slowly, dragging a large handcart behind them.

"Maybe you should talk to them, Sturm," Tanis said softly. "We need information about the road ahead. But be careful, my friend."

"I'll be careful." Sturm said, smiling. "I have no intention of throwing my life away needlessly."

The knight gripped Tanis's arm a moment in silent apology, then dropped his hand to loosen his sword in its antique scabbard. He walked across to the other side of the road and leaned up against a broken-down wooden fence, head bowed, as though resting. Tanis stood a moment, irresolute, then turned and made his way through the brush, Tasslehoff at his heels.

"What is it?" Caramon grunted as Tanis and Tas appeared. The big warrior shifted his girth, causing his arsenal of weapons to clank loudly. The rest of the companions were huddled together, concealed behind thick clumps of brush, yet able to get a clear view of the road.

"Hush." Tanis knelt down between Caramon and Riverwind, who crouched in the brush a few feet to Tanis's left. "Clerics," he whispered. "A group of them coming down the road. Sturm's going to question them."

"Clerics!" Caramon snorted derisively and settled back comfortably on his heels. But Raistlin stirred restlessly.

"Clerics," he whispered thoughtfully. "I do not like this."

"What do you mean?" asked Tanis.

Raistlin peered at the half-elf from the dark shadows of his hood. All Tanis could see were the mage's golden hourglass eyes, narrow slits of cunning and intelligence.

"Strange clerics," Raistlin spoke with elaborate patience, as one speaks to a child. "The staff has healing, clerical powers—such powers as have not been seen on Krynn since the Cataclysm! Caramon and I saw some of these cloaked and hooded men in Solace. Don't you find it odd, my friend, that these clerics and this staff turned up at the same time, in the same place, when neither has been seen before? Perhaps this staff is truly theirs—by right."

Tanis glanced at Goldmoon. Her face was shadowed with worry. Surely she must be wondering the same thing. He looked back at the road again. The cloaked figures were moving at a crawling pace, pulling the cart. Sturm sat on the fence, stroking his moustaches.

The companions waited in silence. Gray clouds massed overhead, the sky grew darker and soon water began to drip through the branches of the trees.

"There, it's raining," Flint grumbled. "It isn't enough that I have to squat in a bush like a toad, now I get soaked to the skin—"

Tanis glared at the dwarf. Flint mumbled and fell silent. Soon the companions could hear nothing but the rain splatting against the already wet leaves, drumming on shield and helm. It was a cold, steady rain, the kind that seeps through the thickest cloak. It ran off Caramon's dragon helm and trickled down his neck. Raistlin began to shiver and cough, covering his mouth with his hand to muffle the sound as everyone stared at him in alarm.

Tanis looked out to the road. Like Tas, he had never seen anything to compare to these clerics in his hundred years of life on Krynn. They were tall, about six feet in height. Long robes shrouded their bodies, hooded cloaks covered the robes. Even their feet and hands were wrapped in cloth, like bandages covering leprous wounds. As they neared Sturm, they glanced around warily. One of them stared straight into the brush where the companions were hiding. They could see only dark glittering eyes through a swath of cloth.

"Hail, Knight of Solamnia," the lead cleric said in the Common tongue. His voice was hollow, lisping, an inhuman voice. Tanis shivered.

"Greetings, brethren," Sturm answered, also in Common. "I have traveled many miles this day and you are the first travelers I have passed. I have heard strange rumors, and I seek information about the road ahead. Where do you come from?"

"We come from the east originally," the cleric answered. "But today we travel from Haven. It is a chill, bitter day for journeying, knight, which is perhaps why you find the road empty. We ourselves would not undertake such a journey save we are driven by necessity. We did not pass you on the road, so you must be traveling from Solace, Sir Knight."

Sturm nodded. Several of the clerics standing at the rear of the cart turned their hooded faces toward each other, muttering. The lead cleric spoke to them in a strange, guttural language. Tanis looked at his companions. Tasslehoff shook his head, as did the rest of them; none of them had heard it before.

The cleric switched back to Common. "I am curious to hear these rumors you speak of, knight."

"There is talk of armies in the north," Sturm replied. "I am traveling that way, to my homeland of Solamnia. I would not want to run into a war to which I had not been invited."

"We have not heard these rumors," the cleric answered. "So far as we know, the road to the north is clear."

"Ah, that's what comes of listening to drunken companions." Sturm shrugged. "But what is this necessity you speak of that drives the brethren out into such foul weather?"

"We seek a staff," the cleric answered readily. "A blue crystal staff. We heard that it had been sighted in Solace. Do you know aught of it?"

"Yes," Sturm answered. "I heard of such a staff in Solace. I heard of the armies to the north from the same companions. Am I to believe these stories or not?"

This appeared to confound the cleric for a moment. He glanced around, as if uncertain how to react.

"Tell me," said Sturm, lounging back against the fence, "why do you seek a blue crystal staff? Surely one of plain, sturdy wood would suit you reverend gentlemen better."

"It is a sacred staff of healing," the cleric replied gravely. "One of our brothers is sorely ill; he will die without the blessed touch of this holy relic."

"Healing?" Sturm raised his eyebrows. "A sacred staff of healing would be of great value. How did you come to misplace such a rare and wonderful object?"

"We did not misplace it!" the cleric snarled. Tanis saw the man's wrapped hands clench in anger. "It was stolen from our holy order. We tracked the foul thief to a barbarian village in the Plains, then lost his trail. There are rumors of strange doings in Solace, however, and it is there we go." He gestured to the back of the cart. "This dismal journey is but little sacrifice for us compared to the pain and agony our brother endures."

"I'm afraid I cannot help—" Sturm began.

"I can help you!" called a clear voice from beside Tanis. He reached out, but he was too late. Goldmoon had risen from the brush and was walking determinedly to the road, pushing aside tree branches and brambles. Riverwind jumped to his feet and crashed through the shrubbery after her.

"Goldmoon!" Tanis risked a piercing whisper.

"I must know!" was all she said.

The clerics, hearing Goldmoon's voice, glanced at each other knowingly, nodding their hooded heads. Tanis sensed trouble, but before he could say anything, Caramon jumped to his feet.

"The Plainsmen are not leaving me behind in a ditch while they have all the fun!" Caramon stated, plunging through the thicket after Riverwind.

"Has everyone gone mad?" Tanis growled. He grabbed Tasslehoff by his shirt collar, dragging the kender back as he was about to leap joyfully after Caramon. "Flint, watch the kender. Raistlin—"

"No need to worry about me, Tanis," the mage whispered. "I have no intention of going out there."

"Right. Well, stay here." Tanis rose to his feet and slowly started forward, an "eerie feeling" creeping over him.

SEARCH FOR TRUTH.
UNEXPECTED ANSWERS.

8

I can help you." Goldmoon's clear voice rang out like a pure, silver bell. The Chieftain's Daughter saw Sturm's shocked face; she understood Tanis's warning.

But this was not the act of a foolish, hysterical woman. Goldmoon was far from that. She had ruled her tribe in all but name for ten years, ever since sickness had struck her father like a lightning bolt, leaving him unable to speak clearly or to move his right arm and leg. She had led her people in times of war with neighboring tribes and in times of peace. She had confounded attempts to wrest her power from her. She knew that what she was doing now was dangerous. These strange clerics filled her with loathing. But they obviously knew something about this staff, and she had to know the answer.

"I am the bearer of the blue crystal staff," Goldmoon said, approaching the leader of the clerics, her head held proudly. "But we did not steal it; the staff was given to us."

Riverwind stepped to one side of her, Sturm to the other. Caramon came charging through the brush and stood behind her, his hand on his sword hilt, an eager grin on his face.

"So you say," the cleric said in a soft, sneering voice. He stared at the plain brown staff in her hand with avid, black, gleaming eyes, then reached out his wrapped hand to take it. Goldmoon swiftly clasped the staff to her body.

"The staff was carried out of a place of great evil," she said. "I will do what I can to help your dying brother, but I will not relinquish this staff to you or to anyone else until I am firmly convinced of your rightful claim to it."

The cleric hesitated, glanced back at his fellows. Tanis saw them make nervous, tentative gestures toward the wide cloth belts they wore tied around their flowing robes. Unusually wide belts, Tanis noticed, with strange bulges beneath them—not, he was sure, made by prayer books. He swore in frustration, wishing Sturm and Caramon were paying attention. But Sturm seemed completely relaxed and Caramon was nudging him as though sharing a private joke. Tanis raised his bow cautiously and put an arrow to the string.

The cleric finally bowed his head in submission, folding his hands in his sleeves. "We will be grateful for whatever aid you can give our poor brother," he said, his voice muffled. "And then I hope you and your companions will return with us to Haven. I promise you that you will be convinced that the staff has come into your possession wrongly."

"We'll go where we've a mind to, brother," Caramon growled.

Fool! Tanis thought. The half-elf considered shouting a warning, then decided to remain hidden in case his growing fears were realized.

Goldmoon and the leader of the cloaked men passed the cart, Riverwind next to her. Caramon and Sturm remained near the front of it, watching with interest. As Goldmoon and the cleric reached the back, the cleric put out a wrapped hand and drew Goldmoon toward the cart. She pulled away from his touch and stepped forward by herself. The cleric bowed humbly, then lifted up a cloth covering the back of the cart. Holding the staff in front of her, Goldmoon peered in.

Tanis saw a flurry of movement. Goldmoon screamed. There was a flash of blue light and a cry. Goldmoon sprang backward as Riverwind jumped in front of her. The cleric lifted a horn to his lips and blew long, wailing notes.

"Caramon! Sturm!" Tanis called, raising his bow. "It's a tra—"
A great weight dropped on the half-elf from above, knocking him

to the ground. Strong hands groped for his throat, shoving his face deep into the wet leaves and mud. The man's fingers found their hold and began squeezing. Tanis fought to breathe, but his nose and mouth were filled with mud. Seeing starbursts, he tore frantically at the hands that were trying to crush his windpipe. The man's grip was incredibly strong. Tanis felt himself losing consciousness. He tensed his muscles for one final, desperate struggle, then he heard a hoarse cry and a bone-crushing thump. The hands relaxed their grip and the heavy weight was dragged off him.

Tanis staggered to his knees, his breath coming in painful gasps. Wiping mud from his face, he looked up to see Flint with a log in his hand. But the dwarf's eyes were not on him. They were on the body at his feet.

Tanis followed the astonished dwarf's gaze, and the half-elf recoiled in horror. It wasn't a man! Leathery wings sprang from its back. It had the scaly flesh of a reptile; its large hands and feet were clawed, but it walked upright in the manner of men. The creature wore sophisticated armor that allowed it the use of its wings. It was the creature's face, however, that made him shudder, it was not the face of any living being he had ever seen before, either on Krynn or in his darkest nightmares. The creature had the face of a man, but it was as if some malevolent being had twisted it into that of a reptile!

"By all the gods," Raistlin breathed, creeping up to Tanis. "What is that?"

Before Tanis could answer, he saw out of the corner of his eye a brilliant flash of blue light and he heard Goldmoon calling.

For one instant, as Goldmoon had looked into the cart, she had wondered what terrible disease could turn a man's flesh into scales. She had moved forward to touch the pitiful cleric with her staff, but at that moment the creature sprang out at her, grasping for the staff with a clawed hand. Goldmoon stumbled backward, but the creature was swift and its clawed hand closed around the staff. There was a blinding flash of blue light. The creature shrieked in pain and fell back, wringing its blackened hand. Riverwind, sword drawn, had leaped in front of his Chieftain's Daughter.

But now she heard him gasp and she saw his sword arm drop weakly. He staggered backward, making no effort to defend himself. Rough wrapped hands grabbed her from behind. A horrible scaled hand was clapped over her mouth. Struggling to free herself, she caught a glimpse of Riverwind. He was staring wide-eyed in terror at the thing in the cart, his face deathly white, his breathing swift and shallow—a man who wakes from a nightmare to discover it is reality.

Goldmoon, strong child of a warrior race, kicked backward at the cleric holding her, her foot aiming for his knee. Her skillful kick caught her opponent off guard and crushed his kneecap. The instant the cleric eased his grip on her, Goldmoon whirled around and struck him with her staff. She was amazed to see the cleric slump to the ground, seemingly felled by a blow even the mighty Caramon might have envied. She looked at her staff in astonishment, the staff that now glowed a bright blue. But there was no time to wonder—other creatures surrounded her. She swung her glistening staff in a wide arc, holding them at bay. But for how long?

"Riverwind!"

Goldmoon's cry woke the Plainsman from his terror. Turning, he saw her backing into the forest, keeping the cloaked clerics away with the staff. He grabbed one of the clerics from behind and threw him heavily to the ground. Another jumped at him while a third sprang toward Goldmoon.

There was a blinding blue flash.

A moment ahead of Tanis's cry, Sturm had realized the clerics had set a trap and drew his sword. He had seen, through the slats of the old wooden cart, a clawed hand grabbing for the staff. Lunging forward, he had gone to back up Riverwind. But the knight was totally unprepared for the Plainsman's reaction at sight of the creature in the cart. Sturm saw Riverwind stagger backward, helpless, as the creature grabbed a battle-axe in its uninjured hand and sprang directly at the barbarian. Riverwind made no move to defend himself. He just stared, his weapon dangling in his hand.

Sturm plunged his sword into the creature's back. The thing screamed and whirled around to attack, wrenching the sword from the knight's hand. Slavering and gurgling in its dying rage, the creature wrapped its arms around the startled knight and bore him into the muddy road. Sturm knew the thing that grasped him was dying and fought to beat down the terror and revulsion he felt at the touch of its slimy skin. The screaming stopped, and he felt the creature go rigid. The knight shoved the body over and quickly started to pull his sword from the creature's back. The weapon didn't budge! He stared at it in disbelief, then yanked on the sword with all his might, even putting his booted foot against the body to gain leverage. The weapon was stuck fast. Furious, he beat at the creature with his hands, then drew back in fear and loathing. The thing had turned to stone!

"Caramon!" Sturm yelled as another of the strange clerics leaped toward him, swinging an axe. Sturm ducked, felt a slashing pain, and then was blinded when blood flowed into his eyes. He stumbled, unable to see, and a crushing weight bore him to the ground.

Caramon, standing near the front of the cart, started to go to Goldmoon's aid when he heard Sturm's cry. Then two of the creatures bore down on him. Swinging his shortsword to force them to keep their distance, Caramon drew his dagger with his left hand. One cleric jumped for him and Caramon slashed out, his blade biting deep into flesh. He smelled a foul, rotting stench and saw a sickly green stain appear on the cleric's robes, but the wound appeared just to enrage the creature. It kept coming, saliva dripping from jaws that were the jaws of a reptile—not a man. For a moment, panic engulfed Caramon. He had fought trolls and goblins, but these horrible clerics completely unnerved him. He felt lost and alone, then he heard a reassuring whisper next to him.

"I am here, my brother." Raistlin's calm voice filled his mind.

"About time," Caramon gasped, threatening the creature with his sword. "What sort of foul clerics are these?"

"Don't stab them!" Raistlin warned swiftly. "They'll turn to stone. They're not clerics. They are some sort of reptile man. That is the reason for the robes and hoods."

Though different as light and shadow, the twins fought well as a team. They exchanged few words during battle, their thoughts

merging faster than tongues could translate. Caramon dropped his sword and dagger and flexed his huge arm muscles. The creatures, seeing Caramon drop his weapons, charged forward. Their rags had fallen loose and fluttered about them grotesquely. Caramon grimaced at the sight of the scaled bodies and clawed hands.

"Ready," he said to his brother.

"*Ast tasark simiralan krynawi*," said Raistlin softly, and he threw a handful of sand into the air. The creatures stopped their wild rush, shook their heads groggily as magical sleep stole over them . . . but then blinked their eyes. Within moments, they had regained their senses and started forward again!

"Magic resistant!" Raistlin murmured in awe. But that brief interlude of near sleep was long enough for Caramon. Encircling their scrawny, reptilian necks with his huge hands, the warrior swept their heads together. The bodies tumbled to the ground— lifeless statues. Caramon looked up to see two more clerics crawling over the stony bodies of their brethren, curved swords gleaming in their wrapped hands.

"Stand behind me," ordered Raistlin in a hoarse whisper. Caramon reached down and grabbed dagger and sword. He dodged behind his brother, fearful for his twin's safety, yet knowing Raistlin could not cast his spell if he stood in the way.

Raistlin stared intently at the creatures, who—recognizing a magic-user—slowed and glanced at each other, hesitant to approach. One dropped to the ground and crawled under the cart. The other sprang forward, sword in hand, hoping to impale the mage before his spell was cast, or at least break the concentration that was so necessary to the spellcaster. Caramon bellowed. Raistlin seemed not to hear or see any of them. Slowly he raised his hands. Placing his thumbs together, he spread his thin fingers in a fanlike pattern and spoke, "*Kair tangus miopiar*." Magic coursed through his frail body, and the creature was engulfed in flame.

Tanis, recovering from his initial shock, heard Sturm's yell and crashed through the brush out onto the road. He swung the flat of his sword blade like a club and struck the creature that had Sturm pinned to the ground. The cleric fell over with a shriek and Tanis was able to drag the wounded knight into the brush.

"My sword," Sturm mumbled, dazed. Blood poured down his face; he tried unsuccessfully to wipe it away.

"We'll get it," Tanis promised, wondering how. Looking down the road, he could see more creatures swarming out of the woods and heading toward them. Tanis's mouth was dry. We've got to get out of here, he thought, fighting down panic. He forced himself to pause and draw a deep breath. Then he turned to Flint and Tasslehoff who had run up behind him.

"Stay here and guard Sturm," he instructed. "I'm going to get everyone together. We'll head back into the woods."

Not waiting for an answer, Tanis dashed out into the road, but then the flames from Raistlin's spell flared out and he was forced to fling himself to the ground.

The cart began to smoke as the straw pallet the creature had been lying on inside caught fire.

"Stay here and guard Sturm. Humpf!" Flint muttered, getting a firm grip on his battle-axe. For the moment, the creatures coming down the road did not seem to notice the dwarf or the kender or the wounded knight lying in the shadows of the trees. Their attention was on the two small knots of battling warriors. But Flint knew it was only a matter of time. He planted his feet more firmly. "Do something for Sturm," he said to Tas irritably. "Make yourself useful for once."

"I'm trying," Tasslehoff replied in a hurt tone. "But I can't get the bleeding stopped." He wiped the knight's eyes with a moderately clean handkerchief. "There, can you see now?" he asked anxiously.

Sturm groaned and tried to sit up, but pain flashed through his head and he sank back. "My sword," he said.

Tasslehoff looked over to see Sturm's two-handed weapon sticking out of the back of the stone cleric. "That's fantastic!" the wide-eyed kender said. "Look, Flint! Sturm's sword—"

"I know, you fog-brained idiot kender!" Flint roared as he saw a creature running toward them, its blade drawn.

"I'll just go get it," Tas said cheerfully to Sturm as he knelt beside him. "I won't be a moment."

"No—" Flint yelled, realizing the attacking cleric was out of Tas's line of vision. The creature's wicked, curved sword lashed out in a flashing arc, aimed for the dwarf's neck. Flint swung his axe, but at that moment, Tasslehoff—his eyes on Sturm's sword—rose to his feet. The kender's hoopak staff struck the dwarf in the back of the knees, causing Flint's legs to buckle beneath him. The creature's sword whistled harmlessly overhead as the dwarf gave a startled yell and fell over backward on top of Sturm.

Tasslehoff, hearing the dwarf shout, looked back, astonished at an odd sight: a cleric was attacking Flint and, for some reason, the dwarf was lying on his back, legs flailing, when he should have been up fighting.

"What *are* you doing, Flint?" Tas shouted. He nonchalantly struck the creature in the midsection with his hoopak, struck it again on the head as it toppled forward, and watched it fall to the ground, unconscious.

"There!" he said irritably to Flint. "Do I have to fight your battles for you?" The kender turned and headed back toward Sturm's sword.

"Fight! For me!" The dwarf, sputtering with rage, struggled wildly to stand up. His helm had slipped over his eyes, blinding him. Flint shoved it back just as another cleric bowled into him, knocking the dwarf off his feet again.

Tanis found Goldmoon and Riverwind standing back to back, Goldmoon fending off the creatures with her staff. Three of them lay dead at her feet, their stony remains blackened from the staff's blue flame. Riverwind's sword was caught fast in the guts of another statue. The Plainsman had unslung his only remaining weapon—his short bow—and had an arrow nocked and ready. The creatures were, for the moment, hanging back, discussing their strategy in low, indecipherable tones. Knowing they must rush the Plainsmen in a moment, Tanis leaped toward them and smote one of the creatures from behind, using the flat of his sword, then made a backhand swing at another.

"Come on!" he shouted to the Plainsmen. "This way!"

Some of the creatures turned at this new attack; others hesitated. Riverwind fired an arrow and felled one, then he grabbed Goldmoon's hand and together they ran toward Tanis, jumping over the stone bodies of their victims.

Margaret Weis & Tracy Hickman

Tanis let them get past him, fending off the creatures with the flat of his sword. "Here, take this dagger!" he shouted to Riverwind as the barbarian ran by. Riverwind grabbed it, reversed it, and struck one of the creatures in the jaw. Jabbing upward with the hilt, he broke its neck. There was another flash of blue flame as Goldmoon used her staff to knock another creature out of the way. Then they were into the woods.

The wooden cart was burning fiercely now. Peering through the smoke, Tanis caught glimpses of the road. A shiver ran through him as he saw dark winged forms floating to the ground about a half mile away on either side of them. The road was cut off in both directions. They were trapped unless they escaped into the woods immediately.

He reached the place where he had left Sturm. Goldmoon and Riverwind were there, so was Flint. Where was everyone else? He stared around in the thick smoke, blinking back tears.

"Help Sturm," he told Goldmoon. Then he turned to Flint, who was trying unsuccessfully to yank his axe out of the chest of a stone creature. "Where are Caramon and Raistlin? And where's Tas? I told him to stay here—"

"Blasted kender nearly got me killed!" Flint exploded. "I hope they carry him off! I hope they use him for dog meat! I hope—"

"In the name of the gods!" Tanis swore in exasperation. He made his way through the smoke toward where he had last seen Caramon and Raistlin and stumbled across the kender, dragging Sturm's sword back along the road. The weapon was nearly as big as Tasslehoff and he couldn't lift it, so he was dragging it through the mud.

"How did you get that?" Tanis asked in amazement, coughing in the thick smoke that boiled around them.

Tas grinned, tears streaming down his face from the smoke in his eyes. "The creature turned to dust," he said happily. "Oh, Tanis, it was wonderful. I walked up and pulled on the sword and it wouldn't come out, so I pulled again and—"

"Not now! Get back to the others!" Tanis grabbed the kender and shoved him forward. "Have you seen Caramon and Raistlin?"

But just then he heard the warrior's voice boom out of the smoke. "Here we are," Caramon panted. He had his arm around his brother, who was coughing uncontrollably. "Have we destroyed them all?" the big man asked cheerfully.

"No, we haven't," Tanis replied grimly. "In fact, we've got to get away through the woods to the south." He put his arm around Raistlin and together they hurried back to where the others were huddled by the road, choking in the smoke, yet thankful for its enveloping cover.

Sturm was on his feet, his face pale, but the pain in his head was gone and the wound had quit bleeding.

"The staff healed him?" Tanis asked Goldmoon.

She coughed. "Not completely. Enough so that he can walk."

"It has . . . limits," Raistlin said, wheezing.

"Yes—" Tanis interrupted. "Well, we're heading south, into the woods."

Caramon shook his head. "That's Darken Wood—" he began.

"I know—you'd rather fight the living," Tanis interrupted. "How do you feel about that now?"

The warrior did not answer.

"More of those creatures are coming from both directions. We can't fight off another assault. But we won't enter Darken Wood if we don't have to. There's a game trail not far from here we can use to reach Prayer's Eye Peak. There we can see the road to the north, as well as all other directions."

"We could go north as far as the cave. The boat's hidden there." Riverwind suggested.

"No!" yelled Flint in a strangled voice. Without another word, the dwarf turned and plunged into the forest, running south as fast as his short legs could carry him.

FLIGHT! THE WHITE STAG.

9

The companions stumbled through the thick woods as fast as they could and soon reached the game trail. Caramon took the lead, sword in hand, eyeing every shadow. His brother followed, one hand on Caramon's shoulder, his lips set in grim determination. The rest came after, their weapons drawn.

But they saw no more of the creatures.

"Why aren't they chasing us?" Flint asked after they had traveled about an hour.

Tanis scratched his beard—he had been wondering about the same thing. "They don't need to," he said finally. "We are trapped. They've undoubtedly blocked all the exits from this forest. With the exception of Darken Wood . . ."

"Darken Wood!" Goldmoon repeated softly. "Is it truly necessary to go that way?"

"It may not be," Tanis said. "We'll get a look around from Prayer's Eye Peak."

Suddenly they heard Caramon, walking ahead of them, shout. Running forward, Tanis found Raistlin had collapsed.

"I'll be all right," the mage whispered. "But I must rest."

"We can all use rest," Tanis said.

No one answered. All sank down wearily, catching their breath in quick, sharp gasps. Sturm closed his eyes and leaned against a moss-covered rock. His face was a ghastly shade of grayish white. Blood had matted his long moustaches and caked his hair. The wound was a jagged slash, turning slowly purple. Tanis knew that the knight would die before he said a word of complaint.

"Don't worry," Sturm said harshly. "Just give me a moment's peace." Tanis gripped the knight's hand briefly, then went to sit beside Riverwind.

Neither spoke for long minutes, then Tanis asked, "You've fought those creatures before, haven't you?"

"In the broken city." Riverwind shuddered. "It all came back to me when I looked inside the cart and saw that thing leering at me! At least—" He paused, shook his head. Then he gave Tanis a half-smile. "At least I know now that I'm not going insane. Those horrible creatures really do exist—I had wondered sometimes."

"I can imagine," Tanis murmured. "So these creatures are spreading all over Krynn, unless your broken city was near here."

"No. I came into Que-shu out of the east. It was far from Solace, beyond the Plains of my homeland."

"What do you suppose those creatures meant, saying they had tracked you to our village?" Goldmoon asked slowly, laying her cheek on his leather tunic sleeve, slipping her hand around his arm.

"Don't worry," Riverwind said, taking her hand in his. "The warriors there would deal with them."

"Riverwind, do you remember what you were going to say?" she prompted.

"Yes, you are right," Riverwind replied, stroking her silver-gold hair. He looked at Tanis and smiled. For an instant, the expressionless mask was gone and Tanis saw warmth deep within the man's brown eyes. "I give my thanks to you, Half-Elven, and to all of you." His glance flickered over everyone. "You have saved our lives more than once and I have been ungrateful. But"—he paused—"it's all so strange!"

"It's going to get stranger." Raistlin's voice was ominous.

The companions were drawing nearer Prayer's Eye Peak. They had been able to see it from the road, rising above the forests. Its split peak looked like two hands pressed together in prayer—thus the name. The rain had stopped. The woods were deathly quiet. The companions began to think that the forest animals and birds had vanished from the land, leaving an eerie, empty silence behind. All of them felt uneasy—except perhaps Tasslehoff, and kept peering over their shoulders or drawing their swords at shadows.

Sturm insisted on walking rear guard, but he began lagging behind as the pain in his head increased. He was becoming dizzy and nauseated. Soon he lost all conception of where he was and what he was doing. He knew only that he must keep walking, placing one foot in front of the other, moving forward like one of Tas's automatons.

How did Tas's story go? Sturm tried to remember it through a haze of pain. These automatons served a wizard who had summoned a demon to carry the kender away. It was nonsense, like all the kender's stories. Sturm put one foot in front of the other. Nonsense. Like the old man's stories—the old man in the Inn. Stories of the White Stag and ancient gods—Paladine. Stories of Huma. Sturm clasped his hands on his throbbing temples as if he could hold his splitting head together. Huma . . .

As a boy, Sturm had fed on stories of Huma. His mother, daughter of a Knight of Solamnia, married to a Knight—had known no other stories to tell her son. Sturm's thoughts turned to his mother, his pain making him think of her tender ministrations when he was sick or hurt. Sturm's father had sent his wife and their son into exile because the boy—his only heir—was a target for those who would see the Knights of Solamnia banished forever from the face of Krynn. Sturm and his mother took refuge in Solace. Sturm made friends readily, particularly with one other boy, Caramon, who shared his interest in all things military. But Sturm's proud mother considered the people beneath her. And so, when the fever consumed her, she had died alone except for her teenage son. She had commended the boy to his father—if his father still lived, which Sturm was beginning to doubt.

After his mother's death, the young man became a seasoned warrior under the guidance of Tanis and Flint, who adopted Sturm as they had unofficially adopted Caramon and Raistlin. Together with Tasslehoff, the travel-loving kender, and, on occasion, the twins' wild and beautiful half-sister, Kitiara, Sturm and his friends escorted Flint on his journeys through the lands of Abanasinia, plying his trade as metalsmith.

Five years ago, however, the companions decided to separate to investigate reports of evil growing in the land. They vowed to meet again at the Inn of the Last Home.

Sturm had traveled north to Solamnia, determined to find his father and his heritage. He found nothing, and only narrowly escaped with his life—and his father's sword and armor. The journey to his homeland was a harrowing experience. Sturm had known the Knights were reviled, but he had been shocked to realize just how deep the bitterness against them ran. Huma, Lightbringer, Knight of Solamnia, had driven back the darkness years ago, during the Age of Dreams, and thus began the Age of Might. Then came the Cataclysm, when the gods abandoned man, according to the popular belief. The people had turned to the Knights for help, as they had turned to Huma in the past. But Huma was long dead. The Knights could only watch helplessly as terror rained down from heaven and Krynn was smote asunder. The people had cried to the Knights, but they could do nothing, and the people had never forgiven them. Standing in front of his family's ruined castle, Sturm vowed that he would restore the honor of the Knights of Solamnia—if it meant that he must sacrifice his life in the attempt.

But how could he do that fighting a bunch of clerics, he wondered bitterly, the trail dimming before his eyes. He stumbled, caught himself quickly. Huma had fought dragons. Give me dragons, Sturm dreamed. He lifted his eyes. The leaves blurred into a golden mist and he knew he was going to faint. Then he blinked. Everything came sharply into focus.

Before him rose Prayer's Eye Peak. He and his companions had arrived at the foot of the old, glacial mountain. He could see trails twisting and winding up the wooded slope, trails used by Solace residents to reach picnic spots on the eastern side of the Peak. Next to one of the well-worn paths stood a white stag. Sturm stared. The stag was the most magnificent animal the knight had ever seen. It was huge, standing several hands taller than any other stag the knight had hunted. It held its head proudly, its splendid rack gleaming like a crown. Its eyes were deep brown against its pure white fur, and it gazed at the knight intently, as if it knew him. Then, with a slight shake of its head, the stag bounded away to the southwest.

"Stop!" the knight called out hoarsely.

The others whirled around in alarm, drawing weapons. Tanis came running back to him. "What is it, Sturm?"

The knight involuntarily put his hand to his aching head.

"I'm sorry, Sturm," Tanis said. "I didn't realize you were as sick as this. We can rest. We're at the foot of Prayer's Eye Peak. I'm going to climb the mountain and see—"

"No! Look!" The knight gripped Tanis's shoulder and turned him around. He pointed. "See it? The white stag!"

"The white stag?" Tanis stared in the direction the knight indicated. "Where? I don't—"

"There," Sturm said softly. He took a few steps forward, toward the animal who had stopped and seemed to be waiting for him. The stag nodded its great head. It darted away again, just a few steps, then turned to face the knight once more. "He wants us to follow him," Sturm gasped. "Like Huma!"

The others had gathered around the knight now, regarding him with expressions that ranged from deeply concerned to obviously skeptical.

"I see no stag of any color," Riverwind said, his dark eyes scanning the forest.

"Head wound." Caramon nodded like a charlatan cleric. "C'mon, Sturm, lie down and rest while—"

"You great blithering idiot!" the knight snarled at Caramon. "With your brains in your stomach, it is just as well you do not see the stag. You would probably shoot it and cook it! I tell you this—we must follow it!"

"The madness of the head wound," Riverwind whispered to Tanis. "I have seen it often."

"I'm not sure," Tanis said. He was silent for a few moments. When he spoke, it was with obvious reluctance. "Though I have not seen the white stag myself, I have been with one who has and I have followed it, like in the old man's story." His hand absently fingered the ring of twisted ivy leaves that he wore on his left hand, his thoughts with the golden-haired elfmaiden who wept when he left Qualinesti.

"You're suggesting we follow an animal we can't even see?" Caramon said, his jaw going slack.

"It would not be the strangest thing we have done," Raistlin commented sarcastically in his whispering voice. "Though, remember, it was the old man who told the tale of the White Stag and the old man who got us into this—"

"It was our own choice got us into this," Tanis snapped. "We could have turned the staff over to the High Theocrat and talked our way out of the predicament; we've talked our way out of worse. I say we follow Sturm. He has been chosen, apparently, just as Riverwind was chosen to receive the staff—"

"But it's not even leading us in the right direction!" Caramon argued. "You know as well as I do there are no trails through the western part of the woods. No one ever goes there."

"All the better," Goldmoon said suddenly. "Tanis said those creatures must have the paths blocked. Maybe this is a way out. I say we follow the knight." She turned and started off with Sturm, not even glancing back at the others—obviously accustomed to being obeyed. Riverwind shrugged and shook his head, scowling darkly, but he walked after Goldmoon and the others followed.

The knight left the well-trodden paths of Prayer's Eye Peak behind, moving in a southwesterly direction up the slope. At first it appeared Caramon was right—there were no trails. Sturm was crashing through the brush like a madman. Then, suddenly, a smooth wide trail opened up ahead of them. Tanis stared at it in amazement.

"What or who cleared this trail?" he asked Riverwind, who was also examining it with a puzzled expression.

"I don't know," the Plainsman said. "It's old. That felled tree has lain there long enough to sink over halfway into the dirt and it's covered with moss and vines. But there are no tracks—other than Sturm's. There's no sign of anyone or any animal passing through here. Yet why isn't it overgrown?"

MARGARET WEIS & TRACY HICKMAN

Tanis couldn't answer and he couldn't take time to think about it. Sturm forged ahead rapidly; all the party could do was try to keep him in sight.

"Goblins, boats, lizard men, invisible stags—what next?" complained Flint to the kender.

"I wish I could see the stag," Tas said wistfully.

"Get hit on the head." The dwarf snorted. "Although with you, we probably couldn't tell the difference."

The companions followed Sturm, who was climbing with a wild kind of elation, his pain and wound forgotten. Tanis had difficulty catching up with the knight. When he did, he was alarmed at the feverish gleam in Sturm's eye. But the knight was obviously being guided by something. The trail led them up the slope of Prayer's Eye Peak. Tanis saw that it was taking them to the gap between the "hands" of stone, a gap that as far as he knew no one had ever entered before.

"Wait a moment," he gasped, running to catch up with Sturm. It was nearly midday, he guessed, though the sun was still hidden by jagged gray clouds. "Let's rest. I'm going to take a look at the land from over there." He pointed to a rock ledge that jutted out from the side of the peak.

"Rest . . ." repeated Sturm vaguely, stopping and catching his breath. He stared ahead for a moment, then turned to Tanis. "Yes. We'll rest." His eyes gleamed brightly.

"Are you all right?"

"Fine," Sturm said absently and paced around the grass, gently stroking and smoothing his moustaches. Tanis looked at him a moment, irresolute, then went back to the others who were just coming over the crest of a small rise.

"We're going to rest here," the half-elf said. Raistlin breathed a sigh of relief and sank down in the wet leaves.

"I'm going to have a look north, see what's moving back on the road to Haven," Tanis added.

"I'll come with you," Riverwind offered.

Tanis nodded and the two left the path, heading for the rock ledge. Tanis glanced at the tall warrior as they walked together. He was beginning to feel comfortable with the stern, serious

Plainsman. A deeply private person himself, Riverwind respected the privacy of others and would never think of probing the boundaries Tanis set around his soul. This was as relaxing to the half-elf as a night's unbroken sleep. He knew that his friends—simply because they were his friends and had known him for years—were speculating on his relationship with Kitiara. Why had he chosen to break it off so abruptly five years ago? And why, then, his obvious disappointment when she failed to join them? Riverwind, of course, knew nothing about Kitiara, but Tanis had the feeling that if he did, it would be all the same to the Plainsman: it was Tanis's business, not his.

When they were within sight of the Haven Road, they crawled the last few feet, inching their way along the wet rock until they came to the rim of the ledge. Tanis, looking below and to the east, could see the old picnic paths disappearing around the side of the mountain. Riverwind pointed, and Tanis realized there were creatures moving along the picnic trails! That explained the uncanny hush in the forest. Tanis pressed his lips together grimly. The creatures must be waiting to ambush them. Sturm and his white stag had probably saved their lives. But it wouldn't take the creatures long to find this new trail. Tanis glanced below him and blinked—there was no trail! There was nothing but thick, impenetrable forest. The trail had closed behind them! I must be imagining things, he thought, and he turned his eyes back to Haven Road and the many creatures moving along it. It hadn't taken them long to get organized, he thought. He gazed farther to the north and saw the still, peaceful waters of Crystalmir Lake. Then his glance traveled to the horizon.

He frowned. There was something wrong. He couldn't place it immediately, so he said nothing to Riverwind but stared at the skyline. Storm clouds massed in the north more thickly than ever, long gray fingers raking the land. And reaching up to meet them—that was it! Gripping Riverwind's arm, Tanis stabbed his finger northward. Riverwind looked, squinting, seeing nothing at first. Then he saw it, black smoke drifting into the sky. His thick, heavy brows contracted.

"Campfires," Tanis said.

"Many hundred campfires," Riverwind amended softly. "The fires of war. That is an army encampment."

"So the rumors are confirmed," Sturm said when they returned. "There *is* an army to the north."

"But what army? Whose? And why? What are they going to attack?" Caramon laughed incredulously. "No one would send an army after this staff." The warrior paused. "Would they?"

"The staff is but a part of this," Raistlin hissed. "Remember the fallen stars!"

"Children's stories!" Flint sniffed. He upended the empty wineskin, shook it, and sighed.

"My stories are not for children," Raistlin said viciously, twisting up from the leaves like a snake. "And you would do well to heed my words, dwarf!"

"There it is! There's the stag!" Sturm said suddenly, his eyes staring straight at a large boulder—or so it seemed to his companions. "It is time to go."

The knight began walking. The others hastily gathered their gear together and hurried after him. As they climbed ever farther up the trail—which seemed to materialize before them as they went—the wind switched and began blowing from the south. It was a warm breeze, carrying with it the fragrance of late-blooming autumn wildflowers. It drove back the storm clouds and just as they came to the cleft between the two halves of the Peak, the sun broke free.

It was well past midday when they stopped to rest for one more brief period before attempting the climb through the narrow gap between the walls of Prayer's Eye Peak through which Sturm said they must go. The stag had led the way, he insisted.

"It'll be suppertime soon," Caramon said. He heaved a gusty sigh, staring at his feet. "I could eat my boots!"

"They're beginning to look good to me, too," Flint said grumpily. "I wish that stag was flesh and blood. It might be useful for something besides getting us lost!"

"Shut up!" Sturm turned on the dwarf in a sudden rage, his fists clenched. Tanis rose quickly, put his hand on the knight's shoulder, holding him back.

Sturm stood glaring at the dwarf, moustaches quivering, then he jerked away from Tanis. "Let's go," he muttered.

As the companions entered the narrow defile, they could see clear blue sky on the other side. The south wind whistled across the steep white walls of the Peak soaring above them. They walked carefully, small stones causing their feet to slip more than once. Fortunately, the way was so narrow that they could easily regain their balance by catching themselves against the steep walls.

After about thirty minutes of walking, they came out on the other side of Prayer's Eye Peak. They halted, staring down into a valley. Lush, grassy meadowland flowed in green waves below them to lap on the shores of a light-green aspen forest far to the south. The storm clouds were behind them, and the sun shone brightly in a clear, azure sky.

For the first time, they found their cloaks too heavy, except for Raistlin who remained huddled in his red, hooded cape. Flint had spent the morning complaining about the rain and now started in on the sunshine, it was too bright, glaring into his eyes. It was too hot, beating down on his helm.

"I say we throw the dwarf off the mountain," growled Caramon to Tanis.

Tanis grinned. "He'd rattle all the way down and give away our position."

"Who's down there to hear him?" Caramon said, gesturing toward the valley with his broad hand. "I bet we're the first living beings to set eyes on this valley."

"First *living* beings," Raistlin breathed. "You are right there, my brother. For you look on Darken Wood."

No one spoke. Riverwind shifted uncomfortably; Goldmoon crept over to stand beside him, staring down into the green trees, her eyes wide. Flint cleared his throat and fell silent, stroking his long beard. Sturm regarded the forest calmly. So did Tasslehoff. "It doesn't look bad at all," the kender said cheerfully. Sitting cross-legged on the ground, a sheaf of parchment spread out on his knees, he was drawing a map with a bit of charcoal, attempting to trace their way up Prayer's Eye Peak.

"Looks are as deceptive as light-fingered kender," Raistlin whispered harshly.

Tasslehoff frowned, started to retort, then caught Tanis's eye and went back to his drawing. Tanis walked over to Sturm. The knight stood out on a ledge, the south wind blowing back his long hair and whipping his frayed cape about him.

"Sturm, where is the stag? Do you see it now?"

"Yes," Sturm answered. He pointed downward. "It walked across the meadow; I can see its trail in the tall grass. It has gone into the aspens there."

"Gone into Darken Wood," Tanis murmured.

"Who says that is Darken Wood?" Sturm turned to face Tanis.

"Raistlin."

"Bah!"

"He is magi," Tanis said.

"He is crazed," Sturm replied. Then he shrugged. "But stay here rooted on the side of the Peak if you like, Tanis. I will follow the stag—as did Huma—even if it leads me into Darken Wood." Wrapping his cloak around him, Sturm climbed down the ledge and began to walk along a winding trail that led down the mountainside.

Tanis returned to the others. "The stag's leading him on a straight path right into the forest," he said. "How certain are you that this forest is Darken Wood, Raistlin?"

"How certain is one of anything, Half-Elven?" the mage replied. "I am not certain of drawing my next breath. But go ahead. Walk into the wood that no living man has ever walked out of. Death is life's one great certainty, Tanis."

The half-elf felt a sudden urge to throw Raistlin off the side of the mountain. He stared after Sturm, who was nearly halfway down into the valley.

"I'm going with Sturm," he said suddenly. "But I'll be responsible for no one else in this decision. The rest of you may follow as you choose."

"I'm coming!" Tasslehoff rolled his map up and slipped it into his scroll case. He scrambled to his feet, sliding in the loose rock.

"Ghosts!" Flint scowled at Raistlin, snapped his fingers derisively, then stumped over to stand beside the half-elf. Goldmoon followed unhesitatingly, though her face was pale. Riverwind joined the group more slowly, his face thoughtful. Tanis was relieved—the barbarians had many frightening legends of Darken Wood, he knew. And finally, Raistlin moved forward so rapidly he took his brother completely by surprise.

Tanis regarded the mage with a slight smile. "Why do you come?" he couldn't help asking.

"Because you will need me, Half-Elven," the mage hissed. "Besides, where would you have us go? You have allowed us to be led this far, there can be no turning back. It is the Ogre's Choice you offer us, Tanis—'Die fast or die slow.' " He set off down the side of the Peak. "Coming, brother?"

The others glanced uneasily at Tanis as the brothers passed. The half-elf felt like a fool. Raistlin was right, of course. He'd let this go far beyond his control, then made it seem as if it were their decision, not his, allowing him to go forward with a clear conscience. Angrily he picked up a rock and hurled it far down the mountainside. Why was it his responsibility in the first place? Why had he gotten involved, when all he had wanted was to find Kitiara and tell her his mind was made up—he loved her and wanted her. He could accept her human frailties as he had learned to accept his own.

But Kit hadn't come back to him. She had a "new lord." Maybe that's why he'd—

"Ho, Tanis!" The kender's voice floated up to him.

"I'm coming," he muttered.

The sun was just beginning to dip into the west when the companions reached the edge of the forest. Tanis figured they had at least three or four hours of daylight left. If the stag continued to lead them on smooth, clear trails, they might be able to get through this forest before darkness fell.

Sturm waited for them beneath the aspens, resting comfortably in the leafy, green shade. The companions left the meadow slowly, none of them in any hurry to enter the woods.

"The stag entered here," Sturm said, rising to his feet and pointing into the tall grass.

Tanis saw no tracks. He took a drink of water from his nearly empty waterskin and stared into the forest. As Tasslehoff had said, the wood did not seem sinister. In fact, it looked cool and inviting after the harsh brilliance of the autumn sunshine.

"Maybe there'll be some game in here," Caramon said, rocking back on his heels. "Not stags, of course," he added hastily. "Rabbits, maybe."

"Shoot nothing. Eat nothing. Drink nothing in Darken Wood," Raistlin whispered.

Tanis looked at the mage, whose hourglass eyes were dilated. The metallic skin shone a ghastly color in the strong sunlight. Raistlin leaned upon his staff, shivering as if from a chill.

"Children's stories," Flint muttered, but the dwarf's voice lacked conviction. Although Tanis knew Raistlin's flair for the dramatic, he had never seen the mage affected like this before.

"What do you sense, Raistlin?" he asked quietly.

"There is a great and powerful magic laid on this wood," whispered Raistlin.

"Evil?" asked Tanis.

"Only to those who bring evil in with them," the mage stated.

"Then you are the only one who need fear this forest," Sturm told the mage coldly.

Caramon's face flushed an ugly red; his hand fumbled for his sword. Sturm's hand went to his blade. Tanis gripped Sturm's arm as Raistlin touched his brother. The mage stared at the knight, his golden eyes glimmering.

"We shall see," Raistlin said, the words nothing more than hissing sounds flicking between his teeth. "We shall see." Then, leaning heavily upon his staff, Raistlin turned to his brother. "Coming?"

Caramon glared angrily at Sturm, then entered the wood, walking beside his twin. The others moved after them, leaving only Tanis and Flint standing in the long, waving grass.

"I'm getting too old for this, Tanis," the dwarf said suddenly.

"Nonsense," the half-elf replied, smiling. "You fought like a—"

"No, I don't mean the bones or the muscles"—the dwarf looked at his gnarled hands—"though they're old enough. I mean the spirit. Years ago, before the others were born, you and I would have walked into a magicked wood without giving it a second thought. Now . . ."

"Cheer up," Tanis said. He tried to sound light, though he was deeply disturbed by the dwarf's unusual somberness. He studied Flint closely for the first time since meeting outside Solace. The dwarf looked old, but then Flint had always looked old. His face, what could be seen through the mass of gray beard and moustaches and overhanging white eyebrows, was brown and wrinkled and cracked like old leather. The dwarf grumbled and complained, but then Flint had always grumbled and complained. The change was in the eyes. The fiery luster was gone.

"Don't let Raistlin get to you," Tanis said. "We'll sit around the fire tonight and laugh at his ghost stories."

"I suppose so." Flint sighed. He was silent a moment, then said, "Someday I'll slow you up, Tanis. I don't ever want you to think, why do I put up with this grumbling old dwarf?"

"Because I need you, grumbling old dwarf," Tanis said, putting his hand on the dwarf's heavy-set shoulder. He motioned into the wood, after the others. "I need you, Flint. They're all so . . . so young. You're like a solid rock that I can set my back against as I wield my sword."

Flint's face flushed in pleasure. He tugged at his beard, then cleared his throat gruffly. "Yes, well, you were always sentimental. Come along. We're wasting time. I want to get through this confounded forest as fast as possible." Then he muttered, "Just glad it's daylight."

DARKEN WOOD.
THE DEAD WALK. RAISTLIN'S MAGIC.

10

The only thing Tanis felt on entering the forest was relief at being out of the glare of the autumn sun. The half-elf recalled all the legends he had heard about Darken Wood— stories of ghosts told around the fire at night—and he kept in mind Raistlin's foreboding. But all Tanis felt was that the forest was so much more alive than any other he had ever entered.

There was no deathly hush as they had experienced earlier. Small animals chattered in the brush. Birds fluttered in the high branches above them. Insects with gaily colored wings flitted past. Leaves rustled and stirred, flowers swayed though no breeze touched them—as if the plants reveled in being alive.

All of the companions entered the forest with their hands on their weapons, wary and watchful and distrustful. After a time of trying to avoid making leaves crunch, Tas said it seemed "kind of silly," and they relaxed—all except Raistlin.

They walked for about two hours, traveling at a smooth but rapid easy pace along a smooth and clear trail. Shadows lengthened as the sun made its downward slide. Tanis felt at peace in this forest. He had no fear that the awful, winged creatures could follow them here. Evil seemed out of place, unless, as Raistlin said, one brought one's own evil into the wood. Tanis looked at the mage. Raistlin walked alone, his head bowed. The shadows of the forest trees seemed to gather thickly around the young mage. Tanis shivered and realized that the air was turning cool as the sun dropped below the treetops. It was time to begin thinking about making camp for the night.

Tanis pulled out Tasslehoff's map to study it once more before the light faded. The map was of elven design and written across the forest in flowing script were the words "Darken Wood." But the woods themselves were only vaguely outlined, and Tanis couldn't be certain if the words pertained to this forest or one farther south. Raistlin must be wrong, Tanis decided—this can't be Darken Wood. Or, if so, its evil was simply a product of the mage's imagination. They walked on.

Soon it was twilight, that time of evening when the dying light makes everything most vivid and distinct. The companions began to lag. Raistlin limped, and his breath came in wheezing gasps. Sturm's face turned ashen. The half-elf was just about to call a halt for the night when—as if anticipating his wishes—the trail led them right to a large, green glade. Clear water bubbled up from underground and trickled down smooth rocks to form a shallow brook. The glade was blanketed with thick, inviting grass; tall trees stood guard duty on the edges. As they saw the glade, the sun's light reddened, then faded, and the misty shades of night crept around the trees.

"Do not leave the path," Raistlin intoned as his companions started to enter the glade.

Tanis sighed. "Raistlin," he said patiently—"we'll be all right. The path is in plain sight, not ten feet away. Come on. You've got to rest. We all do. Look"—Tanis held out the map—"I don't think this is Darken Wood. According to this—"

Raistlin ignored the map with disdain. The rest of the companions ignored the mage and, moving off the path, began setting up camp. Sturm sank down against a tree, his eyes closed in pain, while Caramon stared at the smaller, fleeting shadows with a hungry eye. At a signal from Caramon, Tasslehoff slipped off into the forest after firewood.

Watching them, the mage's face twisted in a sardonic smile. "You are all fools. This is Darken Wood, as you will see before the night is ended." He shrugged. "But, as you say, I need rest. However, I will not leave the path." Raistlin sat down on the trail, his staff beside him.

Caramon flushed in embarrassment as he saw the others exchanging amused glances. "Aw, Raist," the big man said, "join us. Tas has gone for wood and maybe I can shoot a rabbit."

"*Shoot* nothing!" Raistlin actually spoke above a whisper, making everyone start. "*Harm* nothing in Darken Wood! Neither plant nor tree, bird nor animal!"

"I agree with Raistlin," Tanis said. "We have to spend the night here and I don't want to kill any animal in this forest if we don't have to."

"Elves never want to kill period," Flint grumbled. "The magician scares us to death and you starve us. Well, if anything does attack us tonight, I hope it's edible!"

"You and me both, dwarf." Caramon heaved a sigh, went over to the creek, and began trying to assuage his hunger by drowning it.

Tasslehoff returned with firewood. "I didn't cut it," he assured Raistlin. "I just picked it up."

But even Riverwind couldn't make the wood catch fire. "The wood's wet," he stated finally and tossed his tinderbox back into his pack.

"We need light," Flint said uneasily as night's shadows closed in thickly. Sounds in the woods that had been innocent in the daytime now seemed sinister and threatening.

"Surely you do not fear children's stories," Raistlin hissed.

"No!" snapped the dwarf. "I just want to make certain the kender doesn't rifle my pack in the dark."

"Very well," said Raistlin with unusual mildness. He spoke his word of command: "*Shirak.*" A pale, white light shone from the crystal on the tip of the mage's staff. It was a ghostly light and did little to brighten the darkness. In fact, it seemed to emphasize the menace in the night.

"There, you have light," the mage whispered softly. He thrust the bottom of the staff into the wet ground.

It was then Tanis realized his elven vision was gone. He should have been able to see the warm, red outlines of his companions,

MARGARET WEIS & TRACY HICKMAN

but they were nothing more than darker shadows against the starry darkness of the glade. The half-elf didn't say anything to the others, but the peaceful feeling he had been enjoying was pierced by a sliver of fear.

"I'll take the first watch," Sturm offered heavily. "I shouldn't sleep with this head wound, anyway. I once knew a man who did, he never woke up."

"We'll watch in twos," Tanis said. "I'll take first watch with you."

The others opened packs and began making up beds on the grass, except for Raistlin. He remained sitting on the trail, the light of his staff shining on his bowed, hooded head. Sturm settled down beneath a tree. Tanis walked over to the brook and drank thirstily. Suddenly he heard a strangled cry behind him. He drew his sword and stood, all in one motion. The others had their weapons drawn. Only Raistlin sat, unmoving.

"Put your swords away," he said. "They will do you no good. Only a weapon of powerful magic could harm these."

An army of warriors surrounded them. That alone would have been enough to chill anyone's blood. But the companions could have dealt with that. What they couldn't handle was the horror that overwhelmed and numbed their senses. Each one recalled Caramon's flippant comment: "I'll fight the living any day of the week, but not the dead."

These warriors were dead.

Nothing more than fleeting, fragile white light outlined their bodies. It was as if the human warmth that had been theirs while they lived lingered on horribly after death. The flesh had rotted away, leaving behind the body's image as remembered by the soul. The soul apparently remembered other things, too. Each warrior was dressed in ancient, remembered armor. Each warrior carried remembered weapons that could inflict well-remembered death. But the undead needed no weapons. They could kill from fear alone, or by the touch of their grave-cold hands.

How can we fight these things? Tanis thought wildly, he who had never felt such fear in the face of flesh and blood enemies. Panic engulfed him, and he considered yelling for the others to turn and run for it.

Angrily, the half-elf forced himself to calm down, to get a grip on reality. Reality! He almost laughed at the irony. Running was useless; they would get lost, separated. They had to stay and deal with this—somehow. He began to walk toward the ghostly warriors. The dead said nothing, made no threatening moves. They simply stood, blocking the path. It was impossible to count them since some glimmered into being while others faded, only to return when their comrades dimmed. Not that it makes any difference, Tanis admitted to himself, feeling sweat chill his body. One of these undead warriors could kill all of us simply by lifting its hand.

As the half-elf drew nearer to the warriors, he saw a gleam of light—Raistlin's staff. The mage, leaning on his staff, stood in front of the huddle of companions. Tanis came to stand beside him. The pale crystal light reflected on the mage's face, making it seem nearly as ghostly as the faces of the dead before him.

"Welcome to Darken Wood, Tanis," the mage said.

"Raistlin—" Tanis choked. He had to try more than once to get his dry throat to form a sound. "What are these—"

"Spectral minions," the mage whispered without taking his eyes from them. "We are fortunate."

"Fortunate?" Tanis repeated incredulously. "Why?"

"These are the spirits of men who gave their pledge to perform some task. They failed in that pledge, and it is their doom to keep performing the same task over and over until they win their release and find true rest in death."

"How in the name of the Abyss does that make us fortunate?" Tanis whispered harshly, releasing his fear in anger. "Perhaps they pledged to rid the forest of all who entered!"

"That is possible"—Raistlin flickered a glance at the half-elf—"though I do not think it likely. We will find out."

Before Tanis could react, the mage stepped away from the group and faced the spectres.

"Raist!" Caramon said in a strangled voice, starting to shove forward.

"Keep him back, Tanis," Raistlin commanded harshly. "Our lives depend on this."

Gripping the warrior's arm, Tanis asked Raistlin, "What are you going to do?"

"I am going to cast a spell that will enable us to communicate with them. I will perceive their thoughts. They will speak through me."

The mage threw his head back, his hood slipping off. He stretched out his arms and began to speak. "*Ast bilak parbilakar. Suh tangus moipar?*" he murmured, then repeated that phrase three times. As Raistlin spoke, the crowd of warriors parted and a figure more awesome and terrifying than the rest appeared. The spectre was taller than the rest and wore a shimmering crown. His pallid armor was richly decorated with dark jewels. His face showed the most terrible grief and anguish. He advanced upon Raistlin.

Caramon choked and averted his eyes. Tanis dared not speak or cry out, fearful of disturbing the mage and breaking the spell. The spectre raised a fleshless hand, reached out slowly to touch the young mage. Tanis trembled—the spectre's touch meant certain death. But Raistlin, entranced, did not move. Tanis wondered if he even saw the chill hand coming toward his heart. Then Raistlin spoke.

"You who have been long dead, use my living voice to tell us of your bitter sorrow. Then give us leave to pass through this forest, for our purpose is not evil, as you will see if you read our hearts."

The spectre's hand halted abruptly. The pale eyes searched Raistlin's face. Then, shimmering in the darkness, the spectre bowed before the mage. Tanis sucked in his breath; he had sensed Raistlin's power, but this . . !

Raistlin returned the bow, then moved to stand beside the spectre. His face was nearly as pale as that of the ghostly figure next to him. The living dead and the dead living, Tanis thought, shuddering.

When Raistlin spoke, his voice was no longer the wheezing whispering of the fragile mage. It was deep and dark and commanding and rang through the forest. It was cold and hollow and might have come from below the ground. "Who are you who trespass in Darken Wood?"

Tanis tried to answer, but his throat had dried up completely. Caramon, next to him, couldn't even lift his head. Then Tanis felt movement at his side. The kender! Cursing himself, he reached out to grab for Tasslehoff, but it was too late. The small figure, topknot dancing, ran out into the light of Raistlin's staff and stood before the spectre.

Tasslehoff bowed respectfully. "I am Tasslehoff Burrfoot," he said. "My friends"—he waved his small hand at the group—"call me Tas. Who are you?"

"It matters little," the sepulchral voice intoned. "Know only that we are warriors from a time long forgotten."

"Is it true that you broke a pledge and that's how you come to be here?" Tas asked with interest.

"It is. We pledged to guard this land. Then came the smoldering mountain from the heavens. The land was ripped apart. Evil things crept out from the bowels of the earth and we dropped our swords and fled in terror until bitter death overtook us. We have been called to fulfill our oath, as evil once more stalks the land. And here will we remain until evil is driven back and balance is restored again."

Suddenly Raistlin gave a shriek and flung back his head, his eyes rolling upward until the watching companions could see only the whites. His voice became a thousand voices crying out at once. This startled even the kender, who stepped back a pace and looked around uneasily for Tanis.

The spectre raised his hand in a commanding gesture, and the tumult ceased as though swallowed by the darkness. "My men demand to know the reason you enter Darken Wood. If it is for evil, you will find that you have brought evil upon yourselves, for you will not live to see the moons rise."

"No, not evil. Certainly not," Tasslehoff said hurriedly. "It's kind of a long story, you see, but we're obviously not going anywhere in a big hurry and you're obviously not either, so I'll tell it to you.

"To begin with, we were in the Inn of the Last Home in Solace. You probably don't know it. I'm not sure how long it's been there, but it wasn't around during the Cataclysm and it sounds like you were. Well, there we were, listening to the old man talking of Huma and he—the old man, not Huma—told Goldmoon to sing her song and she said what song and then she sang and a Seeker decided to be a music critic and Riverwind, that's the tall man over there—shoved the Seeker into the fire. It was an accident—he didn't mean to. But the Seeker went up like a torch! You should have seen it! Anyway, the old man handed me the staff and said hit him and I did and the staff turned to blue crystal and the flames died and—"

"Blue crystal!" The spectre's voice echoed hollowly from Raistlin's throat as he began to walk toward them. Tanis and Sturm both jumped forward, grabbing Tas and dragging him out of the way. But the spectre seemed intent only on examining the group. His flickering eyes focused on Goldmoon. Raising a pale hand, he motioned her forward.

"No!" Riverwind tried to prevent her from leaving his side, but she pushed away gently and walked over to stand before the spectre, the staff in her hand. The ghostly army encircled them.

Suddenly the spectre drew his sword from its pallid sheath. He held it high overhead and white light tinged with blue flame flickered from the blade.

"Look at the staff!" Goldmoon gasped.

The staff glowed pale blue, as if answering the sword.

The ghostly king turned to Raistlin and reached his pale hand toward the entranced mage. Caramon gave a hoarse bellow and broke free of Tanis's grip. Drawing his sword, he lunged at the undead warrior. The blade pierced the flickering body, but it was Caramon who screamed in pain and dropped, writhing, to the ground. Tanis and Sturm knelt beside him. Raistlin stared ahead, his expression unchanged, unmoving.

"Caramon, where—" Tanis held him, trying frantically to see where the big man was injured.

"My hand!" Caramon rocked back and forth, sobbing, his left hand—his sword hand—thrust tightly under his right arm.

"What's the matter?" Tanis asked. Then, seeing the warrior's sword on the ground, he knew: Caramon's sword was rimed with frost.

Tanis looked up in horror and saw the spectre's hand close tightly around Raistlin's wrist. A shudder wracked the mage's frail body; his face twisted in pain, but he did not fall. The mage's eyes closed, the lines of cynicism and bitterness smoothed away and the peace of death descended on him. Tanis watched in awe, only partially aware of Caramon's hoarse cries. He saw Raistlin's face transform again, this time imbued with ecstasy. The mage's aura of power intensified until it glowed around him with an almost palpable brilliance.

"We are summoned," Raistlin said. The voice was his own and yet like none Tanis had ever heard him use. "We must go."

The mage turned his back on them and walked into the woods, the ghostly king's fleshless hand still grasping his wrist. The circle of undead parted to let him pass.

"Stop them," Caramon moaned. He staggered to his feet.

"We can't!" Tanis fought to restrain him, and finally the big man collapsed in the half-elf's arms, weeping like a child. "We'll follow him. He'll be all right. He's magi, Caramon—we can't understand. We'll follow—"

The eyes of the undead flickered with an unholy light as they watched the companions pass them and enter the forest. The spectral army closed ranks behind them.

The companions stepped into a raging battle. Steel rang; wounded men shrieked for help. So real was the clash of armies in the darkness that Sturm drew his sword reflexively. The tumult deafened him; he ducked and dodged unseen blows that he knew were aimed at him. He swung his sword in desperation at black air, knowing that he was doomed and there was no escape. He began to run, and he suddenly stumbled out of the forest into a barren, wasted glade. Raistlin stood before him, alone.

The mage's eyes were closed. He sighed gently, then collapsed to the ground. Sturm ran to him, then Caramon appeared, nearly knocking Sturm over to reach his brother and gather him tenderly in his arms. One by one, the others ran as if driven into the glade. Raistlin was still murmuring strange, unfamiliar words. The spectres vanished.

"Raist!" Caramon sobbed brokenly.

The mage's eyelids flickered and opened. "The spell . . . drained me. . . ." he whispered. "I must rest. . . ."

"And rest ye shall!" boomed a voice—a living voice!

Tanis breathed a sigh of relief even as he put his hand on his sword. Quickly he and the others jumped protectively in front of Raistlin, turning to face outward, staring into the darkness. Then the silver moon appeared, suddenly, as if a hand had produced it from beneath a black silk scarf. Now they could see the head and shoulders of a man standing amid the trees. His bare shoulders were as large and heavy as Caramon's. A mane of long hair curled around his neck; his eyes were bright and glittered coldly. The companions heard a rustling in the brush and saw the flash of a spear tip being raised, pointing at Tanis.

"Put thy puny weapons down," the man warned. "Ye be surrounded and have not a chance."

"A trick," Sturm growled, but even as he spoke there was a tremendous crashing and cracking of tree limbs. More men appeared, surrounding them, all armed with spears that glinted in the moonlight.

The first man strode forward then, and the companions stared in amazement, their hands on their weapons going slack.

The man wasn't a man at all, but a centaur! Human from the waist up, he had the body of a horse from the waist down. He cantered forward with easy grace, powerful muscles rippling across his barrel chest. Other centaurs moved into the path at his commanding gesture. Tanis sheathed his sword. Flint sneezed.

"Thee must come with us," the centaur ordered.

"My brother is ill," Caramon growled. "He can't go anywhere."

"Place him upon my back," the centaur said coolly. "In fact, if any of you be tired, thee may ride to where we go."

"Where are you taking us?" Tanis asked.

"Thee is in no position to ask questions." The centaur reached out and prodded Caramon's back with his spear. "We travel far and fast. I suggest thee ride. But fear not." He bowed before Goldmoon, extending his foreleg and touching his hand to his shaggy hair. "Harm will not come to thee this night."

"Can I ride, Tanis, please?" begged Tasslehoff.

"Don't trust them!" Flint sneezed violently.

"I *don't* trust them," Tanis muttered, "but we don't seem to have a whole lot of choice in the matter—Raistlin can't walk. Go on, Tas. The rest of you, too."

Caramon, scowling at the centaurs suspiciously, lifted his brother in his arms and set him upon the back of one of the half-man, half-animals. Raistlin slumped forward weakly.

"Climb up," the centaur said to Caramon. "I can bear the weight of thee both. Thy brother will need thy support, for we ride swiftly tonight."

Flushing with embarrassment, the big warrior clambered onto the centaur's broad back, his huge legs dangling almost to the ground. He put an arm around Raistlin as the centaur galloped down the path. Tasslehoff, giggling with excitement, jumped onto a centaur and promptly slid off the other side into the mud. Sturm, sighing, picked up the kender and set him on the centaur's back. Then, before Flint could protest, the knight lifted the dwarf up behind Tas. Flint tried to speak but could only sneeze as the centaur moved away. Tanis rode with the first centaur, who seemed to be the leader.

"Where are you taking us?" Tanis asked again.

"To the Forestmaster," the centaur answered.

"The Forestmaster?" Tanis repeated. "Who is he, one like yourselves?"

"She is the Forestmaster," the centaur replied and began to canter down the trail.

Tanis started to ask another question, but the centaur's quickened pace jolted him, and he nearly bit through his tongue as he came down hard on the centaur's back. Feeling himself start to slide backward as the centaur trotted faster and faster, Tanis threw his arms around the centaur's broad torso.

"Nay, thee doesn't need to squeeze me in two!" The centaur glanced back, his eyes glittering in the moonlight. "It be my job to see thee stays on. Relax. Put thy hands on me rump to balance thyself. There, now. Grip with thy legs."

The centaurs left the trail and plunged into the forest. The moonlight was immediately swallowed up by the dense trees.

Tanis felt branches whip past, swiping at his clothing. The centaur never swerved or slowed in his gallop, however, and Tanis could only assume he knew the trail well, a trail the half-elf couldn't see.

Soon the pace began to slacken and the centaur finally came to a stop. Tanis could see nothing in the smothering darkness. He knew his companions were near only because he could hear Raistlin's shallow breathing, Caramon's jingling armor, and Flint's unabated sneezing. Even the light from Raistlin's staff had died.

"A powerful magic is laid on this forest," the mage whispered weakly when Tanis asked him about it. "This magic dispels all others."

Tanis's uneasiness grew. "Why are we stopping?"

"Because thee art here. Dismount," the centaur ordered gruffly.

"Where is here?" Tanis slid off the centaur's broad back onto the ground. He stared around him but could see nothing. Apparently the trees kept even the smallest glimmer of moonlight or starlight from penetrating through to the trail.

"Thee stands in the center of Darken Wood," the centaur replied. "And now I bid thee farewell—or fare evil, depending on how the Forestmaster judges thee."

"Wait a minute!" Caramon called out angrily. "You can't just leave us here in the middle of this forest, blind as newborn kittens—"

"Stop them!" Tanis ordered, reaching for his sword. But his weapon was gone. An explosive oath from Sturm indicated the knight had discovered the same thing.

The centaur chuckled. Tanis heard hooves beat into soft earth and tree branches rustled. The centaurs were gone.

"Good riddance!" Flint sneezed.

"Are we all here?" Tanis asked, reaching out his hand and feeling Sturm's strong, reassuring grasp.

"I'm here," piped Tasslehoff. "Oh, Tanis, wasn't it wonderful? I—"

"Hush, Tas!" Tanis snapped. "The Plainsmen?"

"We're here," said Riverwind grimly. "Weaponless."

"No one has a weapon?" Tanis asked. "Not that it would do us much good in this cursed blackness," he amended bitterly.

"I have my staff," Goldmoon's low voice said softly.

"And a formidable weapon that is, daughter of Que-shu," came a deep voice. "A weapon for good, intended to combat illness and injury and disease." The unseen voice grew sad. "In these times it will also be used as a weapon against the evil creatures who seek to find and banish it from the world."

THE FORESTMASTER.
A PEACEFUL INTERLUDE.

11

W ho are you?" Tanis called. "Show your-
self!"

"We will not harm you," bluffed Caramon.

"Of course you won't." Now the deep voice was amused. "You
have no weapons. I will return them when the time is propi-
tious. No one brings weapons into Darken Wood, not even a
knight of Solamnia. Do not fear, noble knight. I recognize your
blade as ancient and most valuable! I will keep it safe. Forgive
this apparent lack of trust, but even the great Huma laid the
Dragonlance at my feet."

"Huma!" Sturm gasped. "Who are you?"

"I am the Forestmaster." Even as the deep voice spoke, the
darkness parted. A gasp of awe, gentle as a spring wind, swept
the company as they stared before them. Silver moonlight shone
brightly on a high rock ledge. Standing on the ledge was a
unicorn. She regarded them coolly, her intelligent eyes gleaming
with infinite wisdom.

The unicorn's beauty pierced the heart. Goldmoon felt swift
tears spring to her eyes and she was forced to close them against
the animal's magnificent radiance. Her fur was the silver of
moonlight, her horn was shining pearl, her mane like seafoam.
The head might have been sculpted from glistening marble, but
no human or even dwarven hand could capture the elegance and

grace that lived in the fine lines of the powerful neck and muscular chest. The legs were strong but delicate, the hooves small and cloven like those of a goat. In later days, when Goldmoon walked dark paths and her heart was bleak with despair and hopelessness, she had only to shut her eyes and remember the unicorn to find comfort.

The unicorn tossed her head and then lowered it in grave welcome. The companions, feeling awkward and clumsy and confused, bowed in return. The unicorn suddenly whirled and left the rock ledge, cantering down the rocks toward them.

Tanis, feeling a spell lifted from him, looked around. The bright silver moonlight lit a sylvan glade. Tall trees surrounded them like giant, beneficent guardians. The half-elf was aware of a deep abiding sense of peace here. But there was also a waiting sadness.

"Rest yourselves," the Forestmaster said as she came among them. "You are tired and hungry. Food will be brought and fresh water for cleansing. You may put aside your watchfulness and fears for this evening. Safety exists here, if it exists anywhere in this land tonight."

Caramon, his eyes lighting up at the mention of food, eased his brother to the ground. Raistlin sank into the grass against the trunk of a tree. His face was deathly pale in the silver moonlight, but his breathing was easy. He did not seem ill so much as just terribly exhausted. Caramon sat next to him, looking around for food. Then he heaved a sigh.

"Probably more berries anyway," the warrior said unhappily to Tanis. "I crave meat—roasted deer haunch, a nice sizzling bit of rabbit—"

"Hush," Sturm remonstrated softly, glancing at the Forestmaster. "She'd probably consider roasting you first!"

Centaurs came out of the forest bearing a clean, white cloth, which they spread on the grass. Others placed clear crystal globe lights on the cloth, illuminating the forest.

Tasslehoff stared at the lights curiously. "They're bug lights!"

The crystal globes held thousands of tiny bugs, each one having two brightly glowing spots on its back. They crawled around inside the globes, apparently content to explore their surroundings.

Next, the centaurs brought bowls of cool water and clean white cloths to bathe their faces and hands. The water refreshed their bodies and minds as it washed away the stains of battle. Other centaurs placed chairs, which Caramon stared at dubiously. They were crafted of one piece of wood that curved around the body. They appeared comfortable, except that each chair had only one leg!

"Please be seated," said the Forestmaster graciously.

"I can't sit in that!" the warrior protested. "I'll tip over." He stood at the edge of the tablecloth. "Besides, the tablecloth is spread on the grass. I'll sit on the grass with it."

"Close to the food," muttered Flint into his beard.

The others glanced uneasily at the chairs, the strange crystal bug lamps, and the centaurs. The Chieftain's Daughter, however, knew what was expected of guests. Although the outside world might have considered her people barbarians, Goldmoon's tribe had strict rules of politeness that must be religiously observed. Goldmoon knew that to keep your host waiting was an insult to both the host and his bounty. She sat down with regal grace. The one-legged chair rocked slightly, adjusting to her height, crafting itself for her alone.

"Sit at my right hand, warrior," she said formally, conscious of the many eyes upon them. Riverwind's face showed no emotion, though he was a ludicrous sight trying to bend his tall body to sit in the seemingly fragile chair. But, once seated, he leaned back comfortably, almost smiling in disbelieving approval.

"Thank you all for waiting until I was seated," Goldmoon said hastily, to cover the others' hesitation. "You may all sit now."

"Oh, that's all right," began Caramon, folding his arms across his chest. "I wasn't waiting. I'm not going to sit in these weird chair—" Sturm's elbow dug sharply into the warrior's ribs.

"Gracious lady," Sturm bowed and sat down with knightly dignity.

"Well, if he can do it, so can I," muttered Caramon, his decision hastened by the fact that the centaurs were bringing in food. He helped his brother to a seat and then sat down gingerly, making certain the chair bore his weight.

Four centaurs positioned themselves at each of the four corners of the huge white cloth spread out upon the ground. They lifted the cloth to the height of a table, then released it. The cloth remained floating in place, its delicately embroidered surface as hard and sturdy as one of the solid tables in the Inn of the Last Home.

"How splendid! How do they do that?" Tasslehoff cried, peering underneath the cloth. "There's nothing under there!" he reported, his eyes wide.

The centaurs laughed uproariously and even the Forestmaster smiled. Next the centaurs laid down plates made of beautifully cut and polished wood. Each guest was given a knife and fork fashioned from the horns of a deer. Platters of hot roasted meat filled the air with a tantalizing smoky aroma. Fragrant loaves of bread and huge wooden bowls of fruit glistened in the soft lamplight.

Caramon, feeling secure in his chair, rubbed his hands together. Then he grinned broadly and picked up his fork. "Ahhhh!" He sighed in appreciation as one of the centaurs set before him a platter of roasted deer meat. Caramon plunged his fork in, sniffing in rapture at the steam and juice that gushed forth from the meat. Suddenly he realized everyone was staring at him. He stopped and looked around.

"Wha—?" he asked, blinking. Then his eyes rested on the Forestmaster and he flushed and hurriedly removed his fork. "I . . . I beg your pardon. This deer must have been someone you knew—I mean—one of your subjects."

The Forestmaster smiled gently. "Be at ease, warrior," she said. "The deer fulfills his purpose in life by providing sustenance for the hunter—be it wolf or man. We do not mourn the loss of those who die fulfilling their destinies."

It seemed to Tanis that the Forestmaster's dark eyes went to Sturm as she spoke, and there was a deep sadness in them that filled the half-elf's heart with cold fear. But when he turned back to the Forestmaster, he saw the magnificent animal smiling once more. "My imagination," he thought.

"How do we know, Master," Tanis asked hesitantly, "whether the life of any creature has fulfilled its destiny? I have known the very old to die in bitterness and despair. I have seen young children die before their time but leave behind such a legacy of love and joy that grief for their passing was tempered by the knowledge that their brief lives had given much to others."

"You have answered your own question, Tanis Half-Elven, far better than I could," the Forestmaster said gravely. "Say that our lives are measured not by gain but by giving."

The half-elf started to reply, but the Forestmaster interrupted. "Put your cares aside for now. Enjoy the peace of my forest while you may. Its time is passing."

Tanis glanced sharply at the Forestmaster, but the great animal had turned her attention away from him and was staring far off into the woods, her eyes clouded with sorrow. The half-elf wondered what she meant, and he sat, lost in dark thoughts, until he felt a gentle hand touch his.

"You should eat," Goldmoon said. "Your cares won't vanish with the meal—and, if they do, so much the better."

Tanis smiled at her and began to eat with a sharp appetite. He took the Forestmaster's advice and relegated his worries to the back of his mind for a while. Goldmoon was right: they weren't likely to go away.

The rest of the companions did the same, accepting the strangeness of their surroundings with the aplomb of seasoned travelers. Though there was nothing to drink but water—much to Flint's disappointment—the cool, clear liquid washed the terrors and doubts from their hearts as it had cleansed the blood and dirt from their hands. They laughed, talked, and ate, enjoying each other's companionship. The Forestmaster spoke to them no more but watched each in turn.

Sturm's pale face had regained some color. He ate with grace and dignity. Sitting next to Tasslehoff, he answered the kender's inexhaustible store of questions about his homeland. He also, without calling undue attention to the fact, removed from Tasslehoff's pouch a knife and fork that had unaccountably made their way there. The knight sat as far from Caramon as possible and did his best to ignore him.

The big warrior was obviously enjoying his meal. He ate three times more than anyone else, three times as fast, and three times as loudly. When not eating, he described to Flint a fight with a troll, using the bone he was chewing on as a sword to illustrate his thrusts and parries. Flint ate heartily and told Caramon he was the biggest liar in Krynn.

Raistlin, sitting beside his brother, ate very little, taking nibbles of only the tenderest meat, a few grapes, and a bit of bread he soaked in water first. He said nothing but listened intently to everyone, absorbing all that was said into his soul, storing it for future reference and use.

Goldmoon ate her meal delicately, with practiced ease. The Que-shu princess was accustomed to eating in public view and could make conversation easily. She chatted with Tanis, encouraging him to describe the elven lands and other places he had visited. Riverwind, next to her, was acutely uncomfortable and self-conscious. Although not a boisterous eater like Caramon, the Plainsman was obviously more accustomed to eating at the campfires of his fellow tribesmen than in royal halls. He handled cutlery with awkward clumsiness, and he knew that he appeared crude beside Goldmoon. He said nothing, seeming willing to fade into the background.

Finally everyone began shoving plates away and settling back in the strange wooden chairs, ending their dinner with pieces of sweet shortcake. Tas began to sing his kender trailsong, to the delight of the centaurs. Then suddenly Raistlin spoke. His soft, whispering voice slithered through the laughter and loud talk.

"Forestmaster"—the mage hissed the name—"today we fought loathsome creatures that we have never seen before on Krynn. Can you tell us of these?"

The relaxed and festive mood was smothered as effectively as if covered by a shroud. Everyone exchanged grim looks.

"These creatures walk like men," Caramon added, "but look like reptiles. They have clawed hands and feet and wings and"—his voice dropped—"they turn to stone when they die."

The Forestmaster regarded them with sadness as she rose to her feet. She seemed to expect the question.

"I know of these creatures," she answered. "Some of them entered the Darken Wood with a party of goblins from Haven a week ago. They wore hoods and cloaks, no doubt to disguise their horrible appearance. The centaurs followed them in secret, to make certain they harmed no one before the spectral minions dealt with them. The centaurs reported that the creatures call themselves 'draconians' and speak of belonging to the 'Order of Draco.' "

Raistlin's brow furrowed. "Draco," he whispered, puzzled. "But who are they? What race or species?"

"I do not know. I can tell you only this: they are not of the animal world, and they belong to none of the races of Krynn."

This took a moment for everyone to assimilate. Caramon blinked. "I don't—" he began.

"She means, my brother, that they are not of this world," Raistlin explained impatiently.

"Then where'd they come from?" Caramon asked, startled.

"That's the question, isn't it?" Raistlin said coldly. "Where did they come from—and why?"

"I cannot answer that." The Forestmaster shook her head. "But I can tell you that before the spectral minions put an end to these draconians, they spoke of 'armies to the north.' "

"I saw them." Tanis rose to his feet. "Campfires—" His voice caught in his throat as he realized what the Forestmaster had been about to say. "Armies! Of these draconians? There must be thousands!" Now everyone was standing and talking at once.

"Impossible!" the knight said, scowling.

"Who's behind this? The Seekers? By the gods," Caramon bellowed, "I've got a notion to go to Haven and bash—"

"Go to Solamnia, not to Haven," Sturm advised loudly.

"We should travel to Qualinost," Tanis argued. "The elves—"

"The elves have their own problems," the Forestmaster interrupted, her cool voice a calming influence. "As do the Highseekers of Haven. No place is safe. But I will tell you where you must go to find answers to your questions."

"What do you mean you will tell us where to go?" Raistlin stepped forward slowly, his red robes rippling around him as he walked. "What do you know of us?" The mage paused, his eyes narrowing with a sudden thought.

"Yes, I was expecting you," the Forestmaster replied in answer to Raistlin's thoughts. "A great and shining being appeared to me in the wilderness this day. He told me that the one bearing the blue crystal staff would come this night to Darken Wood. The spectral minions would let the staff-bearer and her companions pass— though they have allowed no human or elf or dwarf or kender to enter Darken Wood since the Cataclysm. I was to give the bearer of the staff this message: 'You must fly straight away across the East-wall Mountains. In two days the staffbearer must be within Xak Tsaroth. There, if you prove worthy, you shall receive the greatest gift given to the world.'"

"Eastwall Mountains!" The dwarf's mouth dropped open. "We'll need to fly all right, to reach Xak Tsaroth in two days time. Shining being! Hah!" He snapped his fingers.

The rest glanced uneasily at each other. Finally Tanis said hesitantly, "I'm afraid the dwarf is right, Forestmaster. The journey to Xak Tsaroth would be long and perilous. We would have to go back through lands we know are inhabited by goblins and these draconians."

"And then we would have to pass through the Plains," Riverwind spoke for the first time since meeting the Forestmaster. "Our lives are forfeit." He gestured toward Goldmoon. "The Queshu are fierce fighters and they know the land. They are waiting. We would never get through safely." He looked at Tanis. "And my people have no love for elves."

"And why go to Xak Tsaroth anyway?" Caramon rumbled. "Greatest gift—what could that be? A powerful sword? A chest of steel coins? That would come in handy, but there's a battle brewing up north apparently. I'd hate to miss it."

The Forestmaster nodded gravely. "I understand your dilemma," she said. "I offer what help is in my power. I will see to it that you reach Xak Tsaroth in two days. The question is, will you go?"

Tanis turned to the others. Sturm's face was drawn. He met Tanis's look and sighed. "The stag led us here," he said slowly, "perhaps to receive this advice. But my heart lies north, in my homeland. If armies of these draconians are preparing to attack, my place is with those Knights who will surely band together to fight this evil. Still, I do not want to desert you, Tanis, or you, lady." He nodded to Goldmoon, then slumped down, his aching head in his hands.

Caramon shrugged. "I'll go anywhere, fight anything, Tanis. You know that. What say you, brother?"

But Raistlin, staring into the darkness, did not answer.

Goldmoon and Riverwind were speaking together in low voices. They nodded to each other, then Goldmoon said to Tanis, "We will go to Xak Tsaroth. We appreciate everything you've done for us—"

"But we ask for no man's help any longer," Riverwind stated proudly. "This is the completion of our quest. As we began alone, so we will finish it alone."

"And you will die alone!" Raistlin said softly.

Tanis shivered. "Raistlin," he said, "a word with you."

The mage turned obediently and walked with the half-elf into a small thicket of gnarled and stunted trees. Darkness closed around them.

"Just like the old days," Caramon said, his eyes following his brother uneasily.

"And look at all the trouble we got into then," Flint reminded him, plopping down onto the grass.

"I wonder what they talk about?" Tasslehoff said. Long ago, the kender had tried to eavesdrop on these private conversations between the mage and the half-elf, but Tanis had always caught him and shooed him away. "And why can't they discuss it with us?"

"Because we'd probably rip Raistlin's heart out," Sturm answered, in a low, pain-filled voice. "I don't care what you say, Caramon, there's a dark side to your brother, and Tanis has seen it. For which I'm grateful. He can deal with it. I couldn't."

Uncharacteristically, Caramon said nothing. Sturm stared at the warrior, startled. In the old days, the fighter would have leaped to his brother's defense. Now he sat silent, preoccupied, his face troubled. So there is a dark side to Raistlin, and now Caramon, too, knows what it is. Sturm shuddered, wondering what had happened in these past five years that cast such a dark shadow across the cheerful warrior.

Raistlin walked close to Tanis. The mage's arms were crossed in the sleeves of his robes, his head bowed in thought. Tanis could feel the heat of Raistlin's body radiate through the red robes, as though he were being consumed by an inner fire. As usual, Tanis felt uncomfortable in the young mage's presence. Yet, right now, he knew of no one else he could turn to for advice. "What do you know of Xak Tsaroth?" Tanis asked.

"There was a temple there—a temple to the ancient gods," Raistlin whispered. His eyes glittered in the eerie light of the red moon. "It was destroyed in the Cataclysm and its people fled, certain that the gods had abandoned them. It passed from memory. I did not know it still existed."

"What did you see, Raistlin?" Tanis asked softly, after a long pause. "You looked far away—what did you see?"

"I am magi, Tanis, not a seer."

"Don't give me that," Tanis snapped. "It's been a long time, but not that long. I know you don't have the gift of foresight. You were thinking, not scrying. And you came up with answers. I want those answers. You've got more brains than all of us put together, even if—" He stopped.

"Even if I am twisted and warped." Raistlin's voice rose with harsh arrogance. "Yes, I am smarter than you—all of you. And someday I will prove it! Someday you—with all your strength and charm and good looks—you, all of you, will call me master!" His hands clenched to fists inside his robes, his eyes flared red in the crimson moonlight. Tanis, who was accustomed to this tirade, waited patiently. The mage relaxed, his hands unclenched. "But for now, I give you my advice. What did I see? These armies, Tanis, armies of draconians, will overrun Solace and Haven and all the lands of your fathers. That is the reason we must reach Xak Tsaroth. What we find there will prove this army's undoing."

"But why are there armies?" Tanis asked. "What would anyone want with control of Solace and Haven and the Plains to the east? Is it the Seekers?"

"Seekers! Hah!" Raistlin snorted. "Open your eyes, Half-Elf. Someone or something powerful created these creatures—these draconians. Not the idiot Seekers. And no one goes to all that trouble to take over two farm cities or even to look for a blue crystal staff. This is a war of conquest, Tanis. Someone seeks to conquer Ansalon! Within two days time, life on Krynn as we have known it will come to an end. This is the portent of the fallen stars. The Queen of Darkness has returned. We face a foe who seeks—at the very least—to enslave us, or perhaps destroy us completely."

"Your advice?" Tanis asked reluctantly. He felt change coming and, like all elves, he feared and detested change.

Raistlin smiled his crooked, bitter smile, reveling in his moment of superiority. "That we go to Xak Tsaroth immediately. That we leave tonight, if possible, by whatever means this Forestmaster has planned. If we do not acquire this gift within two days—the armies of draconians will."

"What do you think the gift might be?" Tanis wondered aloud. "A sword or coins, like Caramon said?"

"My brother's a fool," Raistlin stated coldly. "You don't believe that and neither do I."

"Then what?" Tanis pursued.

Raistlin's eyes narrowed. "I have given you my advice. Act upon it as you will. I have my own reasons for going. Let us leave it at that, Half-Elf. But it will be dangerous. Xak Tsaroth was abandoned three hundred years ago. I do not think it will have remained abandoned long."

"That is true," Tanis mused. He stood silently for long moments. The mage coughed once, softly. "Do you believe we were chosen, Raistlin?" Tanis asked.

The mage did not hesitate. "Yes. So I was given to know in the Towers of Sorcery. So Par-Salian told me."

"But why?" Tanis questioned impatiently. "We are not the stuff of heroes—well, maybe Sturm—"

"Ah," said Raistlin. "But *who* chose us? And for what purpose? Consider that, Tanis Half-Elven!"

The mage bowed to Tanis, mockingly, and turned to walk back through the brush to the rest of the group.

WINGED SLEEP. SMOKE IN THE EAST. DARK MEMORIES.

12

"Xak Tsaroth," Tanis said. "That is my decision."

"Is that what the mage advises?" Sturm asked sullenly.

"It is," Tanis answered, "and I believe his advice is sound. If we do not reach Xak Tsaroth within two days, others will and this 'greatest gift' may be lost forever."

"The greatest gift!" Tasslehoff said, his eyes shining. "Just think, Flint! Jewels beyond price! Or maybe—"

"A keg of ale and Otik's fried potatoes," the dwarf muttered. "And a nice warm fire. But no—Xak Tsaroth!"

"I guess we're all in agreement, then," Tanis said. "If you feel you are needed in the north, Sturm, of course you—"

"I will go with you to Xak Tsaroth." Sturm sighed. "There is nothing in the north for me. I have been deluding myself. The knights of my order are scattered, holed up in crumbling fortresses, fighting off the debt collectors."

The knight's face twisted in agony and he lowered his head. Tanis suddenly felt tired. His neck hurt, his shoulders and back ached, his leg muscles twitched. He started to say something more, then felt a gentle hand touch his shoulder. He looked up to see Goldmoon's face, cool and calm in the moonlight.

"You are weary, my friend," she said. "We all are. But we are glad you are coming, Riverwind and I." Her hand was strong. She looked up, her clear gaze encompassing the entire group. "We are glad all of you are coming with us."

Tanis, glancing at Riverwind, wasn't certain the tall Plainsman agreed with her.

"Just another adventure," Caramon said, flushing with embarrassment. "Eh, Raist?" He nudged his brother. Raistlin, ignoring his twin, looked at the Forestmaster.

"We must leave immediately," the mage said coldly. "You mentioned something about helping us cross the mountains."

"Indeed," the Forestmaster replied, nodding gravely. "I, too, am glad you have made this decision. I hope you find my aid welcome."

The Forestmaster raised her head, looking up into the sky. The companions followed her gaze. The night sky, seen through the canopy of tall trees, glittered brilliantly with stars. Soon the companions became aware of something flying up there, winking out the stars in passing.

"I'll be a gully dwarf," Flint said solemnly. "Flying horses. What next?"

"Oh!" Tasslehoff drew in a deep breath. The kender was transfixed with wonder as he watched the beautiful animals circle above them, descending lower and lower with each turn, their fur radiating blue-white in the moonlight. Tas clasped his hands together. Never in his wildest kender imaginings had he dreamed of flying. This was worth fighting all the draconians on Krynn.

The pegasi dipped to the ground, their feathery wings creating a wind that tossed the tree branches and laid the grass flat. A large pegasus with wings that touched the ground when he walked bowed reverently to the Forestmaster. His bearing was proud and noble. Each of the other beautiful creatures bowed in turn.

"You have summoned us?" the leader asked the Forestmaster.

"These guests of mine have urgent business to the east. I bid you bear them with the swiftness of the winds across the Eastwall Mountains."

The pegasus regarded the companions with astonishment. He walked with stately mien over to stare first at one, then another.

When Tas raised his hand to pet the steed's nose, both of the animal's ears swiveled forward and he reared his great head back. But when he got to Flint, he snorted in disgust and turned to the Forestmaster. "A kender? Humans? And a *dwarf!*"

"Don't do *me* any favors, horse!" Flint sneezed.

The Forestmaster merely nodded and smiled. The pegasus bowed in reluctant assent. "Very well, Master," he replied. With powerful grace, he walked over to Goldmoon and started to bend his foreleg, dipping low before her to assist her in mounting.

"No, do not kneel, noble animal," she said. "I have ridden horses since before I could walk. I need no such assistance." Handing Riverwind her staff, Goldmoon threw her arm around the pegasus's neck and pulled herself astride his broad back. Her silver-gold hair blew feathery white in the moonlight, her face was pure and cold as marble. Now she truly looked like the princess of a barbarian tribe.

She took her staff from Riverwind. Raising it in the air, she lifted her voice in song. Riverwind, his eyes shining with admiration, leaped up behind her on the back of the winged horse. Putting his arms around her, he added his deep baritone voice to hers.

Tanis had no idea what they were singing, but it seemed a song of victory and triumph. It stirred his blood and he would have willingly joined in. One of the pegasi cantered up to him. He pulled himself up and settled himself on his broad back, sitting in front of the powerful wings.

Now all the companions, caught up in the elation of the moment, mounted, Goldmoon's song adding wings to their souls as the pegasi spread their huge wings and caught the wind currents. They soared higher and higher, circling above the forest. The silver moon and the red bathed the valley below and the clouds above in an eerie, beautiful, purplish glow that receded into a deeper purple night. As the forest fell away from them, the last thing the companions saw was the Forestmaster, glimmering like a star fallen from the heavens, shining lost and alone in a darkening land.

One by one, the companions felt drowsiness overcome them.

Tasslehoff fought this magically induced sleep longest. Enchanted by the rush of wind against his face, spellbound by the sight of the tall trees that normally loomed over him reduced to child's toys, Tas struggled to remain awake long after everyone else. Flint's head rested against his back, the dwarf snoring loudly. Goldmoon was cradled in Riverwind's arms. His head drooped over her shoulder. Even in his sleep, he held her protectively. Caramon slumped over his horse's neck, breathing stentoriously. His brother rested against his twin's broad back. Sturm slept peacefully, the lines of pain gone from his face. Even Tanis's bearded face was clear of care and worry and responsibility.

Tas yawned. "No," he mumbled, blinking rapidly and pinching himself.

"Rest now, little kender," his pegasus said in amusement. "Mortals were not meant to fly. This sleep is for your protection. We do not want you to panic and fall off."

"I won't," Tas protested, yawning again. His head sank forward. The pegasus's neck was warm and comfortable, the fur was fragrant and soft. "I won't panic," Tas whispered sleepily. "Never panic . . ." He slept.

The half-elf woke with a start to find that he was lying in a grassy meadow. The leader of the pegasi stood above him, staring off to the east. Tanis sat up.

"Where are we?" he began. "This isn't a city." He looked around. "Why—we haven't even crossed the mountains yet!"

"I am sorry." The pegasus turned to him. "We could not take you as far as the Eastwall Mountains. There is great trouble brewing in the east. A darkness fills the air, such a darkness as I have not felt in Krynn for countless—" He stopped, lowered his head and pawed the ground restlessly. "I dare not travel farther."

"Where are we? " the confused half-elf repeated. "And where are the other pegasi?"

"I sent them home. I remained to guard your sleep. Now that you are awake, I must return home as well." The pegasus gazed sternly at Tanis. "I know not what awakened this great evil on Krynn. I trust it was not you and your companions."

He spread his great wings.

"Wait!" Tanis scrambled to his feet. "What—"

The pegasus leaped into the air, circled twice, then was gone, flying rapidly back to the west.

"What evil?" Tanis asked glumly. He sighed and looked around. His companions were sleeping soundly, lying on the ground around him in various poses of slumber. He studied the horizon, trying to get his bearings. It was nearly dawn, he realized. The sun's light was just beginning to illuminate the east. He was standing on a flat prairie. There was not a tree in sight, nothing but rolling fields of tall grass as far as he could see.

Wondering what the pegasus had meant about trouble to the east, Tanis sat down to watch the sun rise and wait for his friends to wake. He wasn't particularly worried about where he was, for he guessed Riverwind knew this land down to the last blade of grass. So he stretched out on the ground, facing the east, feeling more relaxed after that strange sleep than he had in many nights.

Suddenly he sat upright, his relaxed feeling gone, a tightness clutching at his throat like an unseen hand. For there, snaking up to meet the bright new morning sun, were three thick, twisting columns of greasy, black smoke. Tanis stumbled to his feet. He ran over and shook Riverwind gently, trying to wake the Plainsman without disturbing Goldmoon.

"Hush," Tanis whispered, putting a warning finger on his lips and nodding toward the sleeping woman as Riverwind blinked at the half-elf. Seeing Tanis's dark expression, the barbarian was instantly awake. He stood up quietly and moved off with Tanis, glancing around him.

"What's this?" he whispered. "We're in the Plains of Abanasinia. Still about a half day's journey from the Eastwall Mountains. My village lies to the east—"

He stopped as Tanis pointed silently eastward. Then he gave a shallow, ragged cry as he saw the smoke curling into the sky. Goldmoon jerked awake. She sat up, gazed at Riverwind sleepily, then with growing alarm. Turning, she followed his horrified stare.

"No," she moaned. "No!" she cried again. Quickly rising, she began to gather their possessions. The others woke at her cry.

"What is it?" Caramon jumped up.

"Their village," Tanis said softly, gesturing with his hand. "It's burning. Apparently the armies are moving quicker than we thought."

"No," said Raistlin. "Remember—the draconian clerics mentioned they had traced the staff to a village in the Plains."

"My people," Goldmoon murmured, energy draining from her. She slumped in Riverwind's arms, staring at the smoke. "My father . . ."

"We'd better get going." Caramon glanced around uneasily. "We show up like a jewel in a gypsy dancer's navel."

"Yes," Tanis said. "We've definitely got to get out of here. But where do we go?" he asked Riverwind.

"Que-shu," Goldmoon's tone allowed no contradiction. "It's on our way. The Eastwall Mountains are just beyond my village." She started through the tall grass.

Tanis glanced at Riverwind.

"*Marulina!*" the Plainsman called out to her. Running forward, he caught hold of Goldmoon's arm. "*Nikh pat-takh merilar!*" he said sternly.

She stared up at him, her eyes blue and cold as the morning sky. "No," she said resolutely, "I am going to our village. It is our fault if something has happened. I don't care if there are thousands of those monsters waiting. I will die with our people, as I should have done." Her voice failed her. Tanis, watching, felt his heart ache with pity.

Riverwind put his arm around her and together they began walking toward the rising sun.

Caramon cleared his throat. "I hope I do meet a thousand of those things," he muttered, hoisting his and his brother's packs. "Hey," he said in astonishment. "They're full." He peered in his pack. "Provisions. Several days' worth. And my sword's back in my scabbard!"

"At least that's one thing we won't have to worry about," Tanis said grimly. "You all right, Sturm?"

"Yes," the knight answered. "I feel much better after that sleep."

"Right, then. Let's go. Flint, where's Tas?" Turning, Tanis nearly fell over the kender who had been standing right behind him.

"Poor Goldmoon," Tas said softly. Tanis patted him on the shoulder. "Maybe it won't be as bad as we fear," the half-elf said, following the Plainsmen through the rippling grass. "Maybe the warriors fought them off and those are victory fires."

Tasslehoff sighed and looked up at Tanis, his brown eyes wide. "You're a rotten liar, Tanis," the kender said. He had the feeling it was going to be a very long day.

Twilight. The pale sun set. Shafts of yellow and tan streaked the western sky, then faded into dreary night. The companions sat huddled around a fire that offered no warmth, for there existed no flame on Krynn that would drive the chill from their souls. They did not speak to each other, but each sat staring into the fire, trying to make some sense of what they had seen, trying to make sense of the senseless.

Tanis had lived through much that was horrible in his life. But the ravaged town of Que-shu would always stand out in his mind as a symbol of the horrors of war.

Even so, remembering Que-shu, he could only grasp fleeting images, his mind refusing to encompass the total awful vision. Oddly enough, he remembered the melted stones of Que-shu. He remembered them vividly. Only in his dreams did he recall the twisted and blackened bodies that lay among the smoking stones.

The great stone walls, the huge stone temples and edifices, the spacious stone buildings with their rock courtyards and statuary, the large stone arena—all had melted, like butter on a hot summer day. The rock still smoldered, though it was obvious that the village must have been attacked well over a sunrise ago. It was as if a white-hot, searing flame had engulfed the entire village. But what fire was there on Krynn that could melt rock?

He remembered a creaking sound, remembered hearing it and being puzzled by it, and wondering what it was until locating the source of the only sound in the deathly still town became an obsession. He ran through the ruined village until he located the source. He remembered that he shouted to the others until they came. They stood staring into the melted arena.

Huge stone blocks had poured down from the side of the bowl-shaped depression, forming molten ripples of rock around the bottom of the dish. In the center—on grass that was blackened and charred—stood a crude gibbet. Two stout posts had been driven into the burned ground by unspeakable force, their bases splintered by the impact. Ten feet above the ground, a crosspiece pole was lashed to the two posts. The wood was charred and blistered. Scavenger birds perched on the top. Three chains, made of what appeared to be iron before it had melted and run together, swung back and forth. This was the cause of the creaking sound. Suspended from each chain, apparently by the feet, was a corpse. The corpses were not human; they were hobgoblin. On top of the gruesome structure was a shield stuck to the crosspiece with a broken swordblade. Roughly clawed on the battered shield were words written in a crude form of Common.

"This is what happens to those who take prisoners against my commands. Kill or be killed." It was signed, *Verminaard.*

Verminaard. The name meant nothing to Tanis.

Other images. He remembered Goldmoon standing in the center of her father's ruined house trying to put back together the pieces of a broken vase. He remembered a dog—the only living thing they found in the entire village—curled around the body of a dead child. Caramon stopped to pet the small dog. The animal cringed, then licked the big man's hand. It then licked the child's cold face, looking up at the warrior hopefully, expecting this human to make everything all right, to make his little playmate run and laugh again. He remembered Caramon stroking the dog's soft fur with his huge hands.

He remembered Riverwind picking up a rock, holding it, aimlessly, as he stared around his burned and blasted village.

He remembered Sturm, standing transfixed before the gibbet, staring at the sign, and he remembered the knight's lips moving as though in prayer or perhaps a silent vow.

He remembered the sorrow-lined face of the dwarf, who had seen so much tragedy in his long lifetime, as he stood in the center of the ruined village, patting Tasslehoff gently on the back after finding the kender sobbing in a corner.

He remembered Goldmoon's frantic search for survivors. She crawled through the blackened rubble, screaming out names, listening for faint answers to her calls until she was hoarse and Riverwind finally convinced her it was hopeless. If there were any survivors, they had long since fled.

He remembered standing alone, in the center of the town, looking at piles of dust with arrow heads in them, and recognizing them as bodies of draconians.

He remembered a cold hand touching his arm and the mage's whispering voice. "Tanis, we must leave. There is nothing more we can do and we must reach Xak Tsaroth. Then we will have our revenge."

And so they left Que-shu. They traveled far into the night, none of them wanting to stop, each wanting to push his body to the point of exhaustion so that, when they finally slept, there would be no evil dreams.

But the dreams came anyway.

CHILL DAWN. VINE BRIDGES. DARK WATER.

13

Tanis felt clawed hands clutching at his throat. He struggled and fought, then woke to find Riverwind bending over him in the darkness, shaking him roughly.

"What . . . ?" Tanis sat up.

"You were dreaming," the Plainsman said grimly. "I had to wake you. Your shouts would draw an army down on us."

"Yes, thanks," Tanis muttered. "I'm sorry." He sat up, trying to shake off the nightmare. "What time is it?"

"Still several hours till dawn," Riverwind said wearily. He returned to where he had been sitting, his back against the trunk of a twisted tree. Goldmoon lay sleeping on the ground beside him. She began to murmur and shake her head, making small, soft, moaning cries like a wounded animal. Riverwind stroked her silver-gold hair, and she quieted.

"You should have wakened me earlier," Tanis said. He stood up, rubbing his shoulders and neck. "It's my watch."

"Do you think I could sleep?" asked Riverwind bitterly.

"You've got to," Tanis answered. "You'll slow us up if you don't."

"The men in my tribe can travel for many days without sleep," Riverwind said. His eyes were dull and glazed, and he seemed to stare at nothing.

Tanis started to argue, then sighed and kept quiet. He knew

that he could never truly understand the agony the Plainsman was suffering. To have friends and family—an entire life—utterly destroyed, must be so devastating that the mind shrank from even imagining it. Tanis left him and walked over to where Flint was sitting carving at a piece of wood.

"You might as well get some sleep," Tanis told the dwarf. "I'll watch for a while."

Flint nodded. "I heard you yelling over there." He sheathed his dagger and thrust the piece of wood into a pouch. "Defending Que-shu?"

Tanis frowned at the memory. Shivering in the chill night, he wrapped his cloak around him, drew up his hood. "Any idea where we are?" he asked Flint.

"The Plainsman says we're on a road known as Sageway East," the dwarf answered. He stretched out on the cold ground, dragging a blanket up around his shoulders. "Some old highway. It's been around since before the Cataclysm."

"I don't suppose we'd be fortunate enough to have this road take us into Xak Tsaroth?"

"Riverwind doesn't seem to think so," the dwarf mumbled sleepily. "Says he's only followed it a short distance. But at least it gets us through the mountains." He gave a great yawn and turned over, pillowing his head on his cloak.

Tanis breathed deeply. The night seemed peaceful enough. They hadn't run into any draconians or goblins in their wild flight from Que-shu. As Raistlin said, apparently the draconians had attacked Que-shu in search of the staff, not as part of any preparations for battle. They had struck and then withdrawn. The Forestmaster's time limit still held good, Tanis supposed— Xak Tsaroth within two days. And one day had already passed.

Shivering, the half-elf walked back over to Riverwind. "Do you have any idea how far we have to go and in what direction?" Tanis crouched down next to the Plainsman.

"Yes," Riverwind nodded, rubbing his burning eyes. "We must go to the northeast, toward Newsea. That is where the city is rumored to be. I have never been there—" He frowned, then shook his head. "I've never been there," he repeated.

"Can we reach it by tomorrow?" Tanis asked.

"Newsea is said to be two days' journey from Que-shu." The barbarian sighed. "If Xak Tsaroth exists, we should be able to reach it in a day, though I have heard that the land from here to Newsea is swampy and difficult to travel."

He shut his eyes, his hand absently stroking Goldmoon's hair. Tanis fell silent, hoping the Plainsman would sleep. The half-elf moved quietly to sit beneath the tree, staring into the night. He made a mental note to ask Tasslehoff in the morning if he had a map.

The kender did have a map, but it wasn't much help, dating, as it did, before the Cataclysm. Newsea wasn't on the map since it had appeared after the land had been torn apart and the waters of Turbidus Ocean had rushed in to fill it. Still, the map showed Xak Tsaroth only a short distance from the highway marked Sageway East. They should reach it some time that afternoon, if the territory they had to cross wasn't impassable.

The companions ate a cheerless breakfast, most forcing the food down without appetite. Raistlin brewed his foul-smelling herbal drink over the small fire, his strange eyes lingering on Goldmoon's staff.

"How precious it has become," he commented softly— "now that it has been purchased by the blood of innocents."

"Is it worth it? Is it worth the lives of my people?" Goldmoon asked, staring at the nondescript brown staff dully. She seemed to have aged during the night. Gray circles smudged the skin beneath her eyes.

None of the companions answered, each looking away in awkward silence. Riverwind stood up abruptly and stalked off into the woods by himself. Goldmoon lifted her eyes and stared after him, then her head sank into her hand and she began to weep silently. "He blames himself." She shook her head. "And I am not helping him. It wasn't his fault."

"It's not anyone's fault," Tanis said slowly, walking over to her. He put his hand on her shoulder, rubbing out the tenseness he felt in the bunched muscles of her neck. "We can't understand. We've just got to keep going and hope we find the answer in Xak Tsaroth."

She nodded and wiped her eyes, drew a deep breath, and blew her nose on a handkerchief Tasslehoff handed her.

"You're right," she said, swallowing. "My father would be ashamed of me. I must remember—I am Chieftain's Daughter."

"No," came Riverwind's deep voice from where he stood behind her in the shadows of the trees. "You are Chieftain."

Goldmoon gasped. She twisted to her feet to stare, wide-eyed, at Riverwind. "Perhaps I am," she faltered—"but it is meaningless. Our people are dead—"

"I saw tracks," Riverwind answered. "Some managed to flee. They have probably gone into the mountains. They will return, and you will be their ruler."

"Our people . . . still alive!" Goldmoon's face became radiant.

"Not many. Maybe none now. It would depend on whether or not the draconians followed them into the mountains." Riverwind shrugged. "Still, you are now their ruler"—bitterness crept into his voice—"and I will be husband of Chieftain."

Goldmoon cringed, as though he had struck her. She blinked, then shook her head. "No, Riverwind," she said softly. "I . . . we've talked—"

"Have we?" he interrupted. "I was thinking about it last night. I've been gone so many years. My thoughts were of you, as a woman. I did not realize—" He swallowed and then drew a deep breath. "I left Goldmoon. I returned to find Chieftain's Daughter."

"What choice did I have?" Goldmoon cried angrily. "My father wasn't well. I had to rule or Loreman would have taken over the tribe. Do you know what's it like—being Chieftain's Daughter? Wondering at every meal if this morsel is the one with the poison? Struggling every day to find the money in the treasury to pay the soldiers so that Loreman would have no excuse to take over! And all the time I must act as Chieftain's Daughter, while my father sits and drools and mumbles." Her voice choked with tears.

Riverwind listened, his face stern and unmoving. He stared at a point above her head. "We should get started," he said coldly. "It's nearly dawn."

The companions had traveled only a few miles on the old, broken road when it dumped them, literally, into a swamp. They had noticed that the ground was getting spongier and the tall, sturdy trees of the mountain canyon forests dwindled. Strange, twisted trees rose up before them. A miasma blotted out the sun, and the air became foul to breathe. Raistlin began to cough and he covered his mouth with a handkerchief. They stayed on the broken stones of the old road, avoiding the dank, swampy ground next to it.

Flint was walking in front with Tasslehoff when suddenly the dwarf gave a great shout and disappeared into the muck. They could see only his head.

"Help! The dwarf!" Tas shouted, and the others ran up.

"It's dragging me under!" Flint flailed about the black, oozing mud in panic.

"Hold still," Riverwind cautioned. "You have fallen in death-mirk. Don't go in after him!" he warned Sturm who had leaped forward. "You'll both die. Get a branch."

Caramon grabbed a young sapling, took a deep breath, grunted, and pulled. They could hear its roots snapping and creaking as the huge warrior dragged it out of the ground. Riverwind stretched out flat, extending the branch to the dwarf. Flint, nearly up to his nose in the slimy muck, thrashed about and finally grabbed hold of it. The warrior hauled the tree out of the deathmirk, the dwarf clinging to it.

"Tanis!" The kender clutched at the half-elf and pointed. A snake, as big around as Caramon's arm, slithered into the ooze right where the dwarf had been floundering.

"We can't walk through this!" Tanis gestured at the swamp. "Maybe we should turn back."

"No time," Raistlin whispered, his hourglass eyes glittering.

"And there is no other way," Riverwind said. His voice sounded strange. "And we can get through—I know a path."

"What?" Tanis turned to him. "I thought you said—"

"I've been here," the Plainsman said in a strangled voice. "I can't remember when, but I've been here. I know the way through the swamp. And it leads to—" He licked his lips.

"Leads to a broken city of evil?" Tanis asked grimly when the Plainsman did not finish his sentence.

"Xak Tsaroth!" Raistlin hissed.

"Of course," Tanis said softly. "It makes sense. Where would we go to find answers about the staff—except to the place where the staff was given you?"

"And we must go now!" said Raistlin insistently. "We must be there by midnight tonight!"

The Plainsman took the lead. He found firm ground around the black water and, making them all walk single file, led them away from the road and deeper into the swamp. Trees that he called ironclaw rose out of the water, their roots standing exposed, twisting into the mud. Vines drooped from their branches and trailed across the faint path. The mist closed in, and soon no one could see beyond a few feet. They were forced to move slowly, testing every step. A false move and they would have plunged into the stinking morass that lay foul and stagnant all around them.

Suddenly the trail came to an end in dark swamp water.

"Now what?" Caramon asked gloomily.

"This," Riverwind said, pointing. A crude bridge, made out of vines twisted into ropes, was attached to a tree. It spanned the water like a spider web.

"Who built it?" Tanis asked.

"I don't know," Riverwind said. "But you will find them all along the path, wherever it becomes impassable."

"I told you Xak Tsaroth would not remain abandoned," Raistlin whispered.

"Yes, well—I suppose we shouldn't throw stones at a gift of the gods," replied Tanis. "At least we don't have to swim!"

The journey across the vine bridge was not pleasant. The vines were coated with slimy moss, which made walking precarious. The structure swayed alarmingly when touched, and its motion became erratic when anyone crossed. They made it safely to the other side but had walked only a short distance before they were forced to use another bridge. And always below them and around them was the dark water, where strange eyes watched them hungrily. Then they reached a point where the firm ground ended and there were no vine bridges. Ahead was nothing but slimy water.

"It isn't very deep," Riverwind muttered. "Follow me. Step only where I step."

Riverwind took a step, then another step, feeling his way, the rest keeping right behind him, staring into the water. They stared in disgust and alarm as unknown and unseen things slithered past their legs. When they reached firm ground again, their legs were coated with slime; all of them gagged from the smell. But this last journey seemed, perhaps, to have been the worst. The jungle growth was not as thick, and they could even see the sun shining faintly through a green haze.

The farther north they traveled, the firmer the terrain became. By midday, Tanis called a halt when he found a dry patch of ground beneath an ancient oak tree. The companions sank down to eat lunch and speak hopefully of leaving the swamp behind them. All except Goldmoon and Riverwind. They spoke not at all.

Flint's clothes were sopping wet. He shook with the cold and began complaining about pains in his joints. Tanis grew worried. He knew the dwarf was subject to rheumatism and remembered what Flint had said about fearing to slow them up. Tanis tapped the kender and gestured him over to one side.

"I know you've got something in one of your pouches that would take the chill off the dwarf's bones, if you know what I mean," Tanis said softly.

"Oh, sure, Tanis," Tas said, brightening. He fumbled around, first in one pouch, then another, and finally came up with a gleaming silver flask. "Brandy. Otik's finest."

"I don't suppose you paid for it?" Tanis asked, grinning.

"I will," the kender replied, hurt. "Next time I'm there."

"Sure." Tanis patted him on the shoulder. "Share some with Flint. Not too much," he cautioned. "Just warm him up."

"All right. And we'll take the lead—we mighty warriors." Tas laughed and skipped over to the dwarf as Tanis returned to the others. They were silently packing up the remains of lunch and preparing to move out. All of us could use some of Otik's finest, he thought. Goldmoon and Riverwind had not spoken to each other all morning. Their mood spread a pall on everyone. Tanis could think of nothing to do that would end the torture these two were experiencing. He could only hope that time would salve the wounds.

The companions continued along the trail for about an hour after lunch, moving more quickly since the thickest part of the jungle had been left behind. Just as they thought they had left the swamp, however, the firm ground came abruptly to an end. Weary, sick with the smell, and discouraged, the companions found themselves wading through the muck once again.

Only Flint and Tasslehoff were unaffected by the return to the swamp. These two had ranged far ahead of the others. Tasslehoff soon "forgot" Tanis's warning about drinking only a little of the brandy. The liquid warmed the blood and took the edge off the gloomy atmosphere, so the kender and dwarf passed the flask back and forth many times until it was empty and they were traipsing along, making jokes about what they would do if they encountered a draconian.

"I'd turn it to stone, all right," the dwarf said, swinging an imaginary battle-axe. "Wham!—right in the lizard's gizzard."

"I'll bet Raistlin could turn one to stone with a look!" Tas imitated the mage's grim face and dour stare. They both laughed loudly, then hushed, giggling, peering back unsteadily to see if Tanis had heard them.

"I'll bet Caramon'd stick a fork in one and eat it!" Flint said.

Tas choked with laughter and wiped tears from his eyes. The dwarf roared. Suddenly the two came to the end of the spongy ground. Tasslehoff grabbed hold of the dwarf as Flint nearly plunged head-first into a pool of swamp water so wide that a vine bridge would not span it. A huge ironclaw tree lay across the water, its thick trunk making a bridge wide enough for two people to walk across side-by-side.

"Now *this* is a bridge!" Flint said, stepping back a pace and trying to bring the log into focus. "No more spider crawling on those stupid green webs. Let's go."

"Shouldn't we wait for the others?" Tasslehoff asked mildly. "Tanis wouldn't want to us to get separated."

"Tanis? Humpf!" The dwarf sniffed. "We'll show him."

"All right," Tasslehoff agreed cheerfully. He leaped up onto the fallen tree. "Careful," he said, slipping slightly, then easily catching his balance. "It's slick." He took a few quick steps, arms outstretched, his feet pointed out like a rope walker he'd seen once at a summer fair.

The dwarf clambered up after the kender, Flint's thick boots clumping clumsily on the log. A voice in the unbrandied part of Flint's mind told him he could never have done this cold sober. It also told him he was a fool for crossing the bridge without waiting for the others, but he ignored it. He was feeling positively young again.

Tasslehoff, enchanted with pretending he was Mirgo the Magnificent, looked up and discovered that he did, indeed, have an audience—one of those draconian things leaped onto the log in front of him. The sight sobered Tas up rapidly. The kender was not given to fear, but he was certainly amazed. He had presence of mind enough to do two things. First he yelled out loudly— "Tanis, ambush!" Then he lifted his hoopak staff and swung it in a wide arc.

The move took the draconian by surprise. The creature sucked in its breath and jumped back off the log to the bank below. Tas, momentarily off balance, regained his feet quickly and wondered what to do next. He glanced around and saw another draconian on the bank. They were, he was puzzled to notice, not armed. Before he could consider this oddity, he heard a roar behind him. He had forgotten the dwarf.

"What is it?" Flint shouted.

"Draco-thing-a-ma-jiggers," Tas said, gripping his hoopak and peering through the mists. "Two ahead! Here they come!"

"Well, confound it, get out of my way!" Flint snarled. Reaching behind, he fumbled for his axe.

"Where am I supposed to go?" Tas shouted wildly.

"Duck!" yelled the dwarf.

The kender ducked, throwing himself down on the log as one of the draconians came toward him, its clawed hands outstretched. Flint swung his axe in a mighty blow that would have decapitated the draconian if it had come anywhere near it. Unfortunately, the dwarf miscalculated and the blade whistled harmlessly in front of the draconian who was waving its hands in the air and chanting strange words.

The momentum of Flint's swing spun the dwarf around. His feet slipped on the slimy log, and, with a loud cry, the dwarf tumbled backward into the water.

Tasslehoff, having been around Raistlin for years, recognized that the draconian was casting a magic spell. Lying face down on the log, his hoopak staff clutched in his hand, the kender figured he had about one and a half seconds to consider what to do. The dwarf was gasping and spluttering in the water beneath him. Not inches away, the draconian was clearly reaching a stunning conclusion to his spellcasting. Deciding that anything was better than being magicked, Tas took a deep breath and dove off the log.

"Tanis! Ambush!"

"Blast!" swore Caramon as the kender's voice floated to them out of the mist somewhere ahead.

They all began running toward the sound, cursing the vines and the tree branches that blocked their way. Crashing out through the forest, they saw the fallen ironclaw bridge. Four draconians ran out of the shadows, blocking their path.

Suddenly the companions were plunged into darkness too thick to see their own hands, much less their comrades.

"Magic!" Tanis heard Raistlin hiss. "These are magic-users. Stand aside. You cannot fight them."

Then Tanis heard the mage cry out in agony.

"Raist!" Caramon shouted. "Where—ugh—" There was a groan and the sound of a heavy body thudding to the ground.

Tanis heard the draconians chanting. Even as he fumbled for his sword, he was suddenly covered, head to toe, in a thick, gooey substance that clogged up his nose and mouth. Struggling to free himself, he only enmeshed himself further. He heard Sturm swearing next to him, Goldmoon cried out, Riverwind's voice was choked off, then drowsiness overcame him. Tanis sank to his knees, still fighting to free himself from the weblike substance that glued his hands to his sides. Then he fell forward on his face and sank into an unnatural sleep.

Prisoners of the Draconians.

14

Lying on the ground, panting for breath, Tasslehoff watched as the draconians prepared to carry off his unconscious friends. The kender was well-hidden beneath a bush near the swamp. The dwarf was stretched out next to him, knocked out cold. Tas glanced at him in remorse. He'd had no choice. In his panic, Flint had dragged the kender down in the cold water. If he hadn't clunked the dwarf over the head with his hoopak staff, neither of them would have surfaced alive. He'd hauled the comatose dwarf up out of the water and hidden him beneath a bush.

Then Tasslehoff watched helplessly as the draconians bound his friends magically in what looked like strong spider webs. Tas saw they were all apparently unconscious—or dead—because they didn't struggle or put up a fight.

The kender did get a certain amount of grim amusement out of watching the draconians try to pick up Goldmoon's staff. Evidently they recognized it, for they croaked over it in their guttural language and made gestures of glee. One—presumably the leader—reached out to grasp it. There was a flash of blue light. Giving a screeching cry, the draconian dropped the staff and hopped up and down on the bank, uttering words Tas assumed were impolite. The leader finally came up with an ingenious idea. Pulling a fur blanket from Goldmoon's pack, the draconian laid it down on the ground. The creature picked up a stick and used it to roll the staff onto the blanket. Then it gingerly wrapped the staff in the fur and lifted it up triumphantly. The draconians lifted the webbed bodies of the kender's friends and bore them away. Other draconians followed behind, carrying the companions' packs and their weapons.

As the draconians marched along a path very near the hidden kender, Flint suddenly groaned and stirred. Tas clamped his hand over the dwarf's mouth. The draconians didn't seem to hear and kept moving. Tas could see his friends clearly in the fading afternoon light as the draconians passed. They seemed to be sound asleep. Caramon was even snoring. The kender remembered Raistlin's sleep spell and figured that was what the draconians had used on his friends.

Flint groaned again. One of the draconians near the end of the line stopped and peered into the brush. Tas picked up his hoopak and held it over the dwarf's head—just in case. But it wasn't needed. The draconian shrugged and muttered to itself, then hurried to catch up with its squad. Sighing in relief, Tas took his hand off the dwarf's mouth. Flint blinked and opened his eyes.

"What happened?" The dwarf moaned, his hand on his head.

"You fell off the bridge and hit your head on a log," Tas said glibly.

"I did?" Flint looked suspicious. "I don't remember that. I remember one of those draconian things coming at me and I remember falling into the water—"

"Well, you did, so don't argue," Tas said hurriedly, getting to his feet. "Can you walk?"

"Of course I can walk," the dwarf snapped. He stood up, a little wobbly, but erect. "Where is everybody?"

"The draconians captured them and carried them off."

"All of them?" Flint's mouth fell open. "Just like that?"

"These draconians were magic-users," Tas said impatiently, anxious to get started. "They cast spells, I guess. They didn't hurt them, except for Raistlin. I think they did something terrible to him. I saw him as they passed. He looked awful. But he's the only one." The kender tugged on the dwarf's wet sleeve. "Let's go— we've got to follow them."

"Yeah, sure," Flint mumbled, looking around. Then he put his hand on his head again. "Where's my helm?"

"At the bottom of the swamp," Tas said in exasperation. "Do you want to go in after it?"

The dwarf gave the murky water a horrified glance, shivered, and turned away hurriedly. He put his hand to his head again and felt a large bump. "I sure don't remember hitting my head," he muttered. Then a sudden thought struck him. He felt around his back wildly. "My axe!" he cried.

"Hush!" Tas scolded. "At least you're alive. Now we've got to rescue the others."

"And how do you propose to do that without any weapons except that overgrown slingshot?" Flint grumbled, stumping along after the fast-moving kender.

"We'll think of something," Tas said confidently, though he felt as if his heart were getting tangled up in his feet, it had sunk so low.

The kender picked up the draconians' trail without any trouble. It was obviously an old and well-used trail; it looked as though hundreds of draconian feet had tramped along it. Tasslehoff, examining the tracks, suddenly realized that they might be walking into a large camp of the monsters. He shrugged. No use worrying about such minor details.

Unfortunately, Flint didn't share the same philosophy. "There's a whole army up there!" the dwarf gasped, grabbing the kender by the shoulder.

"Yes, well—" Tas paused to consider the situation. He brightened. "That's all the better. The more of *them* there are, the less chance they'll have of seeing *us*." He started off again. Flint frowned. There was something wrong with that logic, but right now he couldn't figure out what, and he was too wet and chilled to argue. Besides, he was thinking the same thing the kender was: the only other choice they had was to escape into the swamp themselves and leave their friends in the hands of the draconians. And that was no choice at all.

They walked another half hour. The sun sank into the mist, giving it a blood-red tinge, and night fell swiftly in the mirky swamp.

Soon they saw a blazing light ahead of them. They left the trail and sneaked into the brush. The kender moved silently as a mouse; the dwarf stepped on sticks that snapped beneath his feet, ran into trees, and blundered through the brush. Fortunately, the draconian camp was celebrating and probably wouldn't have heard an army of dwarves approaching. Flint and Tas knelt just beyond the firelight and watched. The dwarf suddenly grabbed the kender with such violence that he nearly pulled him over.

"Great Reorx!" Flint swore, pointing. "A dragon!"

Tas was too stunned to say anything. He and the dwarf watched in amazed horror as the draconians danced and prostrated themselves before a giant black dragon. The creature lurked inside the remaining half shell of a crumbled domed ruin. Its head was higher than the treetops, its wing span was enormous. One of the draconians, wearing robes, bent before the dragon, gesturing to the staff as it lay on the ground with the captured weapons.

"There's something strange about that dragon," Tas whispered after watching for a few moments.

"Like they're not supposed to exist?"

"That's just the point," Tas said. "Look at it. The creature isn't moving or reacting to anything. It's just sitting there. I always thought that dragons would be more lively, don't you know?"

"Go up and tickle its foot!" Flint snorted. "Then you'll see lively!"

"I think I'll do that," the kender said. Before the dwarf could say a word, Tasslehoff crept out of the brush, flitting from shadow to shadow as he drew near the camp. Flint could have torn his beard out in frustration, but it would have been disastrous to try and stop him now. The dwarf could do nothing but follow.

"Tanis!"

The half-elf heard someone calling him from across a huge chasm. He tried to answer, but his mouth was stuffed with something sticky. He shook his head. Then he felt an arm around his shoulders, helping him sit up. He opened his eyes. It was night. Judging by the flickering light, a huge fire blazed brightly somewhere. Sturm's face, looking concerned, was near his. Tanis sighed and reached out his hand to clasp the knight's shoulder. He tried to speak and was forced to pull off bits of the sticky substance that clung to his face and mouth like cobwebs.

"I'm all right," Tanis said when he could talk. "Where are we?" He glanced around. "Is everyone here? Anyone hurt?"

"We're in a draconian camp," Sturm said, helping the half-elf stand. "Tasslehoff and Flint are missing and Raistlin's hurt."

"Badly?" Tanis asked, alarmed by the serious expression on Sturm's face.

"Not good," the knight replied.

"Poisoned dart," Riverwind said. Tanis turned toward the Plainsman and got his first clear look at their prison. They were inside a cage made of bamboo. Draconian guards stood outside, their long, curved swords drawn and ready. Beyond the cage, hundreds of draconians milled around a campfire. And above the campfire . . .

"Yes," Sturm said, seeing Tanis's startled expression. "A dragon. More children's stories. Raistlin would gloat."

"Raistlin—" Tanis went over to the mage who was lying in a corner of the cage, covered in his cloak. The young mage was feverish and shaking with chills. Goldmoon knelt beside him, her hand on his forehead, stroking back the white hair. He was unconscious. His head tossed fitfully, and he murmured strange words, sometimes shouting out garbled commands. Caramon, his face nearly as pale as his brother's, sat beside him. Goldmoon met Tanis's questioning gaze and shook her head sadly, her eyes large and gleaming in the reflected firelight. Riverwind came over to stand beside Tanis.

"She found this in his neck," he said, carefully holding up a feathered dart between thumb and forefinger. He glanced at the mage without love but with a certain amount of pity. "Who can say what poison burns in his blood?"

"If we had the staff—" Goldmoon said.

"Right," Tanis said. "Where is it?"

"There," Sturm said, his mouth twisting wryly. He pointed. Tanis peered past hundreds of draconians and saw the staff lying on Goldmoon's fur blanket in front of the black dragon.

Reaching out, Tanis grasped a bar of the cage. "We could break out," he told Sturm. "Caramon could snap this like a twig."

"Tasslehoff could snap it like a twig if he were here," Sturm said. "Of course, then we've only got a few hundred of these creatures to take care of—not to mention the dragon."

"All right. Don't rub it in." Tanis sighed. "Any idea what happened to Flint and Tas?"

"Riverwind said he heard a splash just after Tas yelled out that we were being ambushed. If they were lucky, they dived off the log and escaped into the swamp. If not—" Sturm didn't finish.

Tanis closed his eyes to shut out the firelight. He felt tired—tired of fighting, tired of killing, tired of slogging through the muck. He thought longingly of lying down and sinking back into sleep. Instead, he opened his eyes, stalked over to the cage, and rattled the bars. A draconian guard turned around, sword raised.

"You speak Common?" Tanis asked in the very lowest, crudest form of the Common language used on Krynn.

"I speak Common. Apparently better than you do, elven scum," the draconian sneered. "What do you want?"

"One of our party is injured. We ask that you treat him. Give him an antidote to this poison dart."

"Poison?" The draconian peered into the cage. "Ah, yes, the magic-user." The creature gurgled deep in its throat, a sound obviously meant to be laughter. "Sick, is he? Yes, the poison acts swiftly. Can't have a magic-user around. Even behind bars they're deadly. But don't worry. He won't be lonely—the rest of you will be joining him soon enough. In fact, you should envy him. Your deaths will not be nearly so quick."

The draconian turned its back and said something to its partner, jerking its clawed thumb in the direction of the cage. Both of them croaked their gurgling laughter. Tanis, feeling disgust and rage welling up deep inside of him, looked back at Raistlin.

The mage was rapidly growing worse. Goldmoon put her hand on Raistlin's neck, feeling for the life beat, and then shook her head. Caramon made a moaning sound. Then his glance shifted to the two draconians, laughing and talking together outside.

"Stop—Caramon!" Tanis yelled, but it was too late.

With a roar like a wounded animal, the huge warrior leaped toward the draconians. Bamboo gave way before him, the shards splintering and cutting into his skin. Mad with the desire to kill, Caramon never noticed. Tanis jumped on his back as the warrior crashed past him, but Caramon shook him off as easily as a bear shakes off an annoying fly.

"Caramon, you fool—" Sturm grunted as he and Riverwind both threw themselves on the warrior. But Caramon's rage carried him on.

Whirling, one draconian raised its sword, but Caramon sent the weapon flying. The creature hit the ground, knocked senseless by a blow from the big man's fist. Within seconds, there were six draconians, bows and arrows in their hands, surrounding the warrior. Sturm and Riverwind wrestled Caramon to the ground. Sturm, sitting on him, shoved his face into the mud until he felt Caramon relax beneath him and heard him give a strangled sob.

At that instant, a high-pitched, shrill voice screeched through the camp. "Bring the warrior to me!" said the dragon.

Tanis felt the hair rise on his neck. The draconians lowered their weapons and turned to face the dragon, staring in astonishment and muttering among themselves. Riverwind and Sturm got to their feet. Caramon lay on the ground, choking with sobs. The draconian guards glanced at each other uneasily, while those standing near the dragon backed off hurriedly and formed an immense semicircle around it.

One of the creatures, whom Tanis supposed by the insignia on its armor to be some sort of captain, stalked up to a robed draconian who was staring, open-mouthed, at the black dragon.

"What's going on?" the captain demanded. The draconian spoke in the Common tongue. Tanis, listening closely, realized they were of different species—the robed draconians were apparently the magic-users and the priests. Presumably, the two could not communicate in their own languages. The military draconian was clearly upset.

"Where is that Bozak priest of yours? He must tell us what to do!"

"The higher of my order is not here." The robed draconian quickly regained his composure. "One of *them* flew here and took him to confer with Lord Verminaard about the staff."

"But the dragon never speaks when the priest is not here." The captain lowered his voice. "My boys don't like it. You'd better do something quickly!"

"What is this delay?" The dragon's voice shrieked like a wailing wind. "Bring me the warrior!"

"Do as the dragon says." The robed draconian motioned quickly with a clawed hand. Several draconians rushed over, shoved Tanis and Riverwind and Sturm back into the shattered cage, and lifted the bleeding Caramon up by the arms. They dragged him over to stand before the dragon, his back to the blazing fire. Near him lay the blue crystal staff, Raistlin's staff, their weapons, and their packs.

Caramon raised his head to confront the monster, his eyes blurred with tears and blood from the many cuts the bamboo had inflicted on his face. The dragon loomed above him, seen dimly through the smoke rising from the bonfire.

"We mete out justice swiftly and surely, human scum," the dragon hissed. As it spoke, it beat its huge wings, fanning them slowly. The draconians gasped and began to back up, some stumbling over themselves as they hurried to get out of the monster's way. Obviously they knew what was coming.

Caramon stared at the creature without fear. "My brother is dying," he shouted. "Do what you will to me. I ask only one thing. Give me my sword so that I can die fighting!"

The dragon laughed shrilly; the draconians joined it, gurgling and croaking horribly. As the dragon's wings beat the air, it began to rock back and forth, seemingly preparing to leap on the warrior and devour him.

"This will be fun. Let him have his weapon," the dragon commanded. Its flapping wings caused a wind to whip through the camp, scattering sparks from the fire.

Caramon shoved the draconian guards aside. Wiping his hand across his eyes, he walked over to the pile of weapons and pulled out his sword. Then he turned to face the dragon, resignation and grief etched into his face. He raised his sword.

"We can't let him die out there by himself!" Sturm said harshly, and he took a step forward, prepared to break out.

Suddenly a voice came from the shadows behind them.

"Hssst . . . Tanis!"

The half-elf whirled around. "Flint!" he exclaimed, then glanced apprehensively at the draconian guards, but they were absorbed in watching the spectacle of Caramon and the dragon. Tanis hurried to the back of the bamboo cage where the dwarf stood.

"Get out of here!" the half-elf ordered. "There's nothing you can do. Raistlin's dying, and the dragon—"

"Is Tasslehoff," Flint said succinctly.

"What?" Tanis glared at the dwarf. "Make sense."

"The dragon is Tasslehoff," Flint repeated patiently.

For once Tanis was speechless. He stared at the dwarf.

"The dragon's made of wicker," the dwarf whispered hurriedly. "Tasslehoff sneaked behind it and looked inside. It's rigged! Anyone sitting inside the dragon can make the wings flap and speak through a hollow tube. I guess that's how the priests keep order around here. Anyway, Tasslehoff's the one flapping his wings and threatening to eat Caramon."

Tanis gasped. "But what do we do? There's still a hundred draconians around. Sooner or later they're going to realize what's going on."

"Get over to Caramon, you and Riverwind and Sturm. Grab your weapons and packs and the staff. I'll help Goldmoon carry Raistlin into the woods. Tasslehoff's got something in mind. Just be ready."

Tanis groaned.

"I don't like it any better than you do," the dwarf growled. "Trusting our lives to that rattle-brained kender. But, well, he *is* the dragon, after all."

"He certainly is," Tanis said, eyeing the dragon who was shrieking and wailing and flapping its wings and rocking back and forth. The draconians were staring at it in open-mouthed wonder. Tanis grabbed Sturm and Riverwind and huddled down near Goldmoon, who had not left Raistlin's side. The half-elf explained what was happening. Sturm looked at him as if he were as crazed as Raistlin. Riverwind shook his head.

"Well, have you got a better plan?" Tanis asked.

Both of them looked at the dragon, then back at Tanis, and shrugged.

"Goldmoon goes with the dwarf," Riverwind said.

She started to protest. He looked at her, his eyes expressionless, and she swallowed and fell silent.

"Yes," Tanis said. "Stay with Raistlin, lady, please. We'll bring the staff to you."

"Hurry then," she said through white lips. "He is very nearly gone."

"We'll hurry," Tanis said grimly. "I have a feeling that once things get started out there, we're going to be moving very fast!" He patted her hand. "Come on." He stood up and took a deep breath.

Riverwind's eyes were still on Goldmoon. He started to speak, then shook his head irritably and turned without a word to stand beside Tanis. Sturm joined them. The three crept up behind the draconian guards.

Caramon lifted his sword. It flashed in the firelight. The dragon went into a wild frenzy, and all of the draconians fell back, braying and beating their swords against their shields. Wind from the dragon's wings blew up ashes and sparks from the fire, setting some nearby bamboo huts on fire. The draconians did not notice, so eager were they for the kill. The dragon shrieked and howled, and Caramon felt his mouth go dry and his stomach muscles clench. It was the first time he had ever gone into battle without his brother; the thought made his heart throb painfully. He was about to leap forward and attack when Tanis, Sturm, and Riverwind appeared out of nowhere to stand by his side.

"We will not let our friend die alone!" the half-elf cried defiantly at the dragon. The draconians cheered wildly.

"Get out of here, Tanis!" Caramon scowled, his face flushed and streaked with tears. "This is my fight."

"Shut up and listen!" Tanis ordered. "Get your sword and mine, Sturm. Riverwind, grab your weapons and the packs and any draconian weapons you can pick up to replace those we lost. Caramon, pick up the two staffs."

Caramon stared at him. "What—"

"Tasslehoff's the dragon," Tanis said. "There isn't time to explain. Just do as I say! Get the staff and take it into the woods. Goldmoon's waiting." He laid his hand on the warrior's shoulder. Tanis shoved him. "Go! Raistlin's almost finished! You're his only chance."

This statement reached Caramon's mind. He ran to the pile of weapons and grabbed the blue crystal staff and Raistlin's Staff of Magius, while the draconians yelled. Sturm and Riverwind armed themselves, Sturm bringing Tanis his sword.

"And now, prepare to die, humans!" the dragon screamed. Its wings gave a great lurch and suddenly the creature was flying, hovering in midair. The draconians croaked and cried out in alarm, some breaking for the woods, others hurling themselves flat on the ground.

"Now!" yelled Tanis. "Run, Caramon!"

The big warrior broke for the woods, running swiftly toward where he could see Goldmoon and Flint waiting for him. A draconian appeared in front of him, but Caramon hurled it out of his way with a thrust of his great arm. He could hear a wild commotion behind him, Sturm chanting a Solamnic war cry, draconians yelling. Other draconians leaped at Caramon. He used the blue crystal staff as he had seen Goldmoon use it, swinging it in a wide arc with his huge right hand. It flashed blue flame and the draconians fell back.

Caramon reached the woods and found Raistlin lying at Goldmoon's feet, barely breathing. Goldmoon grabbed the staff from Caramon and laid it on the mage's inert body. Flint watched, shaking his head. "It won't work," muttered the dwarf. "It's used up."

"It has to work," Goldmoon said firmly. "Please," she murmured, "whoever is master of this staff, heal this man. Please." Unknowing, she repeated it over and over. Caramon watched for a moment, blinking his eyes. Then the woods around him were lit by a gigantic burst of flame.

"Name of the Abyss!" Flint breathed. "Look at that!"

Caramon turned just in time to see the great black wicker dragon crash headlong into the blazing bonfire. Flaming logs flew into the air, showering sparks over the camp. The draconians' bamboo huts, some already ablaze, began burning fiercely. The wicker dragon gave a final, horrifying shriek and then it, too, caught fire.

"Tasslehoff!" Flint swore. "That blasted kender—he's inside there!" Before Caramon could stop him, the dwarf ran out into the blazing draconian camp.

"Caramon . . ." Raistlin murmured. The big warrior knelt beside his brother. Raistlin was still pale, but his eyes were open and clear. He sat up, weakly, leaning against his brother, and stared out at the raging fire. "What's going on?"

"I'm not sure," Caramon said. "Tasslehoff turned into a dragon and after that things get real confused. You just rest." The warrior stared into the smoke, his sword drawn and ready in case any draconians came for them.

But the draconians now had little interest in the prisoners. The smaller breed, panic stricken, were fleeing into the forest as their great god-dragon went up in flames. A few of the robed draconians, bigger and apparently more intelligent than the other species, were trying desperately to bring order to the fearful chaos raging around them.

Sturm fought and slashed his way through the draconians without encountering any organized resistance. He had just reached the edge of the clearing, near the bamboo cage, when Flint passed him, running back toward the camp!

"Hey! Where—" Sturm yelled at the dwarf.

"Tas, in the dragon!" The dwarf didn't stop.

Sturm turned and saw the black wicker dragon burning with flames that shot high into the air. Thick smoke boiled up, blanketing the camp, the dank heavy swamp air preventing it from rising and drifting away. Sparks showered down as part of the blazing dragon exploded into the camp. Sturm ducked and batted out sparks that landed on his cape, then ran after the dwarf, catching up with the short-legged Flint easily.

"Flint," he panted, grasping the dwarf's arm. "It's no use. Nothing could live in that furnace! We've got to get back to the others—"

"Let go of me!" Flint roared so furiously that Sturm let go in amazement. The dwarf ran for the burning dragon again. Sturm heaved a sigh and ran after him, his eyes beginning to water in the smoke.

"Tasslehoff Burrfoot!" Flint called. "You idiotic kender! Where are you?"

There was no answer.

"Tasslehoff!" Flint screamed. "If you wreck this escape, I'll murder you. So help me—" Tears of frustration and grief and anger and smoke coursed down the dwarf's cheeks.

The heat was overwhelming. It seared Sturm's lungs, and the knight knew they couldn't breathe much more of this or they would perish themselves. He took hold of the dwarf firmly, intending to knock him out if necessary, when suddenly he saw movement near the edge of the blaze. He rubbed his eyes and looked closer.

The dragon lay on the ground, the head still connected to the blazing body by a long wicker neck. The head had not caught fire yet, but flames were starting to eat into the wicker neck. The head would soon be ablaze, too. Sturm saw the movement again.

"Flint! Look!" Sturm ran toward the head, the dwarf pounding along behind. Two small legs encased in bright blue pants were sticking out of the dragon's mouth, kicking feebly.

"Tas!" Sturm yelled. "Get out! The head's going to burn!"

"I can't! I'm stuck!" came a muffled voice.

Sturm stared at the head, frantically trying to figure out how to free the kender, while Flint just grabbed hold of Tas's legs and pulled.

"Ouch! Stop!" yelled Tas.

"No good," the dwarf puffed. "He's stuck fast."

The inferno crept up the dragon's neck.

Sturm drew his sword. "I may cut off his head," he muttered to Flint, "but it's his only chance." Estimating the size of the kender, guessing where his head would be, and hoping his hands weren't stretched out over his head, Sturm lifted his sword above the dragon's neck.

Flint closed his eyes.

The knight took a deep breath and brought his blade crashing down on the dragon, severing the head from the neck. There was a cry from the kender inside but whether from pain or astonishment, Sturm couldn't tell.

"Pull!" he yelled at the dwarf.

Flint grabbed hold of the wicker head and pulled it away from the blazing neck. Suddenly a tall, dark shape loomed out of the smoke. Sturm whipped around, sword ready, then saw it was Riverwind.

"What are you—" The Plainsman stared at the dragon's head. Perhaps Flint and Sturm had gone mad.

"The kender's stuck in there!" Sturm yelled. "We can't take the head apart out here, surrounded by draconians! We've got to—"

His words were lost in a roar of flame, but Riverwind finally saw the blue legs sticking out of the dragon's mouth. He grabbed hold of one side of the dragon's head, thrusting his hands in one of the eyesockets. Sturm got hold of the other, and together they lifted the head—kender inside—and began running through the camp. Those few draconians they encountered took one look at the terrifying apparition and fled.

"C'mon, Raist," Caramon said solicitously, his arm around his brother's shoulder. "You've got to try and stand. We have to be ready to move out of here. How do you feel?"

"How do I ever feel?" whispered Raistlin bitterly. "Help me up. There! Now leave me in peace for a moment." He leaned against a tree, shivering but standing.

"Sure, Raist," Caramon said, hurt, backing off. Goldmoon glanced at Raistlin in disgust, remembering Caramon's grief when he thought his brother was dying. She turned away to watch for the others, staring through the gathering smoke.

Tanis appeared first, running so fast he crashed into Caramon. The big warrior caught him in his huge arms, breaking the half-elf's forward momentum and keeping him on his feet.

"Thanks!" Tanis gasped. He leaned over, hands on his knees, to catch his breath. "Where are the others?"

"Weren't they with you?" Caramon frowned.

"We got separated." Tanis drew in huge gulps of air, then coughed as the smoke flew down his lungs.

"*SuTorakh!*" interrupted Goldmoon in an awed voice. Tanis and Caramon both spun around in alarm, staring out into the smoke-filled camp to see a grotesque sight emerging from the swirling smoke. A dragon's head with a forked blue tongue was lunging at them. Tanis blinked in disbelief, then he heard a sound behind him that nearly made him leap into a tree in panic. He whirled around, heart in his throat, sword in his hand.

Raistlin was laughing.

Tanis had never heard the mage laugh before, even when Raistlin was a child, and he hoped he would never hear it again. It was weird, shrill, mocking laughter. Caramon stared at his brother in amazement, Goldmoon in horror. Finally the sound of Raistlin's laughter died until the mage was laughing silently, his golden eyes reflecting the glow of the draconian camp going up in flames.

Tanis shuddered and turned back around to see that in fact the dragon's head was carried by Sturm and Riverwind. Flint raced along in front, a draconian helm on his head. Tanis ran forward to meet them.

"What in the name of—"

"The kender's stuck in here!" Sturm said. He and Riverwind dropped the head to the ground, both of them breathing heavily. "We've got to get him out." Sturm eyed the laughing Raistlin warily. "What's the matter with him? Still poisoned?"

"No, he's better," Tanis said, examining the dragon's head.

"A pity," Sturm muttered as he knelt beside the half-elf.

"Tas, are you all right?" Tanis called out, lifting the huge mouth to see inside.

"I think Sturm chopped off my hair!" the kender wailed.

"Lucky it wasn't your head!" Flint snorted.

"What's holding him?" Riverwind leaned down to peer inside the dragon's mouth.

"I'm not sure," Tanis said, swearing softly. "I can't see in all this blasted smoke." He stood up, sighing in frustration. "And we've got to get out of here! The draconians will get organized soon. Caramon, come here. See if you can rip off the top."

The big warrior came over to stand in front of the wicker dragon's head. Bracing himself, he got hold of the two eyesockets, closed his eyes, took a deep breath, then grunted and heaved. For a minute nothing happened. Tanis watched the muscles bulge on the big man's arms, saw his thigh muscles absorb the strain. Blood rushed to Caramon's face. Then there was the ripping and snapping sound of wood splintering. The top of the dragon's head gave way with a sharp crack. Caramon staggered backward as the top half of the head suddenly came off in his hands.

Tanis reached in, grabbed Tas's hand, and jerked him free. "Are you all right?" he asked. The kender seemed wobbly on his feet, but his grin was wide as ever.

"I'm fine," Tas said brightly. "Just a little singed." Then his face darkened. "Tanis," he said, his face crinkling with unusual worry. He felt at his long topknot. "My hair?"

"All there," Tanis said, smiling.

Tas breathed a sigh of relief. Then he began to talk. "Tanis, it was the most wonderful thing—flying like that. And the look on Caramon's face—"

"The story will have to wait," Tanis said firmly. "We've got to get out of here. Caramon? Can you and your brother make it all right?"

"Yeah, go on," Caramon said.

Raistlin stumbled forward, accepting the support of his brother's strong arm. The mage glanced behind at the sundered dragon's head and he wheezed, his shoulders shaking in silent, grim amusement.

ESCAPE. THE WELL.
DEATH ON BLACK WINGS.

15

Smoke from the burning draconian camp hung over the black swamplands, shielding the companions from the eyes of the strange, evil creatures. The smoke floated wraithlike through the swamps, drifting across the silver moon and obscuring the stars. The companions dared not risk a light—even the light from Raistlin's staff—for they could hear horns blowing all around them as the draconian leaders tried to reestablish order.

Riverwind led them. Although Tanis had always prided himself on his own woodland skills, he completely lost all sense of direction in the black misty mire. An occasional fleeting glimpse of the stars, whenever the smoke lifted, showed him that they were bearing north.

They hadn't gone far when Riverwind missed a step and plunged knee-deep into muck. After Tanis and Caramon dragged the Plainsman out of the water, Tasslehoff crept ahead, testing the ground with his hoopak staff. It sank every time.

"We have no choice but to wade," Riverwind said grimly.

Choosing a path where the water seemed shallower, the company left firm ground and splashed into the muck. At first it was only ankle deep, then they sank to their knees. Soon they sank deeper still; Tanis was forced to carry Tasslehoff, the giggling kender grasping him around the neck. Flint steadfastly refused all offers of help, even when the tip of his beard got wet. Then he vanished. Caramon, following him, fished the dwarf out of the water and slung him over his shoulder like a wet sack, the dwarf too tired and frightened to grumble. Raistlin staggered, coughing, through the water, his robes dragging him down. Weary and still sick from the poison, the mage finally collapsed. Sturm grabbed hold of him and half-dragged, half-carried the mage through the swamp.

After an hour of floundering in the icy water, they finally reached firm ground and sank down to rest, shivering with the cold.

The trees began to creak and groan, their branches bending as a sharp wind sprang up from the north. The wind blew the mists into wispy rags. Raistlin, lying on the ground, looked up. The mage caught his breath. He sat up, alarmed.

"Storm clouds." He choked, coughing, and fought to speak. "They come from the north. We have no time. No time! We must reach Xak Tsaroth. Hurry! Before the moon sets!"

Everyone looked up. A gathering darkness was moving out of the north, swallowing up the stars. Tanis could feel the same sense of urgency that was driving the mage. Wearily, he rose to his feet. Without a word, the rest of the group rose and stumbled forward, Riverwind taking the lead. But dark swamp water blocked their path once more.

"Not again!" Flint moaned.

"No, we do not have to wade again. Come look," Riverwind said. He led the way to the water's edge. There, amid many other ruins protruding from the dank ground, lay an obelisk that had either fallen or been pushed over to form a bridge across to the other bank of the swamp.

"I'll go first," Tas volunteered, hopping energetically onto the long stone. "Hey, there's writing on this thing. Runes of some sort."

"I must see!" Raistlin whispered, hurrying over. He spoke his word of command, "*Shirak*," and the crystal on the tip of his staff burst into light.

"Hurry!" Sturm growled. "You've just told everything within a twenty-mile radius we're here."

But Raistlin would not be rushed. He held the light over the spidery runes, studying them intently. Tanis and the others climbed onto the obelisk and joined the mage.

The kender bent down, tracing the runes with his small hand. "What does it say, Raistlin? Can you read it? The language seems very old."

"It is old," the mage whispered. "It dates from before the Cataclysm. The runes say, 'The Great City of Xak Tsaroth, whose beauty surrounds you, speaks to the good of its people and their generous deeds. The gods reward us in the grace of our home.'"

"How awful!" Goldmoon shuddered, looking at the ruin and desolation around her.

"The gods rewarded them indeed," Raistlin said, his lips parting in a cynical smile. No one spoke. Then Raistlin whispered, "*Dulak*," and extinguished the light. Suddenly the night seemed much blacker. "We must keep going," the mage said. "Surely there is more than a fallen monument to mark what this place once stood for."

They crossed the obelisk into thick jungle. At first there seemed to be no trail, then Riverwind, searching diligently, found a trail cut through the vines and the trees. He bent down to study it. His face was grim when he rose.

"Draconians?" Tanis asked.

"Yes," he said heavily. "The tracks of many clawed feet. And they lead north, straight to the city."

Tanis asked in an undertone, "Is this the broken city, where you were given the staff?"

"And where death had black wings," Riverwind added. He closed his eyes, wiping his hand over his face. Then he drew a deep, ragged breath. "I don't know. I can't remember—but I am afraid without knowing why."

Tanis put his hand on Riverwind's arm. "The elves have a saying: 'Only the dead are without fear.'"

Riverwind startled him by suddenly clasping the half-elf's hand with his. "I have never known an elf," the Plainsman said. "My people distrust them, saying that the elves have no care for Krynn or for humans. I think my people may have been mistaken. I am glad I met you, Tanis of Qualinost. I count you as a friend."

Tanis knew enough of Plains lore to realize that, with this statement, Riverwind had declared himself willing to sacrifice everything for the half-elf—even his life. A vow of friendship was a solemn vow among the Plainsmen. "You are my friend, too, Riverwind," Tanis said simply. "You and Goldmoon both are my friends."

Riverwind turned his eyes to Goldmoon who stood near them, leaning on her staff, her eyes closed, her face drawn with pain and exhaustion. Riverwind's face softened with compassion as he looked at her. Then it hardened, pride drawing the stern mask over it again.

"Xak Tsaroth is not far off," he said coolly. "And these tracks are old." He led the way into the jungle. After only a short walk, the northern trail suddenly changed to cobblestones.

"A street!" exclaimed Tasslehoff.

"The outskirts of Xak Tsaroth!" Raistlin breathed.

"About time!" Flint stared all around in disgust. "What a mess! If the greatest gift ever given to man is here, it must be well hidden!"

Tanis agreed. He had never seen a more dismal place. As they walked, the broad street took them into an open-paved courtyard. To the east stood four tall, free-standing columns that supported nothing; the building lay in ruins around them. A huge unbroken circular stone wall rose about four feet above the ground. Caramon, going over to inspect it, announced that it was a well.

"Deep at that," he said. He leaned over and peered down into it. "Smells bad, too."

North of the well stood what appeared to be the only building to have escaped the destruction of the Cataclysm. It was finely constructed of pure white stone, supported by tall, slender columns. Large golden double doors gleamed in the moonlight.

"That was a temple to the ancient gods," Raistlin said, more to himself than anyone else. But Goldmoon, standing near him, heard his soft whisper.

"A temple?" she repeated, staring at the building. "How beautiful." She walked toward it, strangely fascinated.

Tanis and the rest searched the grounds and found no other buildings intact. Fluted columns lay on the ground, their broken pieces aligned to show their former beauty. Statues lay broken and, in some cases, grotesquely defaced. Everything was old, so old it made even the dwarf feel young.

Flint sat down on a column. "Well, we're here." He blinked at Raistlin and yawned. "What now, mage?"

Raistlin's thin lips parted, but before he could reply, Tasslehoff yelled, "Draconian!"

Everyone spun around, weapons in their hands. A draconian, ready to move, was glaring at them from the edge of the well.

"Stop it!" Tanis shouted. "It will alert others!"

But before anyone could reach it, the draconian spread its wings and flew *into* the well. Raistlin, his golden eyes flaring in the moonlight, ran to the well and peered over the edge. Raising his hand as if to cast a spell, he hesitated, then dropped his hand limply to his side. "I can't," he said. "I can't think. I can't concentrate. I must sleep!"

"We're all tired," Tanis said wearily. "If something's down there, it warned it. There's nothing we can do now. We've got to rest."

"It *has* gone to warn something," Raistlin whispered. He huddled in his cloak and stared around, his eyes wide. "Can't you feel it? Any of you? Half-Elf? Evil about to waken and come forth."

Silence fell.

Then Tasslehoff climbed up on the stone wall and peered down. "Look! The draconian is floating down, just like a leaf. His wings don't flap—"

"Be quiet!" Tanis snapped.

Tasslehoff glanced at the half-elf in surprise—Tanis's voice sounded strained and unnatural. The half-elf was staring at the well, his hands clenching nervously. Everything was still. Too still. The storm clouds massed to the north, but there was no wind. Not a branch creaked, not a leaf stirred. The silver moon and the red cast twin shadows that made things seen from the corner of the eye unreal and distorted.

Then, slowly, Raistlin backed away from the well, raising his hands before him as if to ward off some dreadful danger.

"I feel it, too." Tanis swallowed. "What is it?"

"Yes, what is it?" Tasslehoff, leaning over, stared eagerly into the well. It looked as deep and dark as the mage's hourglass eyes.

"Get him away from there!" Raistlin cried.

Tanis, infected by the mage's fear and his own growing sense that something was terribly wrong, started to run for Tas. Even as he began to move, though, he felt the ground shake beneath his feet. The kender gave a startled cry as the ancient stone wall of the well cracked and gave way beneath him. Tas felt himself sliding into the terrible blackness below him. He scrabbled frantically with his hands and feet, trying to clutch the crumbling rocks. Tanis lunged desperately, but he was too far away.

Riverwind had started moving when he heard Raistlin's cry, and the tall man's long, swift strides carried him quickly to the well. Catching hold of Tas by his collar, the Plainsman plucked him from the wall just as the stones and mortar tumbled down into the blackness below.

The ground trembled again. Tanis tried to force his numb mind to figure out what was happening. Then a blast of cold air burst from the well. The wind swept dirt and leaves from the courtyard into the air, stinging his face and eyes.

"Run!" Tanis tried to yell, but he choked on the foul stench erupting from the well.

The columns left standing after the Cataclysm began to shake. The companions stared fearfully at the well. Then Riverwind tore his gaze away. "Goldmoon . . ." he said, looking around. He dropped Tas to the ground. "Goldmoon!" He stopped as a high-pitched shriek rose from the depths of the well. The sound was so loud and shrill that it pierced the head. Riverwind searched frantically for Goldmoon, calling her name.

Tanis was stunned by the noise. Unable to move, he saw Sturm, hand on his sword, slowly back away from the well. He saw Raistlin—the mage's ghastly face glistening metallic yellow, his golden eyes red in the red moon's light—scream something Tanis couldn't hear. He saw Tasslehoff staring at the well in wide-eyed wonder. Sturm ran across the courtyard, scooped up the kender under one arm, and ran on to the trees. Caramon ran to his exhausted brother, caught him up, and headed for cover. Tanis knew some monstrous evil was coming up out of the well, but he could not move. The words "run, fool, run" screamed in his brain.

Riverwind, too, stayed near the well, fighting the fear that was growing within him: he couldn't find Goldmoon! Distracted by rescuing the kender from tumbling into the well, he had not seen Goldmoon approach the unbroken temple. He looked around wildly, struggling to keep his balance as the ground shook beneath his feet. The high-pitched shrieking noise, the throbbing and trembling of the ground, brought back hideous, nightmarish memories. "Death on black wings." He began to sweat and shake, then forced his mind to concentrate on Goldmoon. She needed him; he knew—and he alone knew—that her show of strength only masked her fear, doubt, uncertainty. She would be terribly afraid, and he had to find her.

As the stones of the well began to slide, Riverwind moved away and caught sight of Tanis. The half-elf was shouting and pointing past Riverwind toward the temple. Riverwind knew Tanis was saying something, but he couldn't hear above the shrieking sound. Then he knew! Goldmoon! Riverwind turned to go to her, but he lost his balance and fell to his knees. He saw Tanis start to run toward him.

Then the horror burst from the well, the horror of his fevered nightmares. Riverwind closed his eyes and saw no more.

It was a dragon.

Tanis, in those first few moments when the blood seemed to drain from his body, leaving him limp and lifeless, looked at the dragon as it burst forth from the well and thought, "How beautiful . . . how beautiful. . . ."

Sleek and black, the dragon rose, her glistening wings folded close to her sides, her scales gleaming. Her eyes glowed red-black, the color of molten rock. Her mouth opened in a snarl, teeth flashing white and wicked. Her long, red tongue curled as she breathed the night air. Clear of the well's confines, the dragon spread her wings, blotting out stars, obliterating moonlight. Each wing was tipped with a pure, white claw that shone blood-red in the light of Lunitari.

Fear such as Tanis had never imagined shriveled his stomach. His heart throbbed painfully; he couldn't catch his breath. He could only stare in horror and awe and marvel at the creature's deadly beauty. The dragon circled higher and higher into the night sky. Then, just as Tanis felt the paralyzing fear start to recede, just as he began to fumble for his bow and arrows, the dragon spoke.

One word she said—a word in the language of magic—and a thick, terrible darkness fell from the sky, blinding them all. Tanis instantly lost all grasp on where he was. He only knew there was a dragon above him about to attack. He was powerless to defend himself. All he could do was crouch down, crawl among the rubble, and try desperately to hide.

Deprived of his sense of sight, the half-elf concentrated on his sense of hearing. The shrieking noise had stopped as the darkness fell. Tanis could hear the slow, gentle flap of the dragon's leathery wings and knew it was circling above them, rising gradually. Then he couldn't hear even the flapping anymore; the wings had quit beating. He visualized a great, black bird of prey, hovering alone, waiting.

Then there was a very gentle rustling sound, the sound of leaves shivering as the wind rises before a storm. The sound grew louder and louder until it was the rushing of wind when the storm hits, and then it was the shrieking of the hurricane. Tanis pressed his body close against the crumbled well and covered his head with his arms.

The dragon was attacking.

She could not see through the darkness she had cast, but Khisanth knew that the intruders were still in the courtyard below. Her minions, the draconians, had warned her that a group walked the land, carrying the blue crystal staff. Lord Verminaard wanted that staff, wanted it kept safe with her, never to be seen in human lands. But she had lost it, and Lord Verminaard had not been pleased. She had to get it back. Therefore, Khisanth had waited an instant before casting her darkness spell, studying the intruders carefully, searching for the staff. Unaware that already it had passed beyond her sight, she was pleased. She had only to destroy.

The attacking dragon dropped from the sky, her leathery wings curving back like the blade of a black dagger. She dove straight for the well, where she had seen the intruders running for their lives. Knowing that they would be paralyzed by dragonfear, Khisanth was certain she could kill them all with one pass. She opened her fanged mouth.

Tanis heard the dragon coming nearer. The great rushing sound grew louder and louder, then stopped for an instant. He could hear huge tendons creaking, lifting and spreading giant wings. Then he heard a great gasping sound as of air being drawn into a gaping throat, then a strange sound that reminded him of steam escaping from a boiling kettle. Something liquid splashed near him. He could hear rocks splitting and cracking and bubbling. Drops of the liquid splashed on his hand, and he gasped as a searing pain penetrated his being.

Then Tanis heard a scream. It was a deep-voiced scream, a man's scream—Riverwind. So terrible, so agonized was the scream that Tanis dug his fingernails into his palms to keep from adding his own voice to that horrible wail and revealing himself to the dragon. The screaming seemed to go on and on and then it died into a moan. Tanis felt the rush of a large body swoosh past him in the darkness. The stones he pressed his body against shook. Then the tremor of the dragon's passage sank lower and lower into the depths of the well. Finally the ground was still.

There was silence.

Tanis drew a painful breath and opened his eyes. The darkness was gone. The stars shone; the moons glowed in the sky. For a moment the half-elf could do nothing but breathe and breathe again, trying to calm his shaking body. Then he was on his feet, running toward a dark form lying in the stone courtyard.

Tanis was the first to reach the Plainsman's body. He took one look, then choked and turned away.

What remained of Riverwind no longer resembled anything human. The man's flesh had been seared from his body. The white of bone was clearly visible where skin and muscle had melted from his arms. His eyes ran like jelly down the fleshless, cadaverous cheeks. His mouth gaped open in a silent scream. His ribcage lay exposed, hunks of flesh and charred cloth clinging to the bones. But—most horrible—the flesh on his torso had been burned away, leaving the organs exposed, pulsing red in the garish red moonlight.

Tanis sank down, vomiting. The half-elf had seen men die on his sword. He had seen them hacked to pieces by trolls. But this . . . this was horribly different, and Tanis knew the memory of this would haunt him forever. A strong arm gripped him by the shoulders, offering silent comfort and sympathy and understanding. The nausea passed. Tanis sat back and breathed. He wiped his mouth and nose, then tried to force himself to swallow, gagging painfully.

"You all right?" Caramon asked with concern.

Tanis nodded, unable to speak. Then he turned at the sound of Sturm's voice.

"May the true gods have mercy! Tanis, he's still alive! I saw his hand move!" Sturm choked. He could say no more.

Tanis rose to his feet and walked shakily toward the body. One of the charred and blackened hands had risen from the stones, plucking horribly at the air.

"End it!" Tanis said hoarsely, his throat raw from bile. "End it! Sturm—"

The knight had already drawn his sword. Kissing the hilt, he raised the blade to the sky and stood before Riverwind's body. He closed his eyes and mentally withdrew into an old world where death in battle had been glorious and fine. Slowly and solemnly, he began to recite the ancient Solamnic Death Chant. As he spoke the words that laid hold of the warrior's soul and transported it to realms of peace beyond, he reversed the blade of the sword and held it poised above Riverwind's chest.

"Return this man to Huma's breast
Beyond the wild, impartial skies;
Grant to him a warrior's rest
And set the last spark of his eyes
Free from the smothering clouds of wars,
Upon the torches of the stars.
Let the last surge of his breath
Take refuge in the cradling air
Above the dreams of ravens, where
Only the hawk remembers death.
Then let his shade to Huma rise,
Beyond the wild, impartial skies."

The knight's voice sank.

Tanis felt the peace of the gods wash over him like cool, cleansing water, easing his grief and submerging the horror. Caramon, beside him, wept silently. As they watched, moonlight flashed on the sword blade.

Then a clear voice spoke. "Stop. Bring him to me."

Both Tanis and Caramon sprang up to stand in front of the man's tortured body, knowing that Goldmoon must be spared this hideous sight. Sturm, lost in tradition, came back to reality with a start and reversed his killing stroke. Goldmoon stood, a tall, slender shadow silhouetted against the golden, moonlit doors of the temple. Tanis started to speak, but he felt suddenly the cold hand of the mage grip his arm. Shivering, he jerked away from Raistlin's touch.

"Do as she says," the mage hissed. "Carry him to her."

Tanis's face contorted with fury at the sight of Raistlin's expressionless face, uncaring eyes.

"Take him to her," Raistlin said coldly. "It is not for us to choose death for this man. That is for the gods."

A BITTER CHOICE.
THE GREATEST GIFT.

16

Tanis stared at Raistlin. Not the quiver of an eyelid betrayed his feelings—if the mage had any feelings. Their eyes met and, as always, Tanis felt that the mage saw more than was visible to him. Suddenly Tanis hated Raistlin, hated him with a passion that shocked the half-elf, hated him for not feeling this pain, hated him and envied him at the same time.

"We must do something!" Sturm said harshly. "He's not dead and the dragon may return!"

"Very well," Tanis said, his voice catching in his throat. "Wrap him in a blanket. . . . But give me a moment alone with Goldmoon."

The half-elf walked slowly across the courtyard. His footsteps echoed in the stillness of the night as he climbed marble steps to a wide porch where Goldmoon stood in front of the shining golden doors. Glancing behind him, Tanis could see his friends wrapping blankets from their packs around tree limbs to make a battlefield stretcher. The man's body was nothing more than a dark, shapeless mass in the moonlight.

"Bring him to me, Tanis," Goldmoon repeated as the half-elf came up to her. He took hold of her hand.

"Goldmoon," Tanis said, "Riverwind is horribly injured. He is dying. There is nothing you can do—not even the staff—"

"Hush, Tanis," Goldmoon said gently.

The half-elf fell silent, seeing her clearly for the first time. In astonishment, he realized that the Plainswoman was tranquil, calm, uplifted. Her face in the moonlight was the face of the sailor who has fought the stormy seas in his fragile boat and drifted at last into peaceful waters.

"Come inside the temple, my friend," Goldmoon said, her beautiful eyes looking intently into Tanis's. "Come inside and bring Riverwind to me."

Goldmoon had not heard the approach of the dragon, had not seen its attack on Riverwind. When they entered the broken courtyard of Xak Tsaroth, Goldmoon had felt a strange and powerful force drawing her into the temple. She walked across the rubble and up the stairs, oblivious to everything but the golden doors shimmering in the silver-red moonlight. She approached them and stood before them for a moment. Then she became aware of the commotion behind her and heard Riverwind calling her name. "Goldmoon . . ." She paused, unwilling to leave Riverwind and her friends, knowing a terrible evil was rising from the well.

"Come inside, child," a gentle voice called to her.

Goldmoon lifted her head and stared at the doors. Tears came to her eyes. The voice was her mother's. Tearsong, priestess of Que-shu, had died long ago, when Goldmoon was very young.

"Tearsong?" Goldmoon choked. "Mother—"

"The years have been many and sad for you, my daughter"—her mother's voice was not heard so much as felt in her heart—"and I fear your burden will not soon ease. Indeed, if you continue on you will leave this darkness only to enter a deeper darkness. Truth will light your way, my daughter, though you may find its light shines dimly in the vast and terrible night ahead. Still, without the truth, all will perish and be lost. Come here inside the temple with me, daughter. You will find what you seek."

"But my friends, Riverwind." Goldmoon looked back at the well and saw Riverwind stumble on the shaking cobblestones. "They cannot fight this evil. They will die without me. The staff could help! I cannot leave!" She started to turn back as the darkness fell.

"I can't see them! . . . Riverwind! . . . Mother, help me," she cried in agony.

But there was no answer. This isn't fair! Goldmoon screamed silently, clenching her fists. We never wanted this! We only wanted to love each other, and now—now we may lose that! We have sacrificed so much and none of it has made any difference. I am thirty years old, mother! Thirty and childless. They have taken my youth, they have taken my people. And I have nothing to show in return. Nothing—except this! She shook the staff. And now I am being asked once again to give still more.

Her anger calmed. Riverwind—had he been angry all those long years he searched for answers? All he had found was this staff, and it brought only more questions. No, he hadn't been angry, she thought. His faith is strong. I am the weak one. Riverwind was willing to die for his faith. It seems I must be willing to live—even if it means living without him.

Goldmoon leaned her head against the golden doors, their metal surface cool to her skin. Reluctantly, she made her bitter decision. I will go forward, mother—though if Riverwind dies, my heart dies, too. I ask only one thing: If he dies, let him know, somehow, that I will continue his search.

Leaning upon her staff, the Chieftain of the Que-shu pushed open the golden doors and entered the temple. The doors shut behind her at the precise moment the black dragon burst from the well.

Goldmoon stepped inside soft, enfolding darkness. She could see nothing at first, but a memory of being held very close in her mother's warm embrace played through her mind. A pale light began to shine around her. Goldmoon saw she was under a vast dome that rose high above an intricately inlaid tile floor. Beneath the dome, in the center of the room, stood a marble statue of singular grace and beauty. The light in the room emanated from this statue. Goldmoon, entranced, moved toward it. The statue was of a woman in flowing robes. Her marble face bore an expression of radiant hope, tempered with sadness. A strange amulet hung around her neck.

"This is Mishakal, goddess of healing, whom I serve," said her mother's voice. "Listen to her words, my daughter."

Goldmoon stood directly in front of the statue, marveling at its beauty. But it seemed unfinished, incomplete. Part of the statue was missing, Goldmoon realized. The marble woman's hands were curved, as if they had been holding a long slender pole, but the hands were empty. Without conscious thought, with only the need to complete such beauty, Goldmoon slid her staff into the marble hands.

It began to gleam with a soft blue light. Goldmoon, startled, backed away. The staff's light grew into a blinding radiance. Goldmoon shielded her eyes and fell to her knees. A great and loving power filled her heart. She bitterly regretted her anger.

"Do not be ashamed of your questioning, beloved disciple. It was your questioning that led you to us, and it is your anger that will sustain you through the many trials ahead. You come seeking the truth and you shall receive it.

"The gods have not turned away from man—it is man who turned away from the true gods. Krynn is about to face its greatest trial. Men will need the truth more than ever. You, my disciple, must return the truth and power of the true gods to man. It is time to restore the balance of the universe. Evil now has tipped the scales. For as the gods of good have returned to man, so have the gods of evil—constantly striving for men's souls. The Queen of Darkness has returned, seeking that which will allow her to walk freely in this land once more. Dragons, once banished to the nether regions, walk the land."

Dragons, thought Goldmoon dreamily. She found it difficult to concentrate and grasp the words that flooded her mind. It would not be until later that she would fully comprehend the message. Then she would remember the words forever.

"To gain the power to defeat them, you will need the truth of the gods, this is the greatest gift of which you were told. Below this temple, in the ruins haunted by the glories of ages past, rest the Disks of Mishakal; circular disks made of gleaming platinum. Find the Disks

and you can call upon my power, for I am Mishakal, goddess of healing.

"Your way will not be easy. The gods of evil know and fear the great power of the truth. The ancient and powerful black dragon, Khisanth, known to men as Onyx, guards the Disks. Her lair is in the ruined city of Xak Tsaroth below us. Danger lies ahead of you if you choose to try and recover the Disks. Therefore I bless this staff. Present it boldly, never wavering, and you shall prevail."

The voice faded. It was then Goldmoon heard Riverwind's death cry.

Tanis entered the temple and felt as if he had walked backward into memory. The sun was shining through the trees in Qualinost. He and Laurana and her brother, Gilthanas, were lying on the riverbank, laughing and sharing dreams after some childish game. Happy childhood days had been few for Tanis—the half-elf learned early that he was different from the others. But that day had been a day of golden sunshine and warm friendship. The remembered peace washed over him, easing his grief and horror.

He turned to Goldmoon, standing silently beside him. "What is this place?"

"That is a story whose telling must wait," Goldmoon answered. With a light hand on Tanis's arm, she drew him across the shimmering tile floor until they both stood before the shining marble statue of Mishakal. The blue crystal staff cast a brilliant glow throughout the chamber.

But even as Tanis's lips parted in wonder, a shadow darkened the room. He and Goldmoon turned toward the door. Caramon and Sturm entered, bearing the body of Riverwind between them on the makeshift litter. Flint and Tasslehoff—the dwarf looking old and weary, the kender unusually subdued—stood on either side of the litter, an odd sort of honor guard. The somber procession moved slowly inside. Behind them came Raistlin, his hood pulled over his head, his hands folded in his robes—the spectre of death itself.

They moved across the marble floor, intent on the burden they bore, and came to a halt before Tanis and Goldmoon. Tanis, look-ing down at the body at Goldmoon's feet, shut his eyes. Blood had soaked through the thick blanket, spreading in great dark splotches across the fabric.

"Remove the blanket," Goldmoon commanded. Caramon looked at Tanis pleadingly.

"Goldmoon—" Tanis began gently.

Suddenly, before anyone could stop him, Raistlin bent down and tore the blood-stained blanket from the body.

Goldmoon gave a strangled gasp at the sight of Riverwind's tortured body, turning so pale that Tanis reached out a steadying hand, fearing she might faint. But Goldmoon was the daughter of a strong, proud people. She swallowed, drew a deep, shuddering breath. Then she turned and walked up to the marble statue. She lifted the blue crystal staff carefully from the goddess's hands, then she returned to kneel beside Riverwind's body.

"*Kan-tokah*," she said softly. "My beloved." Reaching out a shaking hand, she touched the dying Plainsman's forehead. The sightless face moved toward her as if he heard. One of the blackened hands twitched feebly, as if he would touch her. Then he gave a great shudder and lay perfectly still. Tears streamed unheeded down Goldmoon's cheeks as she lay the staff across Riverwind's body. Soft blue light filled the chamber. Everyone the light touched felt rested and refreshed. The pain and exhaus-tion from the day's toil left their bodies. The horror of the dragon's attack lifted from their minds, as the sun burns through fog. Then the light of the staff dimmed and faded. Night settled over the temple, lit once more only by the light emanating from the marble statue.

Tanis blinked, trying once more to re-accustom his eyes to the dark. Then he heard a deep voice.

"*Kan-tokah neh sirakan.*"

He heard Goldmoon cry out in joy. Tanis looked down at what should have been Riverwind's corpse. Instead, he saw the Plains-man sit up, holding out his arms for Goldmoon. She clung to him, laughing and crying at the same time.

"And so," Goldmoon told them, coming to the end of her story, "we must find a way down into the ruined city that lies somewhere below the temple, and we must remove the Disks from the dragon's lair."

They were eating a frugal dinner, sitting on the floor in the main chamber of the temple. A quick inspection of the building revealed that it was empty, although Caramon told of finding draconian tracks on the staircase, as well as the tracks of some other creature the warrior couldn't identify.

It was not a large building. Two worship rooms were located on opposite sides of the hallway that led to the main chamber where the statue stood. Two circular rooms branched off the main chamber to the north and south. They were decorated with frescoes that were now covered with fungus and faded beyond recognition. Two sets of golden double doors led to the east. Caramon reported finding a staircase there that led down into the wrecked city below. The faint sound of surf could be heard, reminding them that they were perched on top of a great cliff, overlooking Newsea.

The companions sat, each preoccupied with his own thoughts, trying to assimilate the news Goldmoon had given them. Tasslehoff, however, continued to poke around the rooms, peering into dark corners. Finding little of interest, the kender grew bored and returned to the group, holding an old helmet in his hand. It was too big for him; kenderfolk never wore helmets anyway, considering them bothersome and restrictive. He tossed it to the dwarf.

"What's this?" Flint asked suspiciously, holding it up to the light cast by Raistlin's staff. It was a helm of ancient design, well crafted by a skilled metalsmith. Undoubtedly a dwarf, Flint decided, rubbing his hands over it lovingly. A long tail of animal hair decorated the top. Flint tossed the draconian helm he had been wearing to the floor. Then he put the new-found helm on his head. It fit perfectly. Smiling, he took it off, once more admiring the workmanship. Tanis watched him with amusement.

"That's horsehair," he said, pointing to the tassel.

"No, it's not!" the dwarf protested, frowning. He sniffed at it, wrinkling his nose. Failing to sneeze, he glanced at Tanis in triumph. "It's hair from the mane of a griffon."

Caramon guffawed. "Griffon!" He snorted. "There's about as many griffons on Krynn as there are—"

"Dragons," interjected Raistlin smoothly.

The conversation died abruptly.

Sturm cleared his throat. "We'd better get some sleep," he said. "I'll take first watch."

"No one need keep watch this night," Goldmoon said softly. She sat close to Riverwind. The tall Plainsman had not spoken much since his brush with death. He had stared for a long time at the statue of Mishakal, recognizing the woman in blue light who had given him the staff, but he refused to answer any questions or discuss it.

"We are safe here," Goldmoon affirmed, glancing at the statue.

Caramon raised his eyebrows. Sturm frowned and stroked his moustaches. Both men were too polite to question Goldmoon's faith, but Tanis knew that neither warrior would feel safe if watches weren't set. Yet there weren't many hours left until dawn and they all needed rest. Raistlin was already asleep, wrapped in his robes in a dark corner of the chamber.

"I think Goldmoon is right," Tasslehoff said. "Let's trust these old gods, since it seems we have found them."

"The elves never lost them; neither did the dwarves," Flint protested, scowling. "I don't understand any of this! Reorx is one of the ancient gods, presumably. We have worshiped him since before the Cataclysm."

"Worship?" Tanis asked. "Or cry to him in despair because your people were shut out of the Kingdom under the Mountain. No, don't get mad—" Tanis, seeing the dwarf's face flush an ugly red, held up his hand. "The elves are no better. We cried to the gods when our homeland was laid waste. We know of the gods and we honor their memories—as one would honor the dead. The elven clerics vanished long ago, as did the dwarven clerics. I remember Mishakal the Healer. I remember hearing the stories of her when I was young. I remember hearing stories of dragons, too. Children's tales, Raistlin would say. It seems our childhood has come back to haunt us—or save us, I don't know which. I have seen two miracles tonight, one of evil and one of good. I must believe in both, if I am to trust the evidence of my senses. Yet . . ." The half-elf sighed. "I say we take turns on watch tonight. I am sorry, lady. I wish my faith were as strong as yours."

Sturm took first watch. The rest wrapped themselves in their blankets and lay on the tile floor. The knight walked through the moonlit temple, checking the quiet rooms, more from force of habit than because he felt any threat. He could hear the wind blow chill and fierce outside, sweeping out from the north. But inside it was strangely warm and comfortable—too comfortable.

Sitting at the base of the statue, Sturm felt a sweet peacefulness creep over him. Startled, he sat bolt upright and realized, chagrined, that he had nearly fallen asleep on watch. That was inexcusable! Berating himself severely, the knight determined that he would walk his watch—the full two hours—as punishment. He started to rise, then stopped. He heard singing, a woman's voice. Sturm stared around wildly, his hand on his sword. Then his hand slipped from the hilt. He recognized the voice and the song. It was his mother's voice. Once more Sturm was with her. They were fleeing Solamnia, traveling alone except for one trusted retainer—and he would be dead before they reached Solace. The song was one of those wordless lullabies that were older than dragons. Sturm's mother held her child close, and tried to keep her fear from him by singing this gentle, soothing song. Sturm's eyes closed. Sleep blessed him, blessed all of the companions.

The light from Raistlin's staff glowed brightly, keeping away the darkness.

The Paths of the Dead.
Raistlin's New Friends.

17

The sound of metal crashing against the tile floor jolted Tanis out of a deep sleep. He sat up, alarmed, his hand fumbling for his sword.

"Sorry," Caramon said, grinning shamefacedly. "I dropped my breastplate."

Tanis drew a deep breath that turned into a yawn, stretched, and lay back down on his blanket. The sight of Caramon putting on his armor—with Tasslehoff's help—reminded the half-elf of what they faced today. He saw Sturm buckling his armor on as well, while Riverwind polished the sword he had picked up. Tanis firmly put the thought of what might happen to them today out of his mind.

That was not an easy task, especially for the elven part of Tanis—elves revere life and, although they believe that death is simply a movement into a higher plane of existence, death of any creature is seen to diminish life on this plane. Tanis forced the human side of him to take possession of his soul today. He would have to kill, and perhaps he would have to accept the death of one or more of these people he loved. He remembered how he had felt yesterday, when he thought he might lose Riverwind. The half-elf frowned and sat up suddenly, feeling as if he had awakened from a bad dream.

"Is everyone up?" he asked, scratching his beard.

Flint stumped over and handed him a hunk of bread and some dried strips of venison. "Up and breakfasted," the dwarf grumbled. "You could have slept through the Cataclysm, Half-Elf."

Tanis took a bite of venison without appetite. Then, wrinkling his nose, he sniffed. "What's that funny smell?"

"Some concoction of the mage's." The dwarf grimaced, plopping down next to Tanis. Flint pulled out a block of wood and began carving, hacking away furiously, making chips fly. "He pounded up some sort of powder in a cup and added water. Stirred it up and drank it, but not before it made that gullymudge smell. I'm happier not knowing what it was."

Tanis agreed. He chewed on the venison. Raistlin was now reading his spellbook, murmuring the words over and over until he had committed them to memory. Tanis wondered what kind of spell Raistlin had that might be useful against a dragon. From what little he remembered about dragonlore—learned ages ago from the elven bard, Quivalen Soth—only the spells of the very greatest mages had a chance of affecting dragons, who could work their own magic—as they had witnessed.

Tanis looked at the frail young man absorbed in his spellbook and shook his head. Raistlin might be powerful for his age, and he was certainly devious and clever. But dragons were ancient. They had been in Krynn before the first elves—the oldest of the races—walked the land. Of course, if the plan the companions discussed last night worked out, they wouldn't even encounter the dragon. They hoped simply to find the lair and escape with the Disks. It was a good plan, Tanis thought, and probably worth about as much as smoke on the wind. Despair began to creep over him like a dank fog.

"Well, I'm all set," Caramon announced cheerfully. The big warrior felt immeasurably better in his armor. The dragon seemed a very small annoyance this morning. He tunelessly whistled an old marching song as he stuffed his mud-stained clothing into his pack. Sturm, his armor carefully adjusted, sat apart from the companions, his eyes closed, performing whatever secret ritual knights performed, preparing himself mentally for combat. Tanis stood up, stiff and cold, moving around to get the circulation going and ease the soreness from his muscles. Elves did nothing before battle, except ask forgiveness for taking life.

"We, too, are ready," Goldmoon said. She was dressed in a heavy gray tunic made of soft leather trimmed with fur. She had braided her long silver-gold hair in a twist around her head—a precaution against an enemy using her hair to gain a handhold.

"Let's get this over with." Tanis sighed as he picked up the long-bow and quiver of arrows Riverwind had taken from the draconian camp and slung them over his shoulder. In addition, Tanis was armed with a dagger and his longsword. Sturm had his two-handed sword. Caramon carried his shield, a longsword, and two daggers Riverwind had scrounged. Flint had replaced his lost battle-axe with one from the draconian camp. Tasslehoff had his hoopak and a small dagger he had discovered. He was very proud of it and was deeply wounded when Caramon told him it would be of use if they ran into any ferocious rabbits. Riverwind bore his longsword strapped to his back and still carried Tanis's dagger. Goldmoon bore no weapon other than the staff. We're well armed, Tanis thought gloomily. For all the good it will do us.

The companions left the chamber of Mishakal, Goldmoon coming last. She gently touched the statue of the goddess with her hand as she passed, whispering a silent prayer.

Tas led the way, skipping merrily, his topknot bouncing behind him. He was going to see a real live dragon! The kender couldn't imagine anything more exciting.

Following Caramon's directions, they headed east, passing through two more sets of golden double doors, and came to a large circular room. A tall, slime-coated pedestal stood in the center—so tall not even Riverwind could see what, if anything, was on it. Tas stood beneath it, staring up at it wistfully.

"I tried to climb it last night," he said, "but it was too slippery. I wonder what's up there?"

"Well, whatever it is will have to stay forever beyond the reach of kenders," Tanis snapped irritably. He walked over to investigate the staircase that spiraled down into the darkness. The stairs were broken and covered with rotting plants and fungus.

"The Paths of the Dead," Raistlin said suddenly.

"What?" Tanis started.

"The Paths of the Dead," the mage repeated. "That's what this staircase is called."

"How in the name of Reorx do you know that?" Flint growled.

"I have read something of this city," Raistlin replied in his whispering voice.

"This is the first we've heard of it," Sturm said coldly. "What else do you know that you haven't told us?"

"A great many things, knight," Raistlin returned, scowling. "While you and my brother played with wooden swords, I spent my time in study."

"Yes, study of that which is dark and mysterious," the knight sneered. "What really happened in the Towers of High Sorcery, Raistlin? You didn't gain these wonderful powers of yours without giving something in return. What did you sacrifice in that Tower? Your health—or your soul!"

"I was with my brother in the Tower," Caramon said, the warrior's normally cheerful face now haggard. "I saw him battle powerful mages and wizards with only a few simple spells. He defeated them, though they shattered his body. I carried him, dying, from the terrible place. And I—" The big man hesitated.

Raistlin stepped forward quickly and placed his cold, thin hand on his twin's arm.

"Be careful what you say," he hissed.

Caramon drew a ragged breath and swallowed. "I know what he sacrificed," the warrior said in a husky voice. Then he lifted his head proudly. "We are forbidden to speak of it. But you have known me many years, Sturm Brightblade, and I give you my word of honor, you may trust my brother as you trust me. If ever a time comes when that is not so, may my death—and his—be not far behind."

Raistlin's eyes narrowed at this vow. He regarded his brother with a thoughtful, somber expression. Then Tanis saw the mage's lip curl, the serious mien wiped out by his customary cynicism. It was a startling change. For a moment, the twins' resemblance to each other had been remarkable. Now they were as different as opposite sides of a coin.

Sturm stepped forward and clasped Caramon's hand, gripping it tightly, wordlessly. Then he turned to face Raistlin, unable to regard him without obvious disgust. "I apologize, Raistlin," the knight said stiffly. "You should be thankful you have such a loyal brother."

"Oh, I am," Raistlin whispered.

Tanis glanced at the mage sharply, wondering if he had only imagined sarcasm in the mage's hissing voice. The half-elf licked his dry lips, a sudden, bitter taste in his mouth. "Can you guide us through this place?" he asked abruptly.

"I could have," Raistlin answered, "if we had come here prior to the Cataclysm. The books I studied dated back hundreds of years. During the Cataclysm, when the fiery mountain struck Krynn, the city of Xak Tsaroth was cast down the side of a cliff. I recognize this staircase because it is still intact. As for beyond—" He shrugged.

"Where do the stairs lead?"

"To a place known as the Hall of the Ancestors. Priests and kings of Xak Tsaroth were buried in crypts there."

"Let's get moving," Caramon said gruffly. "All we're doing here is scaring ourselves."

"Yes." Raistlin nodded. "We must go and go quickly. We have until nightfall. By tomorrow, this city will be overrun by the armies moving from the north."

"Bah!" Sturm frowned. "You may know lots of things as you claim, mage, but you can't know that! Caramon is right, though— we have stayed here too long. I will take the lead."

He started down the stairs, moving carefully to keep from slipping on the slimy surface. Tanis saw Raistlin's eyes—narrow, golden slits of enmity—follow Sturm down.

"Raistlin, go with him and light the way," Tanis ordered, ignoring the angry glance Sturm flashed up at him. "Caramon, walk with Goldmoon. Riverwind and I will take rear guard."

"And where does that leave us?" Flint grumbled to the kender as they followed behind Goldmoon and Caramon. "In the middle, as usual. Just more useless baggage—"

"There might be anything up there," Tas said, looking back to the pedestal. He obviously hadn't heard a word of what had been said. "A crystal ball of farseeing, a magic ring like I once had. Did I ever tell you about my magic ring?" Flint groaned. Tanis heard the kender's voice prattling on as the two disappeared down the stairs.

The half-elf turned to Riverwind. "You were here—you must have been. We have seen the goddess who gave you the staff. Did you come down here?"

"I don't know," Riverwind said wearily. "I remember nothing about it. Nothing—except the dragon."

Tanis fell silent. The dragon. It all came down to the dragon. The creature loomed large in everyone's thoughts. And how feeble the small group seemed against a monster who had sprung full grown from Krynn's darkest legends. Why us? Tanis thought bitterly. Was there ever a more unlikely group of heroes—bickering, grumbling, arguing—half of us not trusting the other half. "We were chosen." That thought brought little comfort. Tanis remembered Raistlin's words: "Who chose us—and why?" The half-elf was beginning to wonder.

They moved silently down the steep stairway that curled ever deeper into the hillside. At first it was intensely dark as they spiraled down. Then the way began to get lighter, until Raistlin was able to extinguish the light on his staff. Soon Sturm raised his hand, halting the others behind him. Beyond stretched a short corridor, no more than a few feet long. This led to a large arched doorway that revealed a vast open area. A pale gray light filtered into the corridor, as did the odor of dankness and decay.

The companions stood for long moments, listening carefully. The sound of rushing water seemed to come from below and beyond the door, nearly drowning out all other sounds. Still, Tanis thought he had heard something else—a sharp crack— and he had felt more than heard a thumping and throbbing on the floor. But it didn't last long, and the sharp crack wasn't repeated. Then, more puzzling still, came a metallic scraping sound punctuated by an occasional shrill screech. Tanis glanced at Tasslehoff questioningly.

The kender shrugged. "I haven't a clue," he said, cocking his head and listening closely. "I've never heard anything like it, Tanis, except once—" He paused, then shook his head. "Do you want me to go look?" he asked eagerly.

"Go."

Tasslehoff crept down the short corridor, flitting from shadow to shadow. A mouse running across thick carpet makes more noise than a kender when he wants to escape notice. He reached the door and peered out. Ahead of him stretched what must once have been a vast ceremonial hall. Hall of the Ancestors, that's what Raistlin called it. Now it was a Hall of Ruins. Part of the floor to the east had fallen into a hole from which a foul-smelling white mist boiled up. Tas noticed other huge holes gaping in the floor, while chunks of large stone tile stuck up like grave markers. Carefully testing the floor beneath his feet, the kender stepped out into the hall. Through the mist he could faintly distinguish a dark doorway on the south wall . . . and another on the north. The strange screeching sound came from the south. Tas turned and began walking in that direction.

He suddenly heard the thumping and throbbing sound again to the north, behind him, and felt the floor start to tremble. The kender hurriedly dashed back into the stairwell. His friends had heard the sound and were flattened against the wall, weapons in hand. The thumping sound grew into a loud whoosh. Then ten or fifteen squat, shadowy figures rushed past the arched doorway. The floor shook. They heard hard breathing and an occasional muttered word. Then the figures vanished in the mist, heading south. There was another sharp cracking sound, then silence.

"What in the name of the Abyss was that?" Caramon exclaimed. "Those weren't draconians, unless they've come up with a short, fat breed. And where'd they come from?"

"They came from the north end of the hall," Tas said. "There's a doorway there and one to the south. The weird screeching sounds come from the south, where those things were headed."

"What's east?" Tanis asked.

"Judging by the sound of falling water I could hear, about a thousand-foot drop," the kender replied. "The floor's caved in. I wouldn't recommend walking over there."

Flint sniffed. "I smell something . . . something familiar. I can't place it."

"I smell death," Goldmoon said, shivering, holding her staff close.

"Naw, this is something worse," Flint muttered. Then his eyes opened wide and his face grew red with rage and anger. "I've got it!" he roared. "Gully dwarf!" He unslung his axe. "That's what those miserable little things were. Well, they won't be gully dwarves for long. They'll be stinking corpses!"

He dashed forward. Tanis, Sturm, and Caramon leaped after him just as he reached the end of the corridor and dragged him back.

"Keep quiet!" Tanis ordered the sputtering dwarf. "Now, how sure are you that they are gully dwarves?"

The dwarf angrily shook himself from Caramon's grasp. "Sure!" he started to roar, then dropped it to a loud whisper. "Didn't they hold me prisoner for three years?"

"Did they?" Tanis asked, startled.

"That's why I never told you where I was these last five years," the dwarf said, flushing with embarrassment. His face darkened. "But I swore I'd get revenge. I'll kill every living gully dwarf I come across."

"Wait a minute," Sturm interrupted. "Gully dwarves aren't evil, not like goblins at any rate. What could they be doing living here with draconians?"

"Slaves," Raistlin answered coolly. "Undoubtedly the gully dwarves have lived here many years, probably ever since the city was abandoned. When the draconians were sent, perhaps, to guard the Disks, they found the gully dwarves and used them as slave labor."

"They might be able to help us then," Tanis murmured.

"Gully dwarves!" Flint exploded. "You'd trust those filthy little—"

"No," Tanis said. "We cannot trust them, of course. But nearly every slave is willing to betray his master, and gully dwarves— like most dwarves—feel little loyalty to anyone except their own chieftains. As long as we don't ask them to do anything that

193

might endanger their own dirty skins, we might be able to buy their aid."

"Well, I'll be an ogre's hind end!" Flint said in disgust. He hurled his axe to the ground, tore his pack off, and slumped down against the wall, arms folded. "Go on. Go ask your new friends to help you. I'll not be with you! They'll help you, all right. Help you right up the dragon's snout!"

Tanis and Sturm exchanged concerned glances, remembering the boat incident. Flint could be incredibly stubborn, and Tanis thought it quite likely that this time the dwarf would prove immovable.

"I dunno." Caramon sighed and shook his head. "It's too bad the dwarf's staying behind. If we do get the gully dwarves to help us, who'll keep the scum in line?"

Amazed that Caramon could be so subtle, Tanis smiled and picked up on the warrior's lead. "Sturm, I guess."

"Sturm!" The dwarf bounded to his feet. "A knight who won't stab an enemy in the back? You need someone who knows these foul creatures—"

"You're right, Flint," Tanis said gravely. "I guess you'll have to come with us."

"You bet," Flint grumbled. He grabbed his things and stumped off down the corridor. He turned around. "You coming?"

Hiding their smiles, the companions followed the dwarf out into the Hall of the Ancestors. They kept close to the wall, avoiding the treacherous floor. They headed south, following the gully dwarves, and entered a dimly lit passage that ran south only a few hundred feet, then turned sharply east. Once again they heard the cracking noise. The metallic screeching had stopped. Suddenly, they heard behind them the sound of pounding feet.

"Gully dwarves!" growled Flint.

"Back!" Tanis ordered. "Be ready to jump them. We can't let them raise an alarm!"

Everyone flattened himself against the wall, sword drawn and ready. Flint held his battle-axe, a look of eager anticipation on his face. Staring back into the vast hall, they saw another group of short fat figures running toward them.

Suddenly, the leader of the gully dwarves looked up and saw them. Caramon leaped out in front of the small running figures, his huge arm raised commandingly. "Halt!" he said. The gully dwarves glanced up at him, swarmed around him, and disappeared around the corner to the east. Caramon turned around to stare after them in astonishment.

"Halt . . . " he said half-heartedly.

A gully dwarf popped back around the corner, glared at Caramon, and put a grubby finger to his lips. "Shhhhh!" Then the squat figure vanished. They heard the cracking sound and the screeching noise started up again.

"What do you suppose is going on?" Tanis asked softly.

"Do they all look like that?" Goldmoon said, her eyes wide. "They're so filthy and ragged, and there are sores all over their bodies."

"And they have the brains of a doorknob," Flint grunted.

The group cautiously rounded the corner, hands on their weapons. A long, narrow corridor extended east, lit by torches that flickered and smoked in the stifling air. The light reflected off walls wet with condensed moisture. Arched doorways revealing only blackness opened up off the hallway.

"The crypts," Raistlin whispered.

Tanis shivered. Water dripped on him from the ceiling. The metallic screeching was louder and nearer. Goldmoon touched the half-elf's arm and pointed. Tanis saw, down at the far end of the corridor, a doorway. Beyond the opening was another passageway forming a T-intersection. The corridor was filled with gully dwarves.

"I wonder why the little guys are lined up," Caramon said.

"This is our chance to find out," Tanis said. He was starting forward when he felt the mage's hand on his arm.

"Leave this to me," Raistlin whispered.

"We had better come with you," Sturm stated, "to cover you, of course."

"Of course," Raistlin sniffed. "Very well, but do not disturb me."

Tanis nodded. "Flint, you and Riverwind guard this end of the corridor." Flint opened his mouth to protest, then scowled and fell back to stand opposite the Plainsmen.

"Stay well behind me," Raistlin ordered, then moved down the corridor, his red robes rustling around his ankles, the Staff of Magius thumping softly on the floor at each step. Tanis and Sturm followed, moving along the side of the dripping walls. Cold air flowed from the crypts. Peering inside one, Tanis could see the dark outline of a sarcophagus reflected in the sputtering torchlight. The coffin was elaborately carved, decorated with gold that shone no longer. An oppressive air hung over the crypts. Some of the tombs appeared to have been broken into and plundered. Tanis caught a glimpse of a skull grinning out of the darkness. He wondered if these ancient dead were planning their revenge for having their rest disturbed. Tanis forced himself to return to reality. It was bleak enough.

Raistlin stopped when he neared the end of the corridor. The gully dwarves watched him curiously, ignoring the others behind him. The mage did not speak. He reached into a pouch on his belt and drew out several golden coins. The gully dwarves' eyes brightened. One or two at the front of the line edged toward Raistlin to get a better view. The mage held up a coin so they all could see it. Then he threw it high into the air and . . . it vanished!

The gully dwarves gasped. Raistlin opened his hand with a flourish to reveal the coin. There was scattered applause. The gully dwarves crept closer, mouths gaping in wonder.

Gully dwarves—or Aghar—as their race was known, were truly a miserable lot. The lowest caste in dwarven society, they were to be found all over Krynn, living in filth and squalor in places that had been abandoned by most other living creatures, including animals. Like all dwarves, they were clannish, and several clans often lived together, following the rule of their chieftains or one particularly powerful clan leader. Three clans lived in Xak Tsaroth—the Sluds, the Bulps, and the Glups. Members of all three clans now surrounded Raistlin. There were both males and females, though it was not easy to tell the sexes apart. The females lacked whiskers on their chins but had them on their cheeks. They wore a tattered overskirt wrapped around their waists extending to their bony knees. Otherwise, they were every bit as ugly as their male counterparts. Despite their wretched appearance, gully dwarves generally led a cheerful existence.

Raistlin, with marvelous dexterity, made the coin dance over his knuckles, flipping it in and out of his fingers. Then he made it disappear, only to reappear inside the ear of some startled gully dwarf who stared at the mage in amazement. This last trick produced a momentary interruption in the performance as the Aghar's friends grabbed him and peered intently into his ear, one of them even sticking his finger inside to see if more coins might be forthcoming. This interesting activity ceased, though, when Raistlin reached into another pouch and removed a small scroll of parchment. Spreading it open with his long, thin fingers, the mage began to read from it, chanting softly, *"Suh tangus moipar, ast akular kalipad."* The gully dwarves watched in total fascination.

When the mage finished reading, the spidery-looking words on the scroll began to burn. They flared, then disappeared, leaving traces of green smoke.

"What was that all about?" Sturm asked suspiciously.

"They are now spellbound," Raistlin replied. "I have cast over them a spell of friendship."

The gully dwarves were enthralled and, Tanis noticed, the expressions on their faces had changed from interest to open, unabashed affection for the mage. They reached out and patted him with their dirty hands, jabbering away in their shapeless language. Sturm glanced at Tanis in alarm. Tanis knew what the knight was thinking: Raistlin could have cast that spell on any of them at any time.

Hearing the sound of running feet, Tanis looked quickly back to where Riverwind stood guard. The Plainsman pointed to the gully dwarves, then held up his hands, fingers spread. Ten more were heading their way. Soon, the new Aghar trotted into view, passing Riverwind without so much as a glance. They pulled up short on seeing the commotion around the mage.

"What happening?" said one, staring at Raistlin. The spellbound gully dwarves were gathered around the mage, tugging on his robe and dragging him down the hall.

"Friend. This our friend," they all chattered wildly in a crude form of Common.

"Yes," Raistlin said in a soft and gentle voice, so smooth and winning that Tanis was momentarily taken aback. "You are all my friends," the mage continued. "Now, tell me, my friends, where does this corridor lead?" Raistlin pointed to the east. There was an immediate babble of answers.

"Corridor lead that way," said one, pointing east.

"No, it lead that way!" said another, pointing west.

A scuffle broke out, the gully dwarves pushing and shoving. Soon fists were flying and then one gully dwarf had another on the ground, kicking him, yelling, "That way! That way!" at the top of his lungs.

Sturm turned to Tanis. "This is ridiculous! They'll bring every draconian in the place down on us. I don't know what that crazy magician has done, but you've got to stop him."

Before Tanis could intervene, however, one female gully dwarf took matters into her own hands. Dashing into the melee, she grabbed the two combatants, knocked their heads together smartly, and dumped them on the floor. The others, who had been cheering them on, immediately hushed, and the newcomer turned to Raistlin. She had a thick, bulbous nose and her hair stood up wildly on her head. She wore a patched and ragged dress, thick shoes, and stockings that collapsed around her ankles. But she seemed to be a leader among the gully dwarves, for they all eyed her with respect. This may have been because she carried a huge, heavy bag slung over one shoulder. The bag dragged along the ground as she walked, occasionally tripping her. But the bag was apparently of great importance to her. When one of the other gully dwarves attempted to touch it, she whirled around and smacked him across the face.

"Corridor lead to big bosses," she said, nodding her head toward the east.

"Thank you, my dear," Raistlin said, reaching out to touch her cheek. He spoke a few words, *"Tan-tago, musalah."*

The female gully dwarf watched, fascinated, as he spoke. Then she sighed and gazed up at him in adoration.

"Tell me, little one," Raistlin said. "How many bosses?"

The gully dwarf frowned, concentrating. She raised a grubby hand. "One," she said, holding up one finger. "And one, and one, and one." Looking up at Raistlin triumphantly, she held up four fingers and said, "Two."

"I'm beginning to agree with Flint," Sturm growled.

"Shhhh," Tanis said. Just then the screeching noise stopped. The gully dwarves looked down the corridor uneasily as into the silence came the harsh cracking sound again.

"What is that noise?" Raistlin asked his spellbound adorer.

"Whip," the female gully dwarf said emotionlessly. Reaching out her filthy hand, she took hold of Raistlin's robe and started to pull him toward the east end of the corridor. "Bosses get mad. We go."

"What is it you do for the bosses?" Raistlin asked, holding back.

"We go. You see." The gully dwarf tugged on him. "We down. They up. Down. Up. Down. Up. Come. You go. We give ride down."

Raistlin, being carried along on a tide of Aghar, looked back at Tanis, motioning with his hand. Tanis signaled to Riverwind and Flint, and everyone started moving down the hall behind the gully dwarves. Those Raistlin had charmed remained clustered around him, trying to stay as close as possible, while the rest ran off down the corridor when the whip cracked again. The companions followed Raistlin and the gully dwarves down to the corner, where the screeching noise started up once again, much louder now.

The female gully dwarf brightened as she heard it. She and the rest of the gully dwarves halted. Some of them slouched against the slime-covered walls, others plopped on the floor like sacks. The female stayed near Raistlin, holding the hem of his sleeve in her small hand. "What is it? " he asked. "Why have we stopped?"

"We wait. Not our turn yet," she informed him.

"What will we do when it is our turn?" he asked patiently.

"Go down," she said, staring up at him adoringly.

Raistlin looked at Tanis, shook his head. The mage decided to try a new approach.

"What is your name, little one?" he asked.

"Bupu."

Caramon snorted and quickly clapped his hand over his mouth.

"Now, Bupu," Raistlin said in dulcet tones, "do you know where the dragon's lair is?"

"Dragon?" Bupu repeated, astounded. "You want dragon?"

"No," Raistlin said hastily, "we don't want the dragon—just the dragon's lair, where the dragon lives."

"Oh, me not know that." Bupu shook her head. Then, seeing disappointment on Raistlin's face, she clutched his hand. "But me take you to the great Highbulp. He know everything."

Raistlin raised his eyebrows. "And how do we get to the Highbulp?"

"Down!" she said, grinning happily. The screeching sound stopped. There was a crack of a whip. "It our turn to go down now. You come. You come now. Go see Highbulp."

"Just a moment." Raistlin extricated himself from the gully dwarf's grasp. "I must talk to my friends." He walked over to Tanis and Sturm. "This Highbulp is probably head of the clan, maybe head of several clans."

"If he's as intelligent as this lot, he won't know where his own wash bowl is, let alone the dragon," Sturm growled.

"He'll know, most likely," Flint spoke up grudgingly. "They're not smart, but gully dwarves remember everything they see or hear if you can just get them to put it into words of more than one syllable."

"We better go see the great Highbulp then," Tanis said ruefully. "Now, if we could just figure out what this up and down business is and that squeaking noise—"

"I know!" said a voice.

Tanis looked around. He had completely forgotten about Tasslehoff. The kender came running back in from around the corner, his topknot dancing, eyes shining with merriment. "It's a lift, Tanis," he said. "Like in dwarven mines. I was in a mine, once. It was the most wonderful thing. They had a lift that took rock up and down. And this is just like it. Well, almost like it.

You see—" He was suddenly overcome with giggles and couldn't go on. The rest glaring at him, the kender made a violent effort to control himself

"They're using a giant lard-rendering pot! The gully dwarves that have been standing in line here run out when one of the draco-thing-ama-jiggers cracks this big whip. They all jump into the pot that's attached to a huge chain wrapped around a spoked wheel with teeth that fit into the links of the chain—that's what's squeaking! The wheel turns and down they go, and pretty soon up comes another pot—"

"Big bosses. Pot full of big bosses," Bupu said.

"Filled with draconians!" Tanis repeated in alarm.

"Not come here," Bupu said. "Go that way—" She waved a hand vaguely.

Tanis remained uneasy. "So these are the bosses. How many draconians are there by the pot?"

"Two," said Bupu, holding Raistlin's sleeve securely. "Not more than two."

"Actually, there are four," Tas said with an apologetic glance for contradicting the gully dwarf. "They're the little ones, not the big ones that cast spells."

"Four." Caramon flexed his huge arms. "We can handle four."

"Yes, but we've got to time it so that fifteen more aren't arriv-ing," Tanis pointed out.

The whip cracked again.

"Come!" Bupu tugged urgently on Raistlin's sleeve. "We go. Bosses get mad."

"I'd say this is as good a time as any," Sturm said, shrugging. "Let the gully dwarves run as usual. We'll follow and overwhelm the bosses in the confusion. If one pot is up here waiting to be loaded with gully dwarves, the other has to be on the ground level."

"I suppose," Tanis said. He turned to the gully dwarves. "When you get to the lift—er, pot—don't jump in. Just dodge aside and keep out of the way. All right?"

The gully dwarves stared at Tanis with deep suspicion. The half-elf sighed and looked at Raistlin. Smiling slightly, the mage repeated Tanis's instructions. Immediately the gully dwarves began to smile and nod enthusiastically.

The whip cracked again and the companions heard a harsh voice. "Quit loafing, you scum, or we'll chop your nasty feet off and give you an excuse for being slow!"

"We'll see whose feet get chopped off," Caramon said.

"This be some fun!" said one of the gully dwarves solemnly. The Aghar dashed down the corridor.

Fight at the lift.
Bupu's cure for a cough.

18

Hot mist rose from two large holes in the floor, swirling around whatever was nearby. Between the two holes was a large wheel, around which ran a gigantic chain. A tremendous black iron pot hung suspended from the chain over one of the holes. The other end of the chain disappeared through the other hole. Four armor-clad draconians, two of them swinging leather whips and armed with curved swords, stood around the pot. They were visible only briefly, then mist hid them from view. Tanis could hear the whip crack and a guttural voice bellowing.

"You louse-ridden dwarf vermin! What're you doing, holding back there. Get into this pot before I flay the filthy flesh from your nasty bones! I—ulp!"

The draconian stopped in midsentence, its eyes bulging out of its reptilian head as Caramon emerged from the mist, roaring his battle cry. The draconian let out a yell that changed into a choking gurgle as Caramon grabbed the creature around its scrawny neck, lifted it off its clawed feet, and hurled it back against the wall. Gully dwarves scattered as the body hit the wall with a bone-crushing thump.

Even as Caramon attacked, Sturm—swinging his great two-handed sword—yelled out the knight's salute to an enemy and lopped the head off a draconian who never saw what was coming.

The severed head rolled on the floor with a crunching sound as it changed to stone.

Unlike goblins, who attack anything that moves without strategy or thought, draconians are intelligent and quick-thinking. The two remaining by the pot had no intention of taking on five skilled and well-armed warriors. One of them immediately jumped into the pot, yelling instructions to its companion in their guttural language. The other draconian dashed over to the wheel and freed the mechanism. The pot began to drop through the hole.

"Stop it!" Tanis yelled. "It's going for reinforcements!"

"Wrong!" shouted Tasslehoff, peering over the edge. "The reinforcements are already on the way up in the other pot. There must be twenty of them!"

Caramon ran to stop the draconian operating the lift, but he was too late. The creature left the mechanism turning and dashed toward the pot. With a great bound, it leaped in after its companion. Caramon, on the principle of don't let the enemy get away, jumped right into the pot after it! The gully dwarves cheered and hooted, some dashing over to the edge to get a better view.

"That big idiot!" Sturm swore. Shoving gully dwarves aside to look down, he saw swinging fists and flashing armor as Caramon and the draconians flailed away at each other. Caramon's added weight caused the pot to fall faster.

"They'll cut the lummox to jerky down there," Sturm muttered. "I'm going after him," he yelled to Tanis. Launching himself into the air, he grabbed hold of the chain and slid right down it into the pot.

"Now we've lost both of them!" Tanis groaned. "Flint, come with me. Riverwind, stay up here with Raistlin and Goldmoon. See if you can reverse that damned wheel! No, Tas, not you!"

Too late. The kender, screaming enthusiastically, leaped onto the chain and began shinnying down. Tanis and Flint jumped into the hole, too. Tanis wrapped his arms and legs around the chain, hanging on just above the kender, but the dwarf missed his hold, landing in the pot helmet first. Caramon promptly stepped on him.

The draconians in the pot pinned the warrior against the side. He punched one, sending it slamming to the other side, and drew his dagger on the other as it fumbled for its sword. Caramon stabbed before the draconian could get the sword free, but the warrior's dagger glanced off the creature's armor and was jarred out of Caramon's grasp. The draconian went for his face, trying to gouge his eyes out with its clawed hands. Grabbing the draconian's wrists in a crushing grip, Caramon succeeded in wrenching its hands away from his face. The two powerful beings—human and draconian—struggled against the side of the pot.

The other draconian recovered from Caramon's blow and seized its sword. But its dive for the warrior came to an abrupt halt when Sturm, sliding down the chain, kicked it hard in the face with his heavy boot. The draconian reeled backwards, the sword flying from its grasp. Sturm leaped and tried to club the creature with the flat of his sword, but the draconian thrust the blade aside with its hands.

"Get off me!" Flint roared from the bottom of the pot. Blinded by his helm, he was being slowly crushed by Caramon's big feet. In a spurt of ferocious anger, the dwarf straightened his helm, then heaved himself up, causing Caramon to lose his footing and tumble forward into the draconian. The creature sidestepped while Caramon staggered into the huge chain. The draconian swung its sword wildly. Caramon ducked and the sword clanged uselessly against the chain, notching the blade. Flint hurled himself at the draconian, hitting it squarely in the stomach with his head. The two fell against the side.

The pot gained momentum, swirling the foul mists around them.

Keeping his eyes on the action below, Tanis lowered himself down the chain. "Stay put!" he snarled at Tasslehoff. Letting go his grip, Tanis dropped down and landed in the midst of the melee. Tas, disappointed but reluctant to disobey Tanis, clung to the chain with one hand while he reached into his pouch and pulled out a rock, ready to drop it—on the head of an enemy, he hoped.

The pot began to sway as the combatants fell against the sides in their struggles, all the while dropping lower and lower, causing

205

the other pot—filled with screaming and cursing draconians—to rise higher and higher.

Riverwind, standing at the hole with the gully dwarves, could see very little through the mist. He could, however, hear thumps and curses and groans from the pot holding his friends. Then out of the mist rose the other pot. Draconians stood, swords in their hands, staring, open-mouthed, up at him, their long red tongues panting in anticipation. In moments, he and Goldmoon, Raistlin, and fifteen gully dwarves would be facing about twenty angry draconians!

He spun around, stumbled over a gully dwarf, regained his balance, and ran to the mechanism. Somehow he had to stop that pot from rising. The huge wheel was turning slowly, the chain screeching through the spokes. Riverwind stared at it with the idea of grabbing the chain in his bare hands. A flurry of red shoved him aside. Raistlin watched the wheel for an instant, timing its rotation, then he jammed the Staff of Magius in between the wheel and the floor. The staff shivered for an instant and Riverwind held his breath, fearing the staff would snap. But it held! The mechanism shuddered to a stop.

"Riverwind!" Goldmoon yelled from where she had remained by the hole. The Plainsman ran over to the edge, Raistlin following. The gully dwarves, lined up around the hole, were having a wonderful time, thoroughly enjoying one of the most interesting events to occur in their lives. Only Bupu moved away from the edge—she trotted after Raistlin, grasping his robe whenever possible.

"*Khark-umat!*" breathed Riverwind as he looked down into the swirling mist.

Caramon tossed overboard the draconian he had been fighting. It fell with a shriek into the mist. The big warrior had claw marks on his face and a sword slash on his right arm. Sturm, Tanis, and Flint still battled the second draconian who seemed willing to kill regardless of the consequences. When it finally became clear that hitting was not enough, Tanis stabbed it with his dagger. The creature sank down, immediately turning to rock, holding Tanis's weapon fast in its stony corpse.

Then the pot lurched to a halt, jolting everyone.

"Look out! Neighbors!" yelled Tasslehoff, dropping off the chain. Tanis looked over to see the other pot, filled with draconians, swinging only about twenty feet away. Armed to the teeth, the draconians were preparing a boarding maneuver. Two clambered up onto the edge of the pot, ready to leap across the misty gap. Caramon leaned over the edge of the pot and made a wild and vicious swing with his sword in an attempt to slash one of the boarders. He missed and the momentum of his swing set the pot rotating on its chain.

Caramon lost his balance and fell forward, his great weight tipping the pot dangerously. He found himself staring directly down at the ground far below him. Sturm grabbed hold of Caramon's collar and yanked him back, causing the pot to rock erratically. Tanis slipped, landing on his hands and knees at the bottom of the pot where he discovered that the stone draconian had decayed into dust, allowing him to retrieve his dagger.

"Here they come!" Flint yelled, hauling Tanis to his feet. One draconian launched itself toward them and caught hold of the edge of the pot with its clawed hands. The pot tilted precariously once again.

"Get over there!" Tanis shoved Caramon to the opposite side, hoping the warrior's weight would keep the pot stable. Sturm hacked at the draconian's hands, trying to force it to let go. Then another draconian flew over, gauging its distance better than the first. It landed in the pot next to Sturm.

"Don't move!" Tanis screamed at Caramon as the warrior instinctively charged into combat. The pot tilted. The big man quickly returned to his position. The pot righted itself. The draconian hanging onto the edge, its fingers oozing green, let go, spread its wings, and floated down into the mist.

Tanis spun around to fight the draconian that had landed in the pot and fell over Flint, knocking the dwarf off his feet again. The half-elf staggered against the side. As the pot rocked, he stared down. The mists parted and he saw the ruined city of Xak Tsaroth far below him. When he drew back, feeling sick and disoriented, he saw Tasslehoff fighting the draconian. The little kender crawled up the creature's back and bashed it on the head with a rock. At the bottom of the pot, Flint picked up Caramon's dropped dagger and stabbed the same creature in the leg. The draconian screamed as the blade bit deep. Knowing more draconians were about to fly over, Tanis looked up in despair. But the despair turned to hope when he saw Riverwind and Goldmoon staring down through the mist.

"Bring us back up!" Tanis yelled frantically, then something hit him on the head. The pain was excruciating. He felt himself falling and falling and falling. . . .

Raistlin did not hear Tanis's yell—the mage had already gone into action.

"Come here, my friends," Raistlin said swiftly. The spellbound gully dwarves gathered eagerly around him. "Those bosses down there want to hurt me," he said softly.

The gully dwarves growled. Several frowned darkly. A few shook their fists at the potful of draconians.

"But you can help," Raistlin said. "You can stop them."

The gully dwarves stared at the mage dubiously. Friendship—after all—went only so far.

"All you must do," Raistlin said patiently, "is run over and jump on that chain." He pointed at the chain attached to the draconians' pot.

The gully dwarves' faces brightened. That didn't sound bad. In fact, it was something they did almost daily when they missed catching hold of the pot.

Raistlin waved his arm. "Go!" he ordered.

The gully dwarves—all except Bupu—glanced at each other, then dashed to the edge of the hole and, yelling wildly, flung themselves onto the chain above the draconians, clinging to it with marvelous dexterity.

The mage ran over to the wheel, Bupu trotting along after him. Grabbing the Staff of Magius, he tugged it free. The wheel shivered and began to move once again, turning more and more rapidly as the weight of the gully dwarves caused the draconian pot to plummet back down into the mists.

Several of the draconians who had been perched on the edge about to jump into the other pot were caught off guard by the sudden jolt. They lost their balance and fell. Though their wings stopped their fall, they shrieked in rage as they drifted to the ground below, their cries contrasting oddly with the gleeful shouts of the gully dwarves.

Riverwind leaned out over the edge of the hole and caught hold of the companions' pot as it reached the wheel.

"Are you all right?" Goldmoon asked anxiously, leaning over to help Caramon out. "Tanis is hurt," Caramon said, supporting the half-elf.

"It's just a bump," Tanis protested groggily. He felt a large lump rising on the back of his skull. "I thought I was falling out of that thing." He shuddered at the memory.

"We can't get down that way!" Sturm said, climbing out of the pot. "And we can't stay around up here. It won't take them long to get this lift back in operation and then they'll be after us. We'll have to go back."

"No! Don't go!" Bupu clutched at Raistlin. "I know way to Highbulp!" She tugged at his sleeve, pointing north. "Good way! Secret way! No bosses," she said softly, stroking his hand. "I not let bosses get you. You pretty."

"We don't seem to have much choice. We've got to get down there," Tanis said, wincing when Goldmoon's staff touched him. Then the healing power flowed through his body. He relaxed as the pain eased and sighed. "As you said, they've lived here for years."

Flint growled and shook his head as Bupu started down the corridor, heading north.

"Stop! Listen!" Tasslehoff called softly. They heard the sound of clawed feet coming toward them.

"Draconians!" said Sturm. "We've got to get out of here! Head back west."

"I knew it," Flint grumbled, scowling. "That gully dwarf's led us right into those lizards!"

"Wait!" Goldmoon gripped Tanis's arm. "Look at her!"

The half-elf turned to see Bupu remove something limp and shapeless from the bag she carried over her shoulder. Stepping up to the wall, she waved the thing in front of the stone slab and muttered a few words. The wall shivered, and within seconds, a doorway appeared, leading into darkness.

The companions exchanged uneasy glances.

"No choice," Tanis muttered. The rattle and clank of armored draconians could be heard clearly, marching down the corridor toward them. "Raistlin, light," he ordered.

The mage spoke and the crystal on his staff flared. He and Bupu and Tanis quickly passed through the secret door. The rest followed, and the other door slid shut behind them. The mage's staff revealed a small, square room decorated with wall carvings so covered with green slime that they were impossible to distinguish. They stood in silence as they heard draconians pass in the corridor.

"They must have heard the fight," Sturm whispered. "It won't take them long to get the lift in motion, then we'll have the whole draconian force after us!"

"I know way down." Bupu waved her hand deprecatingly. "No worry."

"How did you open the door, little one?" Raistlin asked curiously, kneeling beside Bupu.

"Magic," she said shyly and she held out her hand. Lying in the gully dwarf's grubby palm was a dead rat, its teeth fixed in a permanent grimace. Raistlin raised his eyebrows, then Tasslehoff touched his arm.

"It's not magic, Raistlin," the kender whispered. "It's a simple, hidden floor lock. I saw it when she pointed at the wall and I was about to say something when she went through this magic rigmarole. She steps on it when she gets close to the door and waves that thing." The kender giggled. "She probably tripped it once, accidentally, while carrying the rat."

Bupu gave the kender a scathing glance. "Magic!" she stated, pouting and stroking the rat lovingly. She popped it back into her bag and said, "Come, you go." She led them north, passing through broken, slime-coated rooms. Finally she came to a halt in a room filled with rock dust and debris. Part of the ceiling had collapsed and the floor was littered with broken tiles. The gully dwarf jabbered and pointed at something in the northeast corner of the room.

"Go down!" she said.

Tanis and Raistlin walked over to inspect. They found a four-foot-wide pipe, one end sticking up out of the crumbling floor. Apparently it had fallen through the ceiling, caving in the northeast section of the room. Raistlin thrust his staff down inside the pipe and peered inside.

"Come, you go!" Bupu said, pointing and tugging at Raistlin's sleeve urgently. "Bosses can't follow."

"That's probably true," Tanis said. "Not with their wings."

"But there's not room enough to swing a sword," Sturm said, frowning. "I don't like it—"

Suddenly everyone stopped talking. They heard the wheel creak and the chain start to screech. The companions looked at each other.

"Me first!" Tasslehoff grinned. Poking his head into the pipe, he crawled forward on his hands and knees.

"Are you sure I'll fit?" Caramon asked, staring at the opening anxiously.

"Don't worry," Tas's voice floated out. "It's so slick with slime you'll slip through like a greased pig."

This cheerful statement did not seem to impress Caramon. He continued to regard the pipe gloomily as Raistlin, led by Bupu, clutched his robes around him and slid inside, his staff lighting the way. Flint climbed in next. Goldmoon followed, grimacing in disgust as her hands slipped in the thick, green slime. Riverwind slid in after her.

"This is insane—I hope you know that!" Sturm muttered in disgust.

Tanis didn't answer. He clapped Caramon on the back. "Your turn," he said, listening to the sound of the chain moving faster and faster.

Caramon groaned. Getting down on his hands and knees, the big warrior crawled forward into the pipe opening. His sword hilt caught on the edge. Backing out, he fumbled to readjust the sword, then he tried again. This time his rump stuck up too far making his back scrape along the top. Tanis planted his foot firmly on the big warrior's rear end and shoved.

"Flatten down!" the half-elf ordered.

Caramon collapsed like a wet sack with another groan. He squirmed in, head first, shoving his shield in front of him, his armor dragging along the metal pipe with a shrill, scraping sound that set Tanis's teeth on edge.

The half-elf reached out and grasped the top of the pipe. Thrusting his legs in first, he began to slide in the foul-smelling slime. He twisted his head around to look back at Sturm, who came last.

"Sanity ended when we followed Tika into the kitchen of the Inn of the Last Home," he said.

"True enough," the knight agreed with a sigh.

Tasslehoff, enthralled by the new experience of crawling down the pipe, suddenly saw dark figures at the bottom end. Scrabbling for a handhold, he slid to a stop.

"Raistlin!" the kender whispered. "Something's coming up the pipe!"

"What is it?" the mage started to ask, but the foul, moist air caught in his throat and he began to cough. Trying to catch his breath, he shone the staff's light down the pipe to see who approached.

Bupu took one look and sniffed. "Gulp-pulphers!" she muttered. Waving her hand, she shouted. "Go back! Go back!"

"We go up—ride lift! Big bosses get mad!" yelled one.

"We go down. See Highbulp!" Bupu said importantly.

At this, the other gully dwarves began backing down, muttering and swearing.

But Raistlin couldn't move for a moment. He clutched his chest, hacking, the sound echoing alarmingly in the stillness of the narrow pipe. Bupu gazed at him anxiously, then thrust her small hand into her bag, fished around for several moments, and came up with an object that she held up to the light, She squinted at it, then sighed and shook her head. "This not what I want," she mumbled.

Tasslehoff, catching sight of a brilliant, colorful flash, crept closer. "What is that?" he asked, even though he knew the answer. Raistlin, too, was staring at the object with wide glittering eyes.

Bupu shrugged. "Pretty rock," she said without interest, searching through the bag once more.

"An emerald!" Raistlin wheezed.

Bupu glanced up. "You like?" she asked Raistlin.

"Very much!" the mage gasped.

"You keep." Bupu put the jewel in the mage's hand. Then, with a cry of triumph, she brought out what she had been searching for. Tas, leaning up close to see the new wonder, drew back in disgust. It was a dead—very dead—lizard. There was a piece of chewed-on leather cord tied around the lizard's stiff tail. Bupu held it toward Raistlin.

"You wear around neck," she said. "Cure cough."

The mage, accustomed to handling much more unpleasant objects than this, smiled at Bupu and thanked her, but declined the cure, assuring her that his cough was much improved. She looked at him dubiously, but he did seem better—the spasm had passed. After a moment, she shrugged and put the lizard back into her bag. Raistlin, examining the emerald with expert eyes, stared coldly at Tasslehoff. The kender, sighing, turned his back and continued down the pipe. Raistlin slipped the stone into one of the secret inner pockets sewn into his robes.

When a branch pipe joined theirs, Tas looked questioningly at the gully dwarf. Bupu hesitantly pointed south, into the new pipe. Tas entered slowly. "This is stee—" he gasped as he began to slide rapidly down. He tried to slow his descent, but the slime was too thick. Caramon's explosive oath, echoing down the pipe from behind him, told the kender that his companions were having the same problem. Suddenly Tas saw light ahead of him. The tunnel was coming to an end, but where? Tas had a vivid vision of bursting out five hundred feet above nothing. But there wasn't anything he could do to stop himself. The light grew brighter, and Tasslehoff shot out the end of the pipe with a small shriek.

Raistlin slid out of the pipe, nearly falling on Bupu. The mage, looking around, thought for an instant that he had tumbled into a fire. Great, billowing clouds of white rolled around the room. Raistlin began to cough and gasp for breath.

"Wha—?" Flint flew out of the end of the pipe, falling on his hands and knees. He peered through the cloud. "Poison?" He gasped crawling over to the mage. Raistlin shook his head, but he couldn't answer. Bupu clutched the mage, dragging him toward the door. Goldmoon slid out on her stomach, knocking the breath from her body. Riverwind tumbled out, twisting his body to avoid hitting Goldmoon. There was a clanging bang as Caramon's shield shot from the pipe. Caramon's spiked armor and broad girth had slowed him enough so that he was able to crawl out of the pipe. But he was bruised and battered and covered with green filth. By the time Tanis arrived, everyone was gagging in the powdery atmosphere.

"What in the name of the Abyss?" Tanis said, astonished, then promptly choked as he inhaled a lungful of the white stuff. "Get out of here," he croaked. "Where's that gully dwarf?"

Bupu appeared in the doorway. She had taken Raistlin out of the room and was now motioning to the others. They emerged thankfully into the unclouded air and slumped down to rest among the ruins of a street. Tanis hoped they weren't waiting for an army of draconians. Suddenly he looked up. "Where's Tas?" he asked in alarm, staggering to his feet.

"Here I am," said a choked and miserable voice.

Tanis whirled around.

Tasslehoff—at least Tanis presumed it was Tasslehoff—stood before him. The kender was covered from topknot to toes in a thick, white, pasty substance. All Tanis could see of him were two brown eyes blinking out of a white mask.

"What happened?" the half-elf asked. He had never seen anyone quite so miserable as the bedraggled kender.

Tasslehoff didn't answer. He just pointed back inside.

Tanis, fearing something disastrous, ran over and peered cautiously through the crumbling doorway. The white cloud had dissipated so that he could see around the room now. Over in one corner—directly opposite the pipe opening—stood a number of large, bulging sacks. Two of them had been split open, spilling a mass of white onto the floor.

Then Tanis understood. He put his hand over his face to hide his smile. "Flour," he murmured.

THE BROKEN CITY.
HIGHBULP PHUDGE I, THE GREAT.

19

The night of the Cataclysm had been a night of horror for the city of Xak Tsaroth. When the fiery mountain struck Krynn, the land split apart. The ancient and beautiful city of Xak Tsaroth slid down the face of a cliff into a vast cavern formed by the huge rents in the ground. Thus, underground, it was lost to the sight of men, and most people believed the city had vanished entirely, swallowed up by Newsea. But it still existed, clinging to the rough sides of the cavern walls, spread out upon the floor of the cavern—there were ruined buildings on several different levels. The building the companions had fallen into, which Tanis assumed must have been a bakery, was on the middle level, caught by rocks and held up against the sheer cliff face. Water from underground streams flowed down the sides of the rock and ran into the street, swirling among the ruins.

Tanis's gaze followed the course of the water. It ran down the middle of the cracked cobblestone street, running past other small shops and houses where people had once lived and gone about their business. When the city fell, the tall buildings that once lined the street toppled against one another, forming a crude archway of broken marble slabs above the cobblestones. Doors and broken shop windows yawned into the street. All was still and quiet, except for the noise of the dripping water. The air was heavy with the odor of decay. It weighed upon the spirit. And though the air was warmer down beneath the ground level than up above, the gloomy atmosphere chilled the blood. No one spoke. They washed the slime from their bodies (and the flour from Tas) as best they could, then refilled their water skins. Sturm and Caramon searched the area but saw no draconians. After a few moments of rest, the companions rose and moved on.

Bupu led them south, down the street, beneath the archway of ruined buildings. The street opened into a plaza—here the water in the streets became a river, flowing west.

"Follow river." Bupu pointed.

Tanis frowned, hearing above the noise of the river another sound, the crashing and roaring of a great waterfall. But Bupu insisted, so the heroes edged their way around the plaza river, occasionally plunging ankle deep in the water. Reaching the end of the street, the companions discovered the waterfall. The street dropped off into air, and the river gushed out from between broken columns to fall nearly five hundred feet into the bottom of the cavern. There rested the remainder of the ruined city of Xak Tsaroth.

They could see by the dim light that filtered through cracks in the cavern roof far above that the heart of the ancient city lay scattered about on the floor of the cavern in many states of decay. Some of the buildings were almost completely intact. Others, however, were nothing but rubble. A chill fog, created by the many waterfalls plunging down into the cavern, hung over the city. Most of the streets had become rivers, which combined to flow into a deep abyss to the north. Peering through the mists, the companions could see the huge chain hanging only a few hundred feet away, slightly north of their present position. They realized that the lift raised and lowered people at least one thousand feet.

"Where does the Highbulp live?" Tanis asked, looking down into the dead city below him.

"Bupu says he lives over there"—Raistlin gestured—"in those buildings on the western side of the cavern."

"And who lives in the reconstructed buildings right below us?" Tanis asked.

"Bosses," Bupu replied, scowling.

"How many bosses?"

"One, and one, and one." Bupu counted until she had used up all her fingers. "Two," she said. "Not more than two."

"Which could be anything from two hundred to two thousand," Sturm muttered. "How do we get to see the Highwhoop."

"Highbulp!" Bupu glared at him. "Highbulp Phudge I. The great."

"How do we get to him, without the bosses catching us?"

In answer, Bupu pointed upward to the rising pot full of draconians. Tanis looked blank, glanced at Sturm who shrugged disgustedly. Bupu sighed in exasperation and turned to Raistlin, obviously considering the others incapable of understanding. "Bosses go up. We go down," she said.

Raistlin stared at the lift through the mist. Then he nodded in understanding. "The draconians probably believe that we are trapped up there with no way to get down into the city. If most of the draconians are up above, that would allow us to move safely below."

"All right," Sturm said. "But how in the name of Istar do we get down? Most of us can't fly!"

Bupu spread her hands. "Vines!" she said. Seeing everyone's look of confusion, the gully dwarf stumped over to the edge of the waterfall and pointed down. Thick, green vines hung over the edge of the rocky cliff like giant snakes. The leaves on the vines were torn, tattered, and, in some places, stripped off entirely, but the vines themselves appeared thick and tough, even if they were slippery.

Goldmoon, unusually pale, crept toward the edge, peered over, and backed away hurriedly. It was a five-hundred-foot drop straight down to a rubble-strewn cobblestone street. Riverwind put his arm around her, comfortingly.

"I've climbed worse," Caramon said complacently.

"Well, I don't like it," said Flint. "But anything's better than sliding down a sewer." Grabbing hold of the vine, he swung himself over the ledge and began to inch slowly down hand over hand. "It's not bad," he shouted up.

Tasslehoff slid down a vine after Flint, traveling rapidly and with such skill that he received a grunt of approbation from Bupu.

The gully dwarf turned to look at Raistlin, pointing at his long, flowing robes and frowning. The mage smiled at her reassuringly. Standing on the edge of the cliff, he said softly, *"Pveathrfall."* The crystal ball on top of his staff flared and Raistlin leaped off the edge of the cliff, disappearing into the mist below. Bupu shrieked. Tanis caught her, fearing the adoring gully dwarf might throw herself over.

"He'll be fine," the half-elf assured her, feeling a flash of pity when he saw the look of genuine anguish on her face. "He is magi," he said. "Magic. You know."

Bupu obviously did *not* know because she stared at Tanis suspiciously, threw her bag around her neck, grabbed hold of a vine, and began scrabbling down the slippery rock. The rest of the companions were preparing to follow when Goldmoon whispered brokenly, "I can't."

Riverwind took her hands. *"Kan-toka,"* he said softly, "it will be all right. You heard what the dwarf said. Just don't look down."

Goldmoon shook her head, her chin quivering. "There must be another way," she said stubbornly. "We will search for it!"

"What's the problem?" Tanis asked. "We should hurry—"

"She's afraid of heights," Riverwind said.

Goldmoon shoved him away. "How dare you tell him that!" she shouted, her face flushed with anger.

Riverwind stared at her coldly. "Why not?" he said, his voice grating. "He's not your subject. You can let him know you're human, that you have human frailties. You have only one subject to impress now, Chieftain, and that is me!"

If Riverwind had stabbed her, he could have inflicted no more terrible pain. The color drained from Goldmoon's lips. Her eyes grew wide and staring, like the eyes of a corpse. "Please secure the staff on my back," she said to Tanis.

"Goldmoon, he didn't mean—" he began.

"Do as I command!" she ordered curtly, her blue eyes blazing in anger.

Tanis, sighing, tied the staff to her back with a length of rope. Goldmoon did not even glance at Riverwind. When the staff was fastened tightly, she started toward the edge of the cliff. Sturm jumped in front of her.

"Allow me to go down the vine ahead of you," he said. "If you slip—"

"If I slip and fall, you'd fall with me. The only thing we'd accomplish would be to die together," she snapped. Leaning down, she took a firm grip on the vine and swung herself over the edge. Almost immediately, her sweating hands slipped. Tanis's breath caught in his throat. Sturm lunged forward, though he knew there wasn't anything he could do. Riverwind stood watching, not a sign of emotion on his face. Goldmoon clutched frantically at the vines and thick leaves. She caught hold and clung to them tightly, unable to breathe, unwilling to move. She pressed her face against the wet leaves, shuddering, her eyes closed to block out the sight of the terrifying drop to the ground below. Sturm went over the edge and climbed down to her.

"Leave me alone," Goldmoon said to him through clenched teeth. She drew a trembling breath, cast a proud, defiant glance at Riverwind, then began to lower herself down the vine.

Sturm stayed near her, keeping an eye on her, as he skillfully climbed down the cliff face. Tanis, standing next to Riverwind, wanted to say something to the Plainsman but feared to do more harm. Saying nothing, therefore, he went over the edge. Riverwind followed silently.

The half-elf found the climb easy, though he slipped the last few feet, landing in an inch of water. Raistlin, he noticed, was shivering with the cold, his cough worsening in the damp air. Several gully dwarves stood around the mage, staring at him with admiring eyes. Tanis wondered how long the charm spell would last.

Goldmoon leaned against the wall, shaking. She did not look at Riverwind as he reached the ground and moved away from her, his face still expressionless.

"Where are we?" Tanis shouted above the noise of the waterfall. The mist was so thick he couldn't see anything except broken columns, overgrown with vines and fungus.

"Great Plaza that way." Bupu urgently jabbed her grubby finger toward the west. "Come. You follow. Go see Highbulp!"

She started off. Tanis reached out his hand and caught hold of her, dragging her to a stop. She glared at him, deeply offended. The half-elf removed his hand. "Please. Just listen a moment! What about the dragon? Where's the dragon?"

Bupu's eyes widened. "You want dragon?" she asked.

"No!" yelled Tanis. "We don't want the dragon. But we need to know if the dragon comes into this part of the city—" He felt Sturm's hand on his shoulder and gave up. "Forget it. Never mind," he said wearily. "Go on."

Bupu regarded Raistlin with deep sympathy for having to put up with these insane people, then she took the mage's hand and trotted off down the street to the west, the other gully dwarves trailing along behind. Half-deafened by the thundering noise of the waterfall, the companions waded after, glancing about them uneasily, dark windows loomed above them, dark doorways threatened. At each moment, they expected scaly, armored draconians to appear. But the gully dwarves did not seem concerned. They sloshed along the street, keeping as close to Raistlin as possible, and jabbering in their uncouth language.

Eventually the sounds of the waterfall faded in the distance. The mist continued to swirl around them, however, and the silence of the dead city was oppressive. Dark water gushed and gurgled past their feet along the cobblestone riverbed. Suddenly the buildings came to an end and the street opened into a huge, circular plaza. Through the water they could see the remnants in the plaza of flagstone paving in an intricate sunburst design. In the center of the plaza, the river was joined by another stream rushing in from the north. They formed a small whirlpool as the waters met and swirled before joining and continuing west between another group of tumble-down buildings.

Here, light streamed into the plaza from a crack in the cavern roof hundreds of feet above, illuminating the ghostly mists, dancing off the surface of the water whenever the mists parted.

"Other side Great Plaza," Bupu pointed.

The companions came to a halt in the shadows of the ruined buildings. All of them had the same thought: The plaza was over one hundred feet across without a scrap of shelter. Once they ventured out, there would be no hiding.

Bupu, trotting along without concern, suddenly realized no one was following her except other gully dwarves. She looked back, irritated at the delay. "You come, Highbulp this way."

"Look!" Goldmoon grasped Tanis's arm.

On the other side of the great flagstone plaza were great, tall marble columns that supported a stone roof. The columns were cracked and shattered, letting the roof sag. The mists parted and Tanis caught a glimpse of a courtyard behind the columns. Dark forms of tall, domed buildings were visible beyond the courtyard. Then the mists closed around them. Though now sunk into degradation and ruin, this structure must have once been the most magnificent in Xak Tsaroth.

"The Royal Palace," Raistlin confirmed, coughing.

"Shhhh!" Goldmoon shook Tanis's arm. "Can't you see? No, wait—"

The mists flowed in front of the pillars. For a moment the companions could not see anything. Then the fog swirled away. The companions shrank back into the dark doorway. The gully dwarves came to a skidding halt in the plaza and, whirling around, raced back to cower behind Raistlin.

Bupu peered at Tanis from under the mage's sleeve. "That dragon," she said. "You want?"

It was the dragon.

Sleek and shining black, her leathery wings folded at her side, Khisanth slithered out from under the roof, ducking her head to fit beneath the sagging stone facade. Her clawed front feet clicked on the marble stairs as she stopped and stared into the floating mist with her bright red eyes. Her back legs and heavy reptilian tail were not visible, the dragon's body extending thirty feet or more back into the courtyard. A cringing draconian walked beside her, the two apparently deep in conversation.

Khisanth was angry. The draconian had brought her disturbing news—it was impossible that any of the strangers could have survived her attack at the well! But now the captain of her guard reported strangers in the city! Strangers who attacked her forces with skill and daring, strangers bearing a brown staff whose description was known to every draconian serving in this part of the Ansalon continent.

"I cannot believe this report! None could have escaped me." Khisanth's voice was soft, almost purring, yet the draconian trembled as he heard it. "The staff was not with them. I would have sensed its presence. You say these intruders are still above, in the upper chambers? Are you certain?"

The draconian gulped and nodded. "There is no way down, royal one, except the lift."

"There are other ways, you lizard," Khisanth sneered. "These miserable gully dwarves crawl around the place like parasites. The intruders have the staff, and they are trying to get down into the city. That means only one thing—they are after the Disks! How could they have learned of them?" The dragon snaked her head around and up and down as if she could see those who threatened her plans through the blinding mists. But the mists swirled past, thicker than ever.

Khisanth snarled in irritation. "The staff! That miserable staff! Verminaard should have foreseen this with those clerical powers he touts so highly, then it could have been destroyed. But, no, he is busy with his war while I must rot here in this dank tomb of a city." Khisanth gnawed a talon as she pondered.

"You could destroy the Disks," the draconian suggested, greatly daring.

"Fool, don't you think we've tried?" Khisanth muttered. She lifted her head. "No, it is far too dangerous to stay here longer. If these intruders know of the secret, others must also. The Disks should be removed to a safe place. Inform Lord Verminaard that I am leaving Xak Tsaroth. I will join him in Pax Tharkas and I will bring the intruders with me for questioning."

"*Inform* Lord Verminaard?" the draconian asked, shocked.

"Very well," Khisanth responded sarcastically. "If you insist on the charade, *ask* my Lord's permission. I suppose you have sent most of the troops up to the top?"

"Yes, royal one." The draconian bowed.

Khisanth considered the matter. "Perhaps you are not such an idiot after all," she mused. "I can handle things below. Concentrate your search in the upper parts of the city. When you find these intruders, bring them straight to me. Do not hurt them any more than necessary to subdue them. And be careful of that staff!"

The draconian fell to its knees before the dragon, who sniffed in derision and crept back into the dark shadows out of which she had come.

The draconian ran down the stairs where it was joined by several more creatures who appeared out of the mist. After a brief, muffled exchange in their own language, the draconians started up the north street. They walked nonchalantly, laughing at some private joke, and soon vanished into the mist.

"They're not worried, are they?" Sturm said.

"No," Tanis agreed grimly. "They think they've got us."

"Let's face it, Tanis. They're right," Sturm said. "This plan we've been discussing has one major flaw. If we sneak in without the dragon knowing, and *if* we get the Disks—we still have to get out of this godforsaken city with draconians crawling all over the upper levels."

"I asked you before and I'll ask you now," Tanis said. "Have you got a better plan?"

"I've got a better plan," Caramon said gruffly. "No disrespect, Tanis, but we all know how elves feel about fighting." The big man gestured toward the palace. "That's obviously where the dragon lives. Let's lure it out as we planned, only this time we'll fight it, not creep around its lair like thieves. When the dragon's disposed of, then we can get the Disks."

"My dear brother," Raistlin whispered, "your strength lies in your sword-arm, not in your mind. Tanis is wise, as the knight said when we started on this little adventure. You would do well to pay attention to him. What do you know of dragons, my brother? You have seen the effects of its deadly breath." Raistlin was overcome by a fit of coughing. He dragged a soft cloth out from the sleeve of his robe. Tanis saw that the cloth was stained with blood.

After a moment, Raistlin continued. "You could defend your-self against that, perhaps, and against the sharp claws and fangs, and the slashing tail, which can knock down those pillars. But what will you use, dear brother, against her magic? Dragons are the most ancient of magic-users. She could charm you as I have charmed my little friend. She could put you to sleep with a word, then murder you while you dreamed."

"All right," Caramon muttered, chagrined. "I didn't know any of that. Damn it, who does know anything about these creatures!"

"There is much lore on the dragons in Solamnia," Sturm said softly.

He wants to fight the dragon, too, Tanis realized. He is think-ing of Huma, the perfect knight, called Dragonbane.

Bupu tugged on Raistlin's robe. "Come. You go. No more bosses. No more dragon." She and the other gully dwarves started splash-ing across the flagstone plaza.

"Well?" Tanis said, looking at the two warriors.

"It seems we have no choice," Sturm said stiffly. "We do not face the enemy, we hide behind gully dwarves! Sooner or later a time must come when we face these monsters!" He spun on his heel and walked off, his back straight, his moustaches bristling. The companions followed.

"Maybe we're worrying needlessly." Tanis scratched his beard, glancing back at the palace that was now obscured by the mist. "Perhaps this is the only dragon left in Krynn—one that survived the Age of Dreams."

Raistlin's lips twisted. "Remember the stars, Tanis," he mur-mured. "The Queen of Darkness has returned. Recall the words of the Canticle: 'swarm of her shrieking hosts.' Her hosts were dragons, according to the ancient ones. She has returned and her hosts have come with her."

"This way!" Bupu clutched at Raistlin, pointing down a street branching off to the north. "This home!"

"At least it's dry," Flint grumbled. Turning right, they left the river behind them. Mist closed in around the companions as they entered another nest of ruined buildings. This section of town must have been the poorer part of the city of Xak Tsaroth, even in its glory days—the buildings were in the last stages of decay and collapse. The gully dwarves began whooping and hollering as they ran down the street. Sturm looked at Tanis in alarm at the noise.

"Can't you get them to be quieter?" Tanis asked Bupu. "So the draconians, er, bosses won't find us."

"Pooh!" She shrugged. "No bosses. They not come here. Afraid of the great Highbulp."

Tanis had his doubts about that, but, glancing around, he couldn't see any signs of the draconians. From what he had observed, the lizardlike men seemed to lead a well-ordered, militaristic life. By contrast, the streets in this part of town were cluttered with trash and filth. The disreputable buildings erupted with gully dwarves. Males, females, and dirty, ragged children stared at them curiously as they walked down the street. Bupu and the other spellbound gully dwarves swarmed around Raistlin, practically carrying him.

The draconians were undeniably smart, Tanis thought. They allowed their slaves to live their private lives in peace—so long as they didn't stir up trouble. A good idea, considering that gully dwarves outnumbered draconians about ten to one. Though they were basically cowards, gully dwarves had a reputation as very nasty fighters when backed into a corner.

Bupu brought the group to a halt in front of one of the darkest, dingiest, filthiest alleys Tanis had ever seen. A foul mist flowed out from it. The buildings leaned over, holding each other up like drunks stumbling out of a tavern. As he watched, small dark creatures skittered out of the alley and gully dwarf children began chasing after them.

"Dinner," shrieked one, smacking his lips.

"Those are rats!" Goldmoon cried in horror.

"Do we have to go in there?" Sturm growled, staring at the tottering buildings.

"The smell alone is enough to knock a troll dead," Caramon added. "And I'd rather die under the dragon's claw than have a gully dwarf hovel fall on top of me."

Bupu gestured down the alley. "The Highbulp!" she said, pointing to the most dilapidated building on the block.

"Stay here and keep watch if you want," Tanis told Sturm. "I'll go talk with the Highbulp."

"No." The knight scowled, gesturing the half-elf into the alley. "We're in this together."

The alley ran several hundred feet to the east, then it twisted north and came suddenly to a dead end. Ahead of them was a decaying brick wall and no way out. Their return was blocked by gully dwarves who had run in after them.

"Ambush!" Sturm hissed and drew his sword. Caramon began to rumble deep in his throat. The gully dwarves, seeing the flash of cold steel, panicked. Falling all over themselves and each other, they whirled and fled back down the alley.

Bupu glared at Sturm and Caramon in disgust. She turned to Raistlin. "You make them stop!" she demanded, pointing to the warriors. "Or I not take to Highbulp."

"Put your sword away, knight," Raistlin hissed, "unless you think you've found a foe worthy of your attention."

Sturm glowered at Raistlin, and for a moment Tanis thought he might attack the mage, but then the knight thrust his sword away. "I wish I knew what your game was, magician," Sturm said coldly. "You were so eager to come to this city, even before we knew about the Disks. Why? What are you after?"

Raistlin did not reply. He stared at the knight malevolently with his strange golden eyes, then turned to Bupu. "They will not trouble you further, little one," he whispered.

Bupu looked around to make certain they were properly cowed, then she walked forward and knocked twice on the wall with her grubby fist. "Secret door," she said importantly.

Two knocks answered Bupu's knock.

"That signal," she said. "Three knocks. Now they let in."

"But she only knocked twice—" Tas began, giggling.

Bupu glared at him.

"Shhh!" Tanis nudged the kender.

Nothing happened. Bupu, frowning, knocked twice more. Two knocks answered. She waited. Caramon, his eyes on the alley opening, began moving restlessly from one foot to the other. Bupu knocked twice again. Two knocks answered.

Finally Bupu yelled at the wall. "I knock secret code knock. You let in!"

"Secret knock five knocks," answered a muffled voice.

"I knock five knocks!" Bupu stated angrily. "You let in!"

"You knock six knocks."

"I count eight knocks," argued another voice.

Bupu suddenly pushed on the wall with both hands. It opened easily. She peered inside. "I knock four knocks. You let in!" she said, raising a clenched fist.

"All right," the voice grumbled.

Bupu shut the door, knocked twice. Tanis, hoping to avoid any more incidents and delays, glared at the kender, who was writhing with suppressed laughter.

The door swung open—again. "You come in," the guard said sourly. "But that not four knocks," he whispered to Bupu loudly. She ignored him as she swept disdainfully past him, dragging her bag along the floor.

"We see Highbulp," she announced.

"You take this lot to Highbulp?" One of the guards gasped, staring at the giant Caramon and the tall Riverwind with wide eyes. His companion began backing up.

"See Highbulp," Bupu said proudly.

The gully dwarf guard, never taking his eyes off the formidable-looking group, backed into a stinking, filthy hallway, then broke into a run. He began shouting at the top of his lungs. "An army! An army has broken in!" They could hear his shouts echo down the hallway.

"Bah!" Bupu sniffed. "Glup-phunger spawn! Come. See Highbulp."

She started down the hallway, clutching her bag to her chest. The companions could still hear the shouts of the gully dwarf echoing down the corridor.

"An army! An army of giants! Save the Highbulp!"

The great Highbulp, Phudge I, was a gully dwarf among gully dwarves. He was almost intelligent, rumored to be fabulously wealthy, and a notorious coward. The Bulps had long been the elite clan of Xak Tsaroth—or "Th" as they called it—ever since Nulph Bulp fell down a shaft one night in a drunken stupor and discovered the city. Upon sobering up the next morning, he claimed it for his clan. The Bulps promptly moved in and, in later years, graciously allowed the clans Slud and Glup to occupy the city as well.

Life was good in the ruined city—by gully dwarf standards, anyway. The outside world left them alone (since the outside world hadn't the foggiest notion they were there and wouldn't have cared if it did). The Bulps had no trouble maintaining their dominance over the other clans, mostly because it was a Bulp (Glunggu) with a scientific turn of mind (certain jealous members of the Slud clan whispered that his mother had been a gnome) who developed the lift, putting to use the two enormous iron pots used by the city's former residents for rendering lard. The lift enabled the gully dwarves to extend their scavenging activities to the jungle above the sunken city, greatly improving their standard of living. Glunggu Bulp became a hero and was proclaimed Highbulp by unanimous decision. The chieftainship of the clans had remained in the Bulp family ever since.

The years passed and then, suddenly, the outside world took an interest in Xak Tsaroth. The arrival of the dragon and the draconians put a sad crimp on the gully dwarf lifestyle. The draconians had initially intended to wipe out the filthy little nuisances, but the gully dwarves—led by the great Phudge—had cringed and cowered and whimpered and wailed and prostrated themselves so abjectly that the draconians were merciful and simply enslaved them.

So it was that the gully dwarves—for the first time in several hundred years of living in Xak Tsaroth—were forced to work. The draconians repaired buildings, put things into military order, and generally made life miserable for the gully dwarves who had to cook and clean and repair things.

Needless to say, the great Phudge was not pleased with this state of affairs. He spent long hours thinking up ways to remove the dragon. He knew the location of the dragon's lair, of course, and had even discovered a secret route leading there. He had actually sneaked in once, when the dragon was away. Phudge had been awestruck by the vast amount of pretty rocks and shining coins gathered in the huge underground room. The great Highbulp had traveled some in his wild youth and he knew that folk in the outside world coveted these pretty rocks and would give vast amounts of colorful and gaudy cloth (Phudge had a weakness for fine clothes) in return. On the spot, the Highbulp drew up a map so he wouldn't forget how to get back to the treasure. He even had the presence of mind to swipe a few of the smaller rocks.

Phudge dreamed of this wealth for months afterward, but he never found another opportunity to return. This was due to two factors: one, the dragon never left again and, two, Phudge couldn't make heads nor tails of his map.

If only the dragon would leave permanently, he thought, or if some hero would come along and conveniently stick a sword into it! These were the Highbulp's fondest dreams, and this was the state of affairs when the great Phudge heard his guards proclaiming that an army was attacking.

Thus it came to pass that—when Bupu finally dragged the great Phudge out from under his bed and convinced him that he was not about to be set upon by an army of giants—Highbulp Phudge I began to believe that dreams could come true.

"And so you're here to kill the dragon," said the great Highbulp, Phudge I, to Tanis Half-Elven.

"No," Tanis said patiently, "we're not."

The companions stood in the Court of the Aghar before the throne of a gully dwarf Bupu had introduced as the great Highbulp. Bupu kept an eye on the companions as they entered the throne room, eagerly anticipating their looks of stunned awe. Bupu was not disappointed. The looks on the companions' faces as they entered might well be described as stunned.

The city of Xak Tsaroth had been stripped of its finery by the early Bulps who used it to decorate the throne room of their lord. Following the philosophy that if one yard of gold cloth is good, forty yards is better, and totally uninhibited by good taste, the gully dwarves turned the throne room of the great Highbulp into a masterpiece of confusion. Heavy, frayed gold cloth swirled and draped every available inch of wall space. Huge tapestries hung from the ceiling (some of them upside-down). The tapestries must have once been beautiful, delicate-colored threads blending to show scenes of city life, or portray stories and legends from the past. But the gully dwarves, wanting to liven them up, painted over the cloth in garish, clashing colors.

Thus Sturm was shocked to the core of his being when confronted by a bright red Huma battling a purple-spotted dragon beneath an emerald-green sky.

Graceful, nude statues, standing in all the wrong places, adorned the room as well. These, too, the gully dwarves had enhanced, considering pure white marble drab and depressing. They painted the statues with enough realism and attention to detail that Caramon—with an embarrassed glance at Goldmoon—flushed bright red and kept his eyes on the floor.

The companions, in fact, had problems maintaining their serious mien when ushered into this gallery of artistic horrors. One failed utterly: Tasslehoff was immediately overcome by the giggles so severely that Tanis was forced to send the kender back to the Waiting Place outside the Court to try and compose himself. The rest of the group bowed solemnly to the great Phudge—with the exception of Flint who stood bolt upright, his hands fingering his battle-axe, without the trace of a smile on his aged face.

The dwarf had laid his hand on Tanis's arm before they entered the court of the Highbulp. "Don't be taken in by this foolery, Tanis," Flint warned. "These creatures can be treacherous."

The Highbulp was somewhat flustered when the companions entered, especially at the sight of the tall fighters. But Raistlin made a few well-chosen remarks that considerably mollified and reassured (if disappointed) the Highbulp.

The mage, interrupted by fits of coughing, explained that they did not want to cause trouble, they simply planned to retrieve an object of religious value from the dragon's lair and leave, preferably without disturbing the dragon.

230

This, of course, didn't fit in with Phudge's plans. He therefore assumed he hadn't heard correctly. Cocooned in gaudy robes, he leaned back in the chipped gold-leaf throne and repeated calmly—"You here. Got swords. Kill dragon."

"No," said Tanis again. "As our friend, Raistlin, explained, the dragon is guarding an object that belongs to our gods. We want to remove the object and escape the city before the dragon is aware that it is gone."

The Highbulp frowned. "How me know you not take all treasure, leave Highbulp only one mad dragon? There be lot of treasure, pretty rocks."

Raistlin looked up sharply, his eyes gleaming. Sturm, fidgeting with his sword, glanced at the mage in disgust.

"We will bring you the pretty rocks," Tanis assured the Highbulp. "Help us and you will get all the treasure. We want only to find this relic of our gods."

It had become obvious to the Highbulp that he was dealing with thieves and liars, not the heroes he had expected. This group was apparently as frightened of the dragon as he was and that gave the Highbulp an idea. "What you want from Highbulp?" he asked, trying to subdue his glee and appear subtle.

Tanis sighed in relief. At last they seemed to be getting somewhere. "Bupu"—he indicated the female gully dwarf clinging to Raistlin's sleeve—"told us that you were the only one in the city who could lead us to the dragon's lair."

"Lead!" The great Phudge lost his composure for a moment and clutched his robes around him. "No lead! Great Highbulp not expendable. People need me!"

"No, no. I didn't mean lead," Tanis amended hastily. "If you had a map or could send someone to show us the way."

"Map!" Phudge mopped the sweat off his brow with the sleeve of his robe. "Should say so in first place. Map. Yes. I send for map. Meantime, you eat. Guests of the Highbulp. Guards take to mess hall."

"No, thank you," Tanis said politely, unable to look at the others. They had passed the gully dwarf mess hall on their way to see the Highbulp. The smell alone had been enough to ruin even Caramon's appetite.

"We have our own food," Tanis continued. "We would like some time to ourselves to rest and discuss our plans further."

"Certainly." The Highbulp scooted forward to the front of the throne. Two of his guards came over to help him down since his feet didn't touch the floor. "Go back to Waiting Place. Sit. Eat. Talk. I send map. Maybe you tell Phudge plans?"

Tanis glanced swiftly at the gully dwarf and saw the Highbulp's squinty eyes gleam with cunning. The half-elf felt cold, suddenly realizing this gully dwarf was no buffoon. Tanis began to wish he had talked more with Flint. "Our plans are hardly formed yet, your majesty," the half-elf said.

The great Highbulp knew better. Long ago he had drilled a hole through the wall of the room known as Waiting Place so that he could eavesdrop on his subjects as they waited for an audience with him, discovering what they intended to bother him about in advance. Thus he knew a great deal about the companions' plans already, so he let the matter drop. The use of the term "your majesty" may have had something to do with this; the Highbulp had never heard anything quite so suitable.

"Your majesty," Phudge repeated, sighing with pleasure. He poked one of his guards in the back. "You remember. From now on, say 'Your Majesty.'"

"Y-yes, y-your, uh, majesty," the gully dwarf stuttered. The great Phudge waved his filthy hand graciously and the companions bowed their way out. Highbulp, Phudge I, stood for a moment beside his throne, smiling in what he considered a charming manner until his guests were gone. Then his expression changed, transforming into a smile so shrewd and devious his guards crowded around him in eager anticipation.

"You," he said to one. "Go to quarters. Bring map. Give to fools in next room."

The guard saluted and ran off. The other guard remained close, waiting in open-mouthed expectation. Phudge glanced around, then drew the guard even nearer, considering exactly how to phrase his next command. He needed some heroes and if he had to create his own out of whatever scum came along, then he would do so. If they died, it was no great loss. If they succeeded in killing the dragon, so much the better. The gully dwarves would get what was—to them—more precious than all the pretty rocks in Krynn: a return to the sweet, halcyon days of freedom! And so, enough of this nonsense about sneaking around.

Phudge leaned over and whispered in the guard's ear. "You go to dragon. Give her best regards of his majesty, Highbulp, Phudge I, and tell her . . . "

THE HIGHBULP'S MAP.
A SPELLBOOK OF FISTANDANTILUS.

I don't trust that little bastard any farther than I can stand the smell of him," Caramon growled.

"I agree," Tanis said quietly. "But what choice do we have? We've agreed to bring him the treasure. He has everything to lose and nothing to gain if he betrays us."

They sat on the floor in the Waiting Place, a filthy antechamber outside the throne room. The decorations in this room were just as vulgar as in the Court. The companions were nervous and tense, speaking little and forcing themselves to eat.

Raistlin refused food. Curled up on the floor apart from the others, he prepared and drank down the strange herbal mixture that eased his cough. Then he wrapped himself in his robes and stretched out, eyes closed, on the floor. Bupu sat curled up near him, munching on something from her bag. Caramon, going over to check on his brother, was horrified to see a tail disappear into her mouth with a slurp.

Riverwind sat by himself. He did not take part in the hushed conversation as the friends went over their plans once again. The Plainsman stared moodily at the floor. When he felt a light touch on his arm, he didn't even lift his head. Goldmoon, her face pale, knelt beside him. She tried to speak, failed, then cleared her throat.

"We must talk," she said firmly in their language.

"Is that a command?" he asked bitterly.

She swallowed. "Yes," she answered, barely audible.

Riverwind rose to his feet and walked over to stand in front of a garish tapestry. He did not look at Goldmoon or even speak to her. His face was drawn into a stern mask, but underneath, Goldmoon could see the searing pain in his soul. She gently laid her hand on his arm.

"Forgive me," she said softly.

Riverwind regarded her in astonishment. She stood before him, her head bowed, an almost childlike shame on her face. He reached out to stroke the silver-gold hair of the one he loved more than life itself. He felt Goldmoon tremble at his touch and his heart ached with love. Moving his hand from her head to her neck, he very gently and tenderly drew the beloved head to his chest and then suddenly clasped her in his arms.

"I've never heard you say those words before," he said, smiling to himself, knowing she could not see him.

"I have never said them," she gulped, her cheek pressed against his leather shirt. "Oh, my beloved, I am sorrier than I can say that you came home to Chieftain's Daughter and not Goldmoon. But I've been so afraid."

"No," he whispered, "I am the one who should ask forgiveness." He raised his hand to wipe away her tears. "I didn't realize what you had gone through. All I could think of was myself and the dangers I had faced. I wish you had told me, heart's dearest."

"I wished you had asked," she replied, looking up at him earnestly. "I have been Chieftain's Daughter so long it is the only thing I know how to be. It is my strength. It gives me courage when I am frightened. I don't think I can let go."

"I don't want you to let go." He smiled at her, smoothing wayward strands of hair from her face. "I fell in love with Chieftain's Daughter the first time I saw you. Do you remember? At the games held in your honor."

"You refused to bow to receive my blessing," she said. "You acknowledged my father's leadership but denied that I was a goddess. You said man could not make gods of other men." Her eyes looked back so many, many years. "How tall and proud and handsome you were, talking of ancient gods that did not exist to me then."

"And how furious you were," he recalled, "and how beautiful! Your beauty was a blessing to me in itself. I needed no other. You wanted me thrown out of the games."

Goldmoon smiled sadly. "You thought I was angry because you had shamed me before the people, but that was not so."

"No? What was it then, Chieftain's Daughter?"

Her face flushed a dusky rose, but she lifted her clear blue eyes to him. "I was angry because I knew when I saw you standing there, refusing to kneel before me, that I had lost part of myself and that, until you claimed it, I would never be whole again."

For reply, the Plainsman pressed her to him, kissing her hair gently.

"Riverwind," she said, swallowing, "Chieftain's Daughter is still here. I don't think she can ever leave. But you must know that Goldmoon is underneath and, if this journey ever ends and we come to peace at last, then Goldmoon will be yours forever and we will banish Chieftain's Daughter to the winds."

A thump at the Highbulp's door caused everyone to start nervously as a gully dwarf guard stumbled into the room. "Map," he said, thrusting a crumpled piece of paper at Tanis.

"Thank you," said the half-elf gravely. "And extend our thanks to the Highbulp."

"His *Majesty*, the Highbulp," the guard corrected with an anxious glance toward a tapestry-covered wall. Bobbing clumsily, he backed into the Highbulp's quarters.

Tanis spread the map flat. Everyone gathered around it, even Flint. After one look, however, the dwarf snorted derisively and walked back to his couch.

Tanis laughed ruefully. "We might have expected it. I wonder if the great Phudge remembers where the 'big secret room' is?"

"Of course not." Raistlin sat up, opening his strange, golden eyes and peering at them through half-closed lids. "That is why he has never returned for the treasure. However, there is one among us who knows where the dragon's lair is located." Everyone followed the mage's gaze.

Bupu glared back at them defiantly. "You right. I know," she said, sulking. "I know secret place. I go there, find pretty rocks. But don't tell Highbulp!"

"Will you tell us?" Tanis asked. Bupu looked at Raistlin. He nodded.

"I tell," she mumbled. "Give map."

Raistlin, seeing the others engrossed in looking at the map, beckoned to his brother.

"Is the plan still the same?" the mage whispered.

"Yes." Caramon frowned. "And I don't like it. I should go with you."

"Nonsense," Raistlin hissed. "You would only be in my way!" Then he added more gently, "I will be in no danger, I assure you." He laid his hand on his twin's arm and drew him close. "Besides"—the mage glanced around—"there is something you must do for me, my brother. Something you must bring me from the dragon's lair."

Raistlin's touch was unusually hot, his eyes burned. Caramon uneasily started to pull back, seeing something in his brother he hadn't seen since the Towers of High Sorcery, but Raistlin's hand clutched at him.

"What is it?" Caramon asked reluctantly.

"A spellbook!" Raistlin whispered.

"So this is why you wanted to come to Xak Tsaroth!" said Caramon. "You knew this spellbook would be here."

"I read about it, years ago. I knew it had been in Xak Tsaroth prior to the Cataclysm, all of the Order knew it, but we assumed it had been destroyed with the city. When I found out Xak Tsaroth had escaped destruction, I realized there might be a chance the book had survived!"

"How do you know it's in the dragon's lair?"

"I don't. I am merely surmising. To magic-users, this book is Xak Tsaroth's greatest treasure. You may be certain that if the dragon found it, she is using it!"

"And you want me to get it for you," Caramon said slowly. "What does it look like?"

"Like my spellbook, of course, except the bone-white parchment is bound in night-blue leather with runes of silver stamped on the front. It will feel deathly cold to the touch."

"What do the runes say?"

"You do not want to know . . ." Raistlin whispered.

"Whose book was it?" Caramon asked suspiciously.

Raistlin fell silent, his golden eyes abstracted as if he were searching inwardly, trying to remember something forgotten. "You have never heard of him, my brother," he said finally, in a whisper that forced Caramon to lean closer. "Yet he was one of the greatest of my order. His name was Fistandantilus."

"The way you describe the spellbook—" Caramon hesitated, fearing what Raistlin would reply. He swallowed and started over. "This Fistandantilus—did he wear the Black Robes?" He could not meet his brother's piercing gaze.

"Ask me no more!" Raistlin hissed. "You are as bad as the others! How can any of you understand me!" Seeing his twin's look of pain, the mage sighed. "Trust me, Caramon. It is not a particularly powerful spellbook, one of the mage's early books, in fact. One he had when he was very young, very young indeed," Raistlin murmured, staring far off. Then he blinked and said more briskly, "But it will be valuable to me, nonetheless. You must get it! You must—" He started to cough.

"Sure, Raist," Caramon promised, soothing his brother. "Don't get worked up. I'll find it."

"Good Caramon. Excellent Caramon," Raistlin whispered when he could speak. He sank back into the corner and closed his eyes. "Now let me rest. I must be ready."

Caramon stood up, looked at his brother a moment, then he turned around and nearly fell over Bupu who was standing behind him, gazing up at him suspiciously with wide eyes.

"What was all that about?" Sturm asked gruffly as Caramon returned to the group.

"Oh, nothing," the big man mumbled, flushing guiltily. Sturm cast an alarmed glance at Tanis.

MARGARET WEIS & TRACY HICKMAN

"What is it, Caramon?" Tanis asked, putting the rolled map in his belt and facing the warrior. "Anything wrong?"

"N-no—" Caramon stuttered. "It's nothing. I—uh—tried to get Raistlin to let me go with him. He said I'd just be in the way."

Tanis studied Caramon. He knew the big man was telling the truth, but Tanis also knew the warrior wasn't telling all the truth. Caramon would cheerfully shed the last drop of his blood for any member of the company, but Tanis suspected he would betray them all at Raistlin's command.

The giant looked at Tanis, silently begging him to ask no more questions.

"He's right, you know, Caramon," Tanis said finally, clapping the big man on the arm. "Raistlin won't be in danger. Bupu will be with him. She'll bring him back here to hide. He's just got to conjure up some of his fancy pyrotechnics, create a diversion to draw the dragon away from her lair. He'll be long gone by the time she gets there."

"Sure, I know that," said Caramon, forcing a chuckle. "You need me anyway."

"We do," Tanis said seriously. "Now is everyone ready?"

Silently, grimly, they stood up. Raistlin rose and came forward, hood over his face, hands folded in his robes. There was an aura around the mage, indefinable, yet frightening—the aura of power derived and created from within. Tanis cleared his throat.

"We'll give you a five hundred count," Tanis said to Raistlin. "Then we'll start. The 'secret place' marked on the map is a trap door located in a building not far from here, according to your little friend. It leads beneath the city to a tunnel that comes up under the dragon's lair, near where we saw her today. Create your diversion in the plaza, then come back here. We'll meet here, give the Highbulp his treasure, and lie low until night. When it's dark, we'll escape."

"I understand," Raistlin said calmly.

I wish I did, Tanis thought bitterly. I wish I understood what was going on in that mind of yours, mage. But the half-elf said nothing.

239

"We go now?" asked Bupu, looking at Tanis anxiously.

"We go now," Tanis said.

Raistlin crept from the shadowy alley and moved swiftly down the street to the south. He saw no signs of life. It was as if all the gully dwarves had been swallowed up by the mist. He found this thought disturbing and kept to the shadows. The frail mage could move silently if there was need. He only hoped he could control his coughing. The pain and congestion in his chest had eased when he drank the herbal mixture whose recipe had been given him by Par-Salian—a kind of apology from the great sorcerer for the trauma the young mage had endured. But the mixture's effect would soon wear off.

Bupu peered out from behind his robes, her beady black eyes squinting down the street leading east to the Great Plaza. "No one," she said and tugged on the mage's robe. "We go now."

No one—thought Raistlin, worried. It didn't make sense. Where were the crowds of gully dwarves? He had the feeling something had gone wrong, but there wasn't time to turn back—Tanis and the others were on their way to the secret tunnel entrance. The mage smiled bitterly. What a fool's quest this was turning out to be. They would probably all die in this wretched city.

Bupu tugged on his robe again. Shrugging, he cast his hood over his head and, together, he and the gully dwarf flitted down the mist-shrouded street.

Two armor-clad figures detached themselves from a dark doorway and slunk quickly after Raistlin and Bupu.

"This is the place," Tanis said softly. Opening a rotting door, he peered in. "It's dark in here. We'll need a light."

There was a sound of flint striking metal and then a flare of light as Caramon lit one of the torches they had borrowed from the Highbulp. The warrior handed one to Tanis and lit one for himself and Riverwind. Tanis stepped inside the building and immediately found himself up to his ankles in water. Holding the torch aloft, he saw water pouring in steady streams down the walls of the dismal room. It swirled around the center of the floor, then ran out through cracks around the edges. Tanis sloshed to the center and held his torch close to the water.

"There it is. I can see it," he said as the others waded into the room. He pointed to a trap door in the floor. An iron pull-ring was barely visible in its center.

"Caramon?" Tanis stood back.

"Bah!" Flint snorted. "If a gully dwarf can open this, I can open it. Stand aside." The dwarf elbowed everyone back, plunged his hand into the water, and heaved. There was a moment's silence. Flint grunted, his face turned red. He stopped, straightened up with a gasp, then reached down and tried again. There wasn't a creak. The door remained shut.

Tanis put his hand on the dwarf's shoulder. "Flint, Bupu says she only goes down during the dry season. You're trying to lift half of Newsea along with the door."

"Well"—the dwarf puffed for breath—"why didn't you say so? Let the big ox try his luck."

Caramon stepped forward. He reached down into the water and gave a heave. His shoulder muscles bulged, and veins in his neck stood out. There was a sucking sound, then the suction was released so suddenly that the big warrior nearly fell over backward. Water drained from the room as Caramon eased the wooden plank door over. Tanis held his torch down to see. A four-foot-square shaft gaped in the floor; a narrow iron ladder descended into the shaft.

"What's the count?" Tanis asked, his throat dry.

"Four hundred and three," answered Sturm's deep voice. "Four hundred and four."

The companions stood around the trap door, shivering in the chill air, hearing nothing but the sound of water pouring down the shaft.

"Four hundred and fifty-one," noted the knight calmly.

Tanis scratched his beard. Caramon coughed twice, as though reminding them of his absent brother. Flint fidgeted and dropped his axe in the water. Tas absent-mindedly chewed on the end of his topknot. Goldmoon, pale but composed, drew near Riverwind, the nondescript brown staff in her hand. He put his arm around her. Nothing was worse than waiting.

"Five hundred," said Sturm finally.

"About time!" Tasslehoff swung himself down onto the ladder. Tanis went next, holding his torch to light the way for Goldmoon, who came after him. The others followed, climbing slowly down into an access shaft of the city sewage system. The shaft ran about twenty feet straight down, then opened up into a five-foot-wide tunnel that ran north and south.

"Check the depth of the water," Tanis warned the kender as Tas was about to let go of the ladder. The kender, hanging onto the last rung with one hand, lowered his hoopak staff into the dark, swirling water below him. The staff sank about half-way.

"Two feet," said Tas cheerfully. He dropped in with a splash, the water hitting him around the thighs. He looked up at Tanis inquiringly.

"That way," Tanis pointed. "South."

Holding his staff in the air, Tasslehoff let the current sweep him along.

"Where's that diversion?" Sturm asked, his voice echoing.

Tanis had been wondering that himself. "We probably won't be able to hear anything down here." He hoped that was true.

"Raist'll come through. Don't worry," Caramon said grimly.

"Tanis!" Tasslehoff fell back into the half-elf. "There's something down here! I felt it go by my feet."

"Just keep moving," Tanis muttered, "and hope it isn't hungry—"

They waded on in silence, the torchlight flickering off the walls, creating illusions in the mind's eye. More than once, Tanis saw something reach out for him, only to realize it was the shadow cast by Caramon's helm or Tas's hoopak.

The tunnel ran straight south for about two hundred feet, then turned east. The companions stopped. Down the eastern arm of the sewer glimmered a column of dim light, filtering from above. This—according to Bupu—marked the dragon's lair.

"Douse the torches!" Tanis hissed, plunging his torch in the water. Touching the slimy wall, Tanis followed the kender—Tas's red outline showing up vividly to his elven eyes—through the tunnel. Behind him he heard Flint complaining about the effects of water on his rheumatism.

"Shhhh," Tanis whispered as they drew near the light. Trying to be silent in spite of clanking armor, they soon stood by a slender ladder that ran up to an iron grating.

"No one ever bothers to lock floor gratings." Tas pulled Tanis close to whisper in his ear. "But I'm sure I can open it, if it is."

Tanis nodded. He didn't add that Bupu had been able to open it as well. The art of picking locks was as much a matter of pride to the kender as Sturm's moustaches were to the knight. They all stood watching, knee-deep in water, as Tas skimmed up the ladder.

"I still don't hear anything outside," Sturm muttered.

"Shhhh!" Caramon growled harshly.

The grating had a lock, a simple one that Tas opened in moments. Then he silently lifted the grating and peered out. Sudden darkness descended on him, darkness so thick and impenetrable it seemed to hit him like a lead weight, nearly making him lose his hold on the grating. Hurriedly he put the grating back into place without making a sound, then slid down the ladder, bumping into Tanis.

"Tas?" the half-elf grabbed him. "Is that you? I can't see. What's going on?"

"I don't know. It just got dark all of a sudden."

"What do you mean, you can't see?" Sturm whispered to Tanis. "What about your elf-talent?"

"Gone," Tanis said grimly, "just as in Darken Wood—and out by the well. . . ."

No one spoke as they stood huddled in the tunnel. All they could hear was the sound of their own breathing and water dripping from the walls.

The dragon was up there—waiting for them.

ABOUT THE AUTHORS

Margaret Weis is the author of fourteen DRAGONLANCE novels, the four-volume galactic fantasy Star of the Guardian, co-author with Don Perrin of *The Doom Brigade*, *Draconian Measures*, *Knights of the Black Earth*, *Robot Blues*, *Hung Out*, and *Brothers in Arms*. She currently lives in a converted barn in southern Wisconsin.

Tracy Hickman started at TSR, Inc. as a game designer, where he helped conceive of the world that became the DRAGONLANCE campaign setting. He has written, in collaboration with Margaret Weis, many DRAGONLANCE novels, the Darksword series, and the Death Gate Cycle. He and his wife Laura are currently at work on a new fantasy series. He lives in Utah with his wife, two daughters, and two sons.

The story begun in
A *Rumor of Dragons* continues in

Night of the Dragons
By Margaret Weis & Tracy Hickman

Available now!

WANT TO KNOW HOW IT ALL BEGAN?

WANT TO KNOW MORE ABOUT THE DRAGONLANCE® WORLD?

FIND OUT IN THIS NEW BOXED SET OF THE FIRST DRAGONLANCE TITLES!

A RUMOR OF DRAGONS
Volume 1

NIGHT OF THE DRAGONS
Volume 2

THE NIGHTMARE LANDS
Volume 3

TO THE GATES OF PALANTHAS
Volume 4

HOPE'S FLAME
Volume 5

A DAWN OF DRAGONS
Volume 6

Gift Set available September 2004
By Margaret Weis & Tracy Hickman
For ages 10 and up

THE NEW ADVENTURES

JOIN A GROUP OF FRIENDS AS THEY UNLOCK MYSTERIES OF THE DRAGONLANCE® WORLD!

TEMPLE OF THE DRAGONSLAYER
Tim Waggoner

Nearra has lost all memory of who she is. With newfound friends, she ventures to an ancient temple where she may uncover her past. Visions of magic haunt her thoughts. And someone is watching.

May 2004

THE DYING KINGDOM
Stephen D. Sullivan

In a near-forgotten kingdom, an ancient evil lurks. As Nearra's dark visions grow stronger, her friends must fight for their lives.

July 2004

THE DRAGON WELL
Dan Willis

Battling a group of bandits, the heroes unleash the mystic power of a dragon well. And none of them will ever be the same.

September 2004

RETURN OF THE SORCERESS
Tim Waggoner

When Nearra and her friends confront the wizard who stole her memory, their faith in each other is put to the ultimate test.

November 2004

For ages 10 and up